A MONSTROUS CLAIM

PART ONE

R.K. PIERCE

A Monstrous Claim: Part One

Copyright © 2022 by R.K. Pierce

All rights reserved.

No part of this book may be reproduced, distributed, or transmitted in any form or by any means, electronic or mechanical, including photocopying, recording, or by any information storage and retrieval system, without permission in writing from the publisher/author.

This is a work of fiction. Names, places, characters, and incidents are either the product of the author's imagination or are used fictitiously, and any resemblance to any actual persons, living or dead, organizations, events, or locales is entirely coincidental.

Cover Design: Crimson Phoenix Creations

Interior & Formatting: Cat Cover Design

Editor: The Fiction Fix

CONTENT WARNING

A Monstrous Claim: Part One is a paranormal why choose romance with themes that may be triggering or disturbing for some readers. This includes (but is not limited to): explicit sexual content, light bondage, monster fucking, tail play, dubious consent, tentacle peen, violence, and gore.

For Krys.
Look, I wrote a book with monster peen.

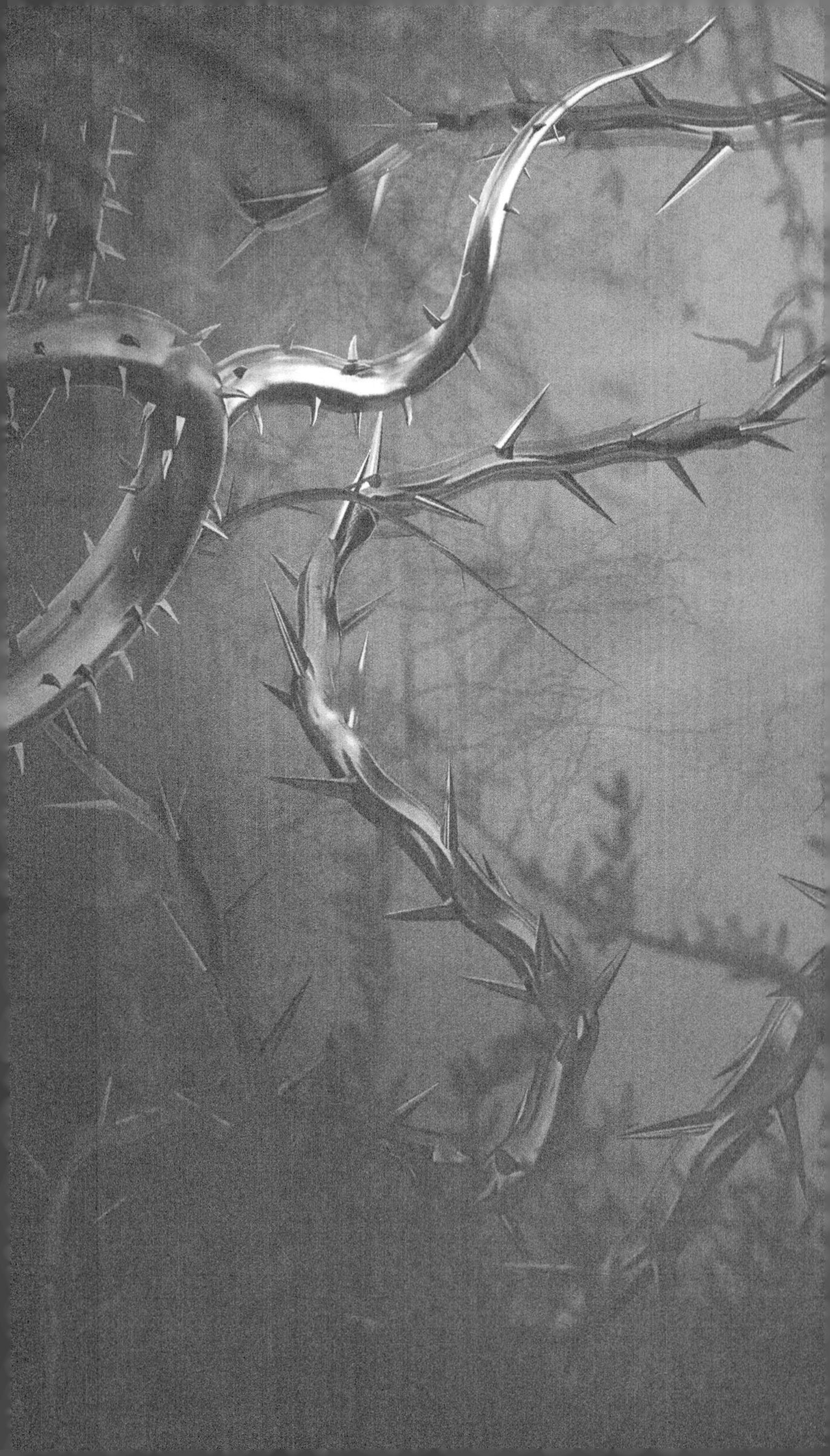

1
DEVYN

"Watch where you're going, jackass!"

Traffic in downtown Atlanta always sucks, but I swear, these drivers took an extra shot of stupid this morning. Gripping the steering wheel with whitened knuckles, I swerve around a red sedan and punch the gas, flipping him off as I pull ahead. He's cussing at me in my rearview mirror, brows pulled low over his eyes as he points a meaty finger at me, but I ignore him. If I don't hurry, I'm going to lose my customers to a taxi, and I can't afford that. My half of the rent is due, and I only need ten more rides to cover it.

Ten more rides.

Easy. I can totally do that.

With any luck I can swing that many in a couple of hours and—

Traffic comes to an abrupt stop again, and I curse, throwing my head back against the headrest and staring at the roof of my ten-year-old Altima. Brown spots dot the material from where I slammed on my brakes last week and slung my coffee everywhere.

I chuckle dryly. At the time, it wasn't funny at all, but when I arrived to pick up customers drenched in caramel macchiato, it made for good conversation. They'd even left me a tip.

Tips. Six months ago, I didn't have to worry about such an inconsistent way of paying my bills. Hell, I hardly had any bills to worry about, considering my ex took care of almost everything. Things had been much simpler, much easier, back then. Now, my entire life depends on spare dollars given to me by strangers.

It's crazy how fast things can change.

I pull down the mirror to check my reflection while I wait for traffic to start moving again and note a few strands of blonde out of place. Running my fingers through my hair to fix them, I check the black liner around my blue eyes and the burgundy stain on my lips. Nothing amiss. Satisfied, I flip the mirror back up and drum my fingers on the steering wheel.

After several minutes of stop-and-go traffic, I finally make it to an exit and veer off the interstate. I hightail it across town, my eyes darting to the GPS on my phone to double-check the directions, and I hardly notice my surroundings as they zip by in a blur. After what feels like much longer than a few minutes, I screech to a stop in front of a ritzy bar and send a message to let the customers know I'm here.

A shaky breath passes my lips as I come off my adrenaline high. Speeding through downtown always spikes my pulse.

I'm not made for hectic city life.

Dipping my head to look through the passenger side window, I scour the sidewalk, searching for anyone who looks like they could be waiting on a ride. My chest flares with panic. I'd waited in a McDonald's parking lot for half an hour before my phone pinged with this job notification, and without it, I won't be any closer to paying my rent.

I wait a few tense minutes, tapping my fingers nervously on the console while my mind flashes with the dismal possibility of not making rent on time.

Our landlord was gracious last month when I lost my job and it took me a few extra days to come up with the money, but I doubt he'll be so understanding a second time. Apartments are nearly impossible to come by in the city, and I'm sure he has a laundry list of renters waiting to swoop in if we get evicted.

I wouldn't be half as stressed if I had a steady job or someone I could ask for help, but borrowing money isn't an option. My mother disappeared when I was a toddler, and I never found out who my father was. Instead of going to live with any relatives, I bounced around the foster system until I aged out and moved in with my ex. Plus, my roommate, Cara, is a full-time student. She doesn't have change to spare most days, so asking her to borrow money is out of the question. If we don't make rent, I won't be the only one getting kicked out.

No. I definitely can't be late again.

I'm just about to give up when two well-dressed

gentlemen turn the corner and head straight for my car, making my heart thrum eagerly.

The first is tall and lean, with blond hair that swoops over a pair of dark blue eyes. He's wearing gray dress pants and a white button-up, a gold watch gleaming on one of his wrists.

The second man is shorter and broader, with shoulder-length brown hair that's pulled into a ponytail, and eyes so dark, they almost look black. His black button-up is pulled taut over bulging muscles, and a neatly trimmed beard defines his jawline.

Separately, they're both breathtaking, but together, they look a little odd—like a CEO and his burly security guard, or a bank teller and a club bouncer.

They pause by my passenger door, and I frantically roll down the window, praying these are the customers I've been waiting on. The blond man bends to peer inside and locks eyes with me before an attractive smirk pulls at his lips.

"Divine?" he asks, his voice a sexy rumble in his throat.

A nervous chuckle pushes past my lips. I've never heard that one before, but damn does it sound incredible when he says it.

"It's Devyn," I correct, finally finding my voice.

His eyes are unnaturally blue, like shards of sapphire—they have to be contacts—and my skin tingles with goosebumps when his smirk widens into a grin.

"Devyn," he says, the name dripping off his tongue.

God, that's even better.

They pile into the back seat, and the combined haze of their cologne creeps in with them, invading my senses and making my thoughts hazy. Whatever they're wearing smells expensive.

And delicious.

Dragging myself back to reality, I look down at the address on my phone and clear my throat. "We're going to Akers Mill Road, correct?"

I'm not familiar with the street, but it's close by. A short trip. I'll be on to my next ride in no time, that much closer to making rent.

Easy peasy. At this rate, I'll be home in time to watch the newest episode of The Intolerable with Cara.

"Actually," the man with dark hair speaks up, cutting off my train of thought. His voice is tinted with an indistinguishable accent. "Would it be a problem if we changed that?"

My hand hesitates on the gearshift, and I meet his eyes in the rearview mirror. The intensity of his gaze burns into me, like he's staring straight through to my jumbled thoughts, and a shiver tumbles down my spine.

This isn't the first time I've carted around attractive men in the city, but these two make me nervous. I don't know if it's because they radiate wealth and power, or if I sense something sinister hovering just below the surface, but they set my blood on fire with a mixture of anxiety and curiosity.

"Where to?" I ask, my eyes still glued to his in the reflection.

"Club 47. Are you familiar?"

I shake my head. I've never heard of it. "No, but I can plug it into the GPS."

My fingers speed across my phone as I type in the new destination. I try to ignore the intimidating gaze of the dark-haired man in the mirror, but I can feel it burrowing under my skin. Uneasiness knots my stomach when the directions come up—Club 47 is nearly an hour away.

"Umm…" I start, not entirely sure how to let these men down.

An hour is way farther than I typically drive, and the thought of being in unfamiliar territory with two strangers—men several times my size who could easily overpower me—makes my skin crawl. There's a taser under the seat that provides the tiniest bit of comfort, but I've never used it before, so I'm not sure how beneficial it would be in a worst-case scenario.

Even in a best-case scenario, I could miss out on several rides in the process, and it'll take that much longer before I can head home for the night.

The good just doesn't seem to outweigh the bad.

"That's a bit farther than I expected." My voice trails off as I struggle with my words.

I've been a people pleaser my entire life, always struggling to set boundaries and tell people no. I never want to be an inconvenience, never want to let people down. You'd think after being let down my entire life that I wouldn't care to extend the feeling to others, but the constant disappointment has had the opposite effect.

I chew my bottom lip, wondering if I'll be able to put my foot down and decline their ride, or if I'll succumb to my life-long habit of putting others' needs before mine.

"We understand if it's an issue." The blond man tugs on the door handle with a frown and eases the door open. "We didn't expect the location of our meeting to change, but we can wait for another ride. Sorry to have wasted your time."

Damn it. As much of an inconvenience as driving them will be, it pales in comparison to the guilt I would feel for making them wait. Who knows how long it will be before someone else comes along? Besides, Cara is counting on me to come up with my half of the rent.

If she were here, she'd tell me to suck it up, and I try to attribute my willingness to that and not my increasing desire to be in their presence. Even if I don't want to acknowledge it, there's something mesmerizing about the men that clouds my thoughts with excitement, and I want to needle them with the pestering questions bouncing around in my mind.

I roll my eyes at myself. One of these days, my curiosity is going to get me in a lot of trouble.

"No." The word rushes past my lips, and I reach for the gearshift again. "It's no problem."

"We really don't want to be a burden," the blond says with a simple shake of his head. "I'm sure we can find a taxi or—"

"It's fine." My tone is a little sharper than I intend, but I don't want to argue. "If you're going to a meeting, you don't want to be late. I can take you."

Our eyes meet in the rearview mirror, and a tiny furrow forms between his brows. I imagine he's trying to guess how long it'll take to best me in a challenge of politeness, but he won't win. He must know it too, because after a beat, he snaps the door shut and tugs his seat belt across his hips.

"Thank you, Miss Devyn." He tips his head in a nod.

We pull away from the curb and slip into traffic. I try not to appear half as annoyed as I am with the bumper-to-bumper madness, and I pinch my bottom lip between my teeth to avoid yelling at incompetent drivers. That isn't the kind of impression I want to leave on customers, especially not when their feedback through the app could lose me my job.

I'm not sure what kind of impression I want to make on them, but it's definitely not one of a screaming mad woman. Can't have that.

As we stop at a red light, the men fall into low conversation. I try to distract myself with the radio, which is playing so quietly I can barely hear it, but their deep, velvety voices transfix me. No matter how hard I try, I can't tune them out.

"The boss is going to kill us," the blond guy says, and my eyes flick to the rearview mirror.

He stares out the window and runs a hand nervously through his hair. I admire the chisel of his jaw, the curve of his cheekbones. He's gorgeous, with the charm of someone who knows just how attractive he is. I imagine trailing my fingers from his jaw to his chest, then quickly scold myself and turn my attention back to the road.

Jesus, what is wrong with me? I ask myself, as though I can answer. The truth is, I have no idea what the hell is going on. I'm clearly sleep deprived or need to drink more water—I don't typically fantasize about strangers.

Hell, I haven't fantasized about anyone in way too long.

"Maybe not," the other says. "Lysander agreed to help us."

"Yeah, but for almost double what Rafe offered. He's gonna be pissed."

"As long as the next deal goes smoothly, he'll be fine." I glance at the mirror again to see the dark-haired man wave away his companion's concerns. "You worry too much, Az."

"Is Az short for something?" The question slips past my lips before I can stop it, and I clamp my mouth shut. It hits me just how rude that was. It's obvious I've been listening.

My insatiable curiosity has always been one of my downfalls.

I should probably stop staring and focus on the job at hand, but I can't help it. Tiny magnets keep tugging my gaze to the mirror so I can soak in as much of them as possible.

The blond man's full lips tug into a smirk, and he leans forward a bit in his seat as he speaks. "Azarius."

My eyes shift, and I glance at the dark-haired man. "And what's yours?"

He hesitates, like he's trying to decide whether he trusts me with the information.

"Elio," he says, his accent distorting the o at the end.

"Are you from around here?" I ask. We're moving again. This street isn't nearly as crowded as before, so I press the gas pedal down further and we speed down the road.

"No," Elio answers. "We're just here on business."

"What do you do?"

A brief moment of silence passes before he answers. "Real estate."

The need to press him further burns in my chest, but his serious tone suggests I need to drop the topic. That's fine. If he doesn't want to talk about it, I won't ask, but I don't plan to stay quiet for the next hour or more. Besides, if I'm lucky, one of them might ask for my number.

It doesn't hurt to hope.

"Is this your only job, Devyn?" Azarius changes the subject. Of the two, he seems the most personable—his tone is friendlier, as are his facial expressions.

"For now." Up until a few weeks ago, I was working at a staffing company. When they were bought out, the entire office department was let go, me included. Being an Uber driver was a quick fix as I waited on my dozens of job applications, praying impatiently for someone to call me back. So far, no one has. "I want something slower paced. Running around and dealing with traffic is no fun."

"It seems fucking awful," Elio mutters.

I nod, my eyes glued to the road, glad we can agree on something. "It is. As soon as I can, I'm moving somewhere peaceful."

"Oh?" Azarius pipes up. I glance at him in the mirror, and his head tilts to the side. "Where do you want to go?"

I shrug. "It doesn't matter. Anywhere but here."

"Are you from Atlanta?" he presses.

"No."

My memory dances with images of Pleasant Grove, the small town where my ex-fiancé, Steven, and I went to high school. After bouncing around from city to city for years, I finally landed there, and I stayed until I turned eighteen. I'd planned to attend a community college, but Steven moved us to Tennessee, hours away from the only place I'd ever really called home.

When I found him balls deep in another woman, I left, no destination in mind. I just had to get away. I slept in my car for a few days while I tried to figure things out, and after exhausting all other options, I somehow got in touch with Cara, a girl I knew from school. Even though we were never friends back then, she agreed to let me move in with her.

It was a nice change of scenery for a few weeks.

Now, I'm growing to resent the place.

"I'm from a tiny town in South Carolina. There are only three stoplights, and you have to drive at least half an hour to find a supercenter. If you blink, you'll probably miss it," I say, shoving all other thoughts from my mind. I try not to think about the past unless it's necessary. There's too much pain and disappointment attached to those memories, even the good ones. They're better left alone in my filing cabinet labeled 'emotional bullshit.'

"Are you in school?" Azarius effortlessly keeps the questions coming, and I wonder if the art of conversation is what led him to real estate. Regardless, our interactions feel natural—almost like I've known him for a long time.

"Nope." I'd already missed the registration deadline by the time I packed up and headed for Atlanta, and even though the idea of applying for next semester has crossed my mind, I'm not sold.

Part of the reason is money. I'll probably never have enough to afford a semester's tuition. Another part, though, is because I have no clue what I want to do for the rest of my life. The idea of picking a single career to last forever feels limiting, constrictive. I crave freedom, and you can't find that in a nine-to-five.

It also can't be found guiding an Uber through frantic, downtown streets, but hopefully, I won't be doing this for much longer. One of the places I applied to is bound to call eventually.

They have to.

"I just don't think college is right for me," I say, pursing my lips. "I'm still figuring things out. I've got plenty of time."

"How old are you?" Elio asks, speaking up for the

first time in a while. The wheels in my head turn as I try to place his accent, but it's unlike anything I've heard before.

"Twenty-three."

He chuckles. "Yeah, you're still young. You have plenty of time. Don't rush it."

Young? Even with his perfect beard, Elio doesn't look much older than me, and neither does Azarius. I give in to my curiosity yet again.

"If I'm young, how old does that make you?" I tease, flashing a cocky smile in the mirror.

"He's twenty-six." Azarius snorts with laughter.

Elio huffs. "Go on, tell her my whole life story while you're at it."

"Don't tempt me." Az's sapphire eyes light up with joy. He clearly enjoys annoying Elio, and it seems he's pretty good at it.

I decide to tempt him, knowing that of the two, Azarius is more likely to answer my prying questions. "Are you guys married?"

Neither answers at first, and I flip my blinker on as we turn onto a busy street.

"No," they both reply, and I can't deny the hint of satisfaction fluttering in my chest. My chances of seeing either of them after this car ride just increased a bit.

"Any girlfriends?" I ask, trying not to sound too eager.

"No," they answer.

My odds just increased again.

Another question forms in my mind, and it falls

out of my mouth before I can stop it. "Are you two a couple?"

It isn't too far-fetched: two single, attractive men traveling alone together and bickering like an old married couple.

Elio chuckles, making my insides melt. After being so brash, his laugh is music to my ears. Maybe he's not as callous as I thought.

"Nah, my taste is much better than this dumbass," he jokes and laughs again.

Azarius scoffs. "As if I'd date your ugly ass."

Laughter bellows through the car.

"Give him some credit, Az," I say. "He isn't that bad."

Elio's gaze grips mine in the mirror, and a smirk flashes over his face. "Do you find me attractive?"

Heat creeps its way into my cheeks, and I look away quickly. I don't know why I'm embarrassed. I did this to myself. I guess I just hadn't expected him to be so straightforward.

Damn him.

I do find him insanely attractive, especially his accent, which I've yet to place. Still, I'm not going to give in that easily. He'll have to fight a little if he wants an answer.

"I didn't say that." I roll my eyes. "I said he could do worse."

Azarius howls with laughter, but Elio hardly seems amused. "Yeah, well, you being a dumbass still stands."

"Whatever." Azarius rolls his eyes. "What about you, Devyn? Are you seeing anyone?"

"No, I'm not."

I'm too embarrassed to admit just how single I am —even Cara is trying to set me up—but my quick reply probably gave it away. Since moving here, I haven't gone out to any bars or clubs, and I haven't downloaded any dating apps. Putting my battered heart back out there isn't in the plans anytime soon—hell, potentially forever.

I doubt anything with Azarius or Elio would be serious; a night of unbridled passion at most, maybe two if the dick is good.

That I can do. No strings attached, no feelings.

"Haven't really found anyone worth my time," I explain with a fake, exasperated sigh, letting my shoulders sag for effect.

"In a big city like this?" Azarius asks, leaning forward in his seat. My eyes are trained ahead, but I can sense his closeness, smell the spice of his cologne. "Surely there's someone who's caught your eye."

"There may have been one or two." I purse my lips to fight a grin. "But men nowadays don't want to take a lady out."

"Ah, I see," he says, his deep voice cueing flutters in my stomach. "Well, maybe if we're ever back in town, we can change that."

My excitement suddenly deflates as his words hit me.

"Back in town?" I ask. "Are you leaving?"

"Tonight, I'm afraid." He sits back and returns to

staring out the window. "Right after we close this deal."

Son of a bitch. I bite back my disappointment and fight to remain unfazed. It shouldn't bother me. After all, I just met them; they could be serial killers for all I know. Still, the pull I feel toward them is unusual, unlike anything I've ever felt before.

Devyn, you've completely lost your fucking marbles.

"Well, if you're ever in town and need a ride, I'm your girl," I say, mustering all my enthusiasm. It's a last-ditch effort to swap numbers with them while I can, and if that doesn't work, I'm never making the first move again.

Club 47 is a sleek, charcoal gray building with blacked-out windows. A bouncer the size of a refrigerator stands outside the glossy black door, despite it being early evening. It's way too early for club goers—it's only four in the afternoon. On a Sunday. I have the sneaking suspicion Azarius and Elio lied about being in real estate—this doesn't seem like the kind of place where people meet to discuss property.

I pull up to the curb and reluctantly put the car in park. Despite my earlier urgency, I don't want them to leave. A strange sensation tugs at my stomach—one I don't quite understand and can't explain. I wish I had more to say to them, or that they had more to say to me.

Azarius unclicks his seat belt and leans forward, poking his head between the front seats.

"For your trouble," he says as he holds a folded hundred-dollar bill neatly between two fingers.

I blanch, my stomach tightening into a knot. A hundred dollars easily covers the rest of my rent, and while a little voice in my head urges me to politely decline, the possibility of being caught up on bills is too strong, so I graciously take it from him. It's probably chump change for them anyway.

"Thank you so much," I say.

His face is only a foot from mine, and when our eyes meet, a tingle starts at the base of my neck, trickling down my spine. He's even more beautiful up close, with flawless skin and impossibly blue eyes—I almost swear they're flecked with bits of purple.

Say something before you never see them again.

My mind goes blank. Perfect fucking timing.

Thankfully, Azarius speaks for me. "If you'd be willing to hang out here until we're done and drive us to our next stop, there's more where that came from."

His eyes fall to the money in my hand, and heat singes my cheeks. More money and more time with them? I can't say no to that.

"How long do you think it will take?" I ask, pretending to check the time, even though it's irrelevant. I plan to stay regardless.

"Longer, if Az makes us late," Elio growls from the back seat.

Azarius ignores him. "It shouldn't take long. What do you say?"

I hesitate, enjoying every moment of making him

wait, but I don't want to be the reason they're late to their meeting. Elio may never forgive me, and that would be a shame.

I nod. "Consider me your chauffeur for the evening."

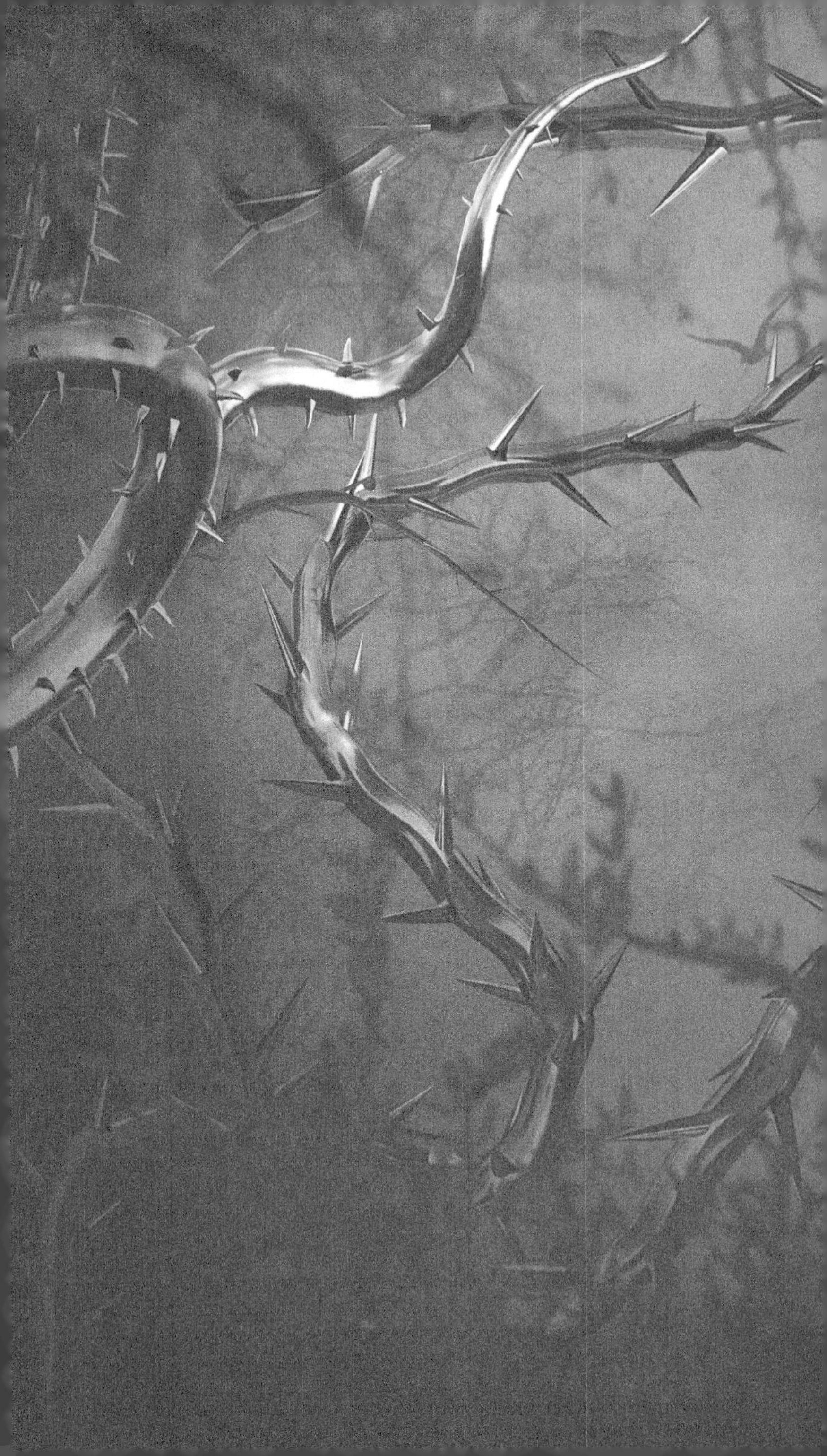

2
DEVYN

Two hours.

I've been sitting outside of Club 47 for two fucking hours, and there's still no sign of Azarius or Elio. My phone has pinged at least a dozen times with people looking for rides, and I've ignored them all to sit here and wait.

I'm questioning my sanity at this point.

After thirty minutes, I killed the engine to conserve gas. After an hour, I got bored and leaned the seat back to—unsuccessfully—attempt a nap.

Now, I'm borderline irate and tempted to leave, but the promise of a decent payday keeps me parked.

This better be worth my fucking time.

I've considered approaching the terrifying bouncer to ask how much longer they'll be, but I can't summon the courage. He hasn't budged from his spot, and his face is fixed with a terrifying scowl that dares anyone to approach.

I doubt anything I have in my arsenal of charm will appeal to him, so I abandon the idea.

Finally, when I've lost almost every shred of patience I possess, the men I'm waiting for come walking around the side of the building and make a beeline for my car. Their steps are brisk, their mouths hardened into thin lines. I barely have time to wonder why they didn't come out the front before Azarius is wrenching open the car door as Elio climbs in on the other side.

"Our apologies," Azarius says with an edge to his voice. "That took way longer than we thought."

"If you would have shut the hell up and stopped trying to kiss Pearson's ass, we would have been in and out," Elio growls.

"You weren't complaining when they were slinging free drinks at you."

I start the car while they snap back and forth at each other before heading toward the road, relieved to finally do something aside from sit still.

"Where to now?" I ask, hoping the distraction will end the argument.

It does—at least momentarily.

"The Château."

Another bar. Go figure. At least I've heard of this one.

I plug the name into the GPS before turning onto the road, and Club 47 shrinks into the distance as we head back downtown. The sun has started to set, turning the sky into a fiery oil painting and drenching the buildings around us in golden light.

"How did your meeting go?" I ask. Considering I waited for two hours, I'm invested. I need to at least know if my patience was worth it.

Not to my surprise, it's Azarius who answers. "Not as well as we'd hoped, but better than it could have gone."

I purse my lips. It isn't the answer I wanted, and their vagueness has me wondering if they're hiding something sinister. Are they members of a cartel? Hitmen? Do they just not want to tell some random girl their business?

My mind races with possibilities, and my eyes flick to my phone. We're seventeen minutes away from our destination. That's seventeen minutes I have to find out anything I can about them. After I drop them off, I may never see them again.

"What's the worst that could have happened?"

Azarius chuckles. "If we came out in body bags."

"Ha. That's a good one." I check Elio in the rearview mirror and see him staring daggers at his companion. "Isn't my idiot partner hilarious? The worst thing that could have happened is that we lost the deal and had to deliver bad news to our boss."

"Oh, right." Azarius drops his voice to a whisper, but I can still hear him. "That's when the body bags come in."

My eyes are on the road, but I hear what sounds like Elio punching Azarius. Someone—my guess is Azarius—sucks in a sharp breath before they both fall quiet again.

"Is this one of those if you tell me, you'll have to

kill me things?" I ask, curiosity getting the better of me.

They answer at the same time.

"Yes."

"No."

Elio sighs forcefully. "This is one of those if we tell you, they'll kill us things. So, the less you know, the better it is for everyone."

I haven't met anyone personally involved with the mafia, but I've seen enough movies to know this definitely sounds like some cartel shit, and I don't want any part of it.

"Fair." Getting someone killed isn't something I'm particularly interested in, but there has to be some nugget of information they can tell me that will satisfy my curiosity. I press on. "You can't tell me where you're from, and you won't tell me what kind of business you're involved in. Are Azarius and Elio even your real names?"

"Yes," Azarius says. "And we are in the real estate business—just not the kind you're familiar with."

I cock my eyebrow. "There's more than one kind?"

He nods but doesn't explain. What kind of real estate spurs all this secrecy?

We pull up in front of a wide building adorned in red and gold. The Château is written in elegant scrawl above the entrance, and a burgundy carpet leads up a short walkway to the door. It's wedged between two towering hotels, and there's a narrow alleyway running to the left of it.

"Thank you, Devyn," Elio says as he reaches for the door. "We appreciate everything you've done for us today."

Azarius leans in close and offers me several folded bills. "Absolutely. If we're ever in the city again, we'll look you up."

My body is numb as I take the money, and I attribute it to the amount of cash in my hand—I won't bother to count it until they're well out of sight, but it's probably enough to cover my bills for the next month.

"Thank you," I mutter, and I attempt a smile.

Deflated. That's how I feel as they climb out of the car, even though I pretend to be unfazed. Azarius winks at me through the passenger window as Elio joins him, and they wave a final time before turning toward the club. I sigh, throwing the car into drive and pulling away from the curb.

I try not to be disappointed. After all, it was a long shot to hope either of these gorgeous and clearly successful men would want anything to do with me. Me. Devyn the Uber driver.

Yeah, it had been a very long shot.

As I roll away, my eyes find the rearview mirror a final time, and I watch the gentlemen disappear into —the alley?

I blink several times to make sure I'm not mistaken as Elio glances back over his shoulder before slipping between the buildings.

What the hell?

I hit the brakes reflexively, and the driver behind

me blares their horn, but I'm too distracted to care. Why the hell are they slinking into the alley instead of heading inside the club?

I shouldn't care.

I know I shouldn't, but that doesn't alleviate the unsettled feeling in my stomach.

What could possibly be down there?

After a second of indecision, I whip the car into a parking space, kill the engine, and reach for my taser. I tuck it into the back pocket of my jeans before jumping out, silently thanking anyone listening that I wore tennis shoes today.

As I move toward the alley, I try to mentally prepare myself for what I'll find there, and my brain runs rampant with possibilities.

Is that where they're meeting their boss?

Are they meeting with members of the cartel?

Is there a secret entrance into The Château for VIP members?

Despite a slew of logical possibilities, an itch crawls over my skin, and it only intensifies as I get closer. Whatever is down there is driving my intuition insane.

I reach the alley and pause, cautiously peering around the corner.

While the street is bathed in orange light from the setting sun, the alley is drenched in darkness. Dumpsters and heaps of trash dot the narrow space, and even from where I'm standing, the smell makes me scrunch my nose. I can vaguely see two figures—

Azarius and Elio—melting into the shadows several yards ahead.

After a second of hesitation, I skitter down the alley after them.

The sounds of the city mask my footsteps as I creep along, closing the distance between us quickly. They're obviously not in a hurry, and while I can hear them talking and laughing, I can't discern what they're saying.

Damn it.

I have to minimize the distance between us if I'm going to catch anything.

We make it a few more yards before a brick wall materializes out of the darkness at the end of the alley. It's a dead end. My stomach drops to the ground. There's nowhere for them to go. There's nowhere for me to go.

Did they come the wrong way? Am I missing something?

I debate turning back and abandoning the whole thing, but a knot in the pit of my stomach urges me on. It's a compulsion so strong, I feel it in my bones.

I slip behind the last dumpster in the alley, cautiously reaching for my pocket, and my fingertips brush the hard edge of the taser. Can't be too careful. I can smooth talk myself out of most situations, but having a weapon adds another layer to my confidence. It's hard to feel entirely helpless when you can conjure 50,000 volts of electricity with the press of a button.

The men freeze in their tracks, and I catch my breath, eyes glued to their movements.

Elio approaches the brick wall and places his hand flat against it. From where I'm hiding, I can't see what he's doing, but after a few seconds, he steps back. The bricks begin to melt away, dissolving like plastic in acid until a six-foot-wide hole gapes before them.

I'm vaguely aware of a deep-settled tug in my bones, begging me to step closer, and a sudden chill makes the hairs on my arms stand on end. Whatever exists within that darkness is calling for me, and every fiber of my being is begging to answer the call.

Neither Azarius nor Elio is fazed, but my heart is racing erratically in my chest as I struggle to process what I've just seen.

Was this magic?

Vandalism?

Before I can give it any more thought, the two men step forward and are swallowed by the impossible blackness in the wall.

My chest lurches.

I'm left staring after them, my eyes trained on the spot where they disappeared, my jaw hanging in disbelief.

Following them seems like a bad idea. Terrible, even. I have no idea where this hole leads, and I'm not sure I want to find out. Maybe they had a good reason for their secrecy after all. Still, the overwhelming pull I feel dragging me toward the black void tugs harder as the seconds trickle by.

As I'm debating, the edges of the hole begin to

quiver, and then it starts to shrink, the brick reappearing, seemingly untouched.

Fuck. It's closing!

If I'm going to follow them, it has to be now.

I jump out from behind the dumpster and break into a sprint, my feet pounding against the unforgiving pavement. The wall is reappearing quickly, but my legs move faster, and just before the hole closes, I leap into the darkness.

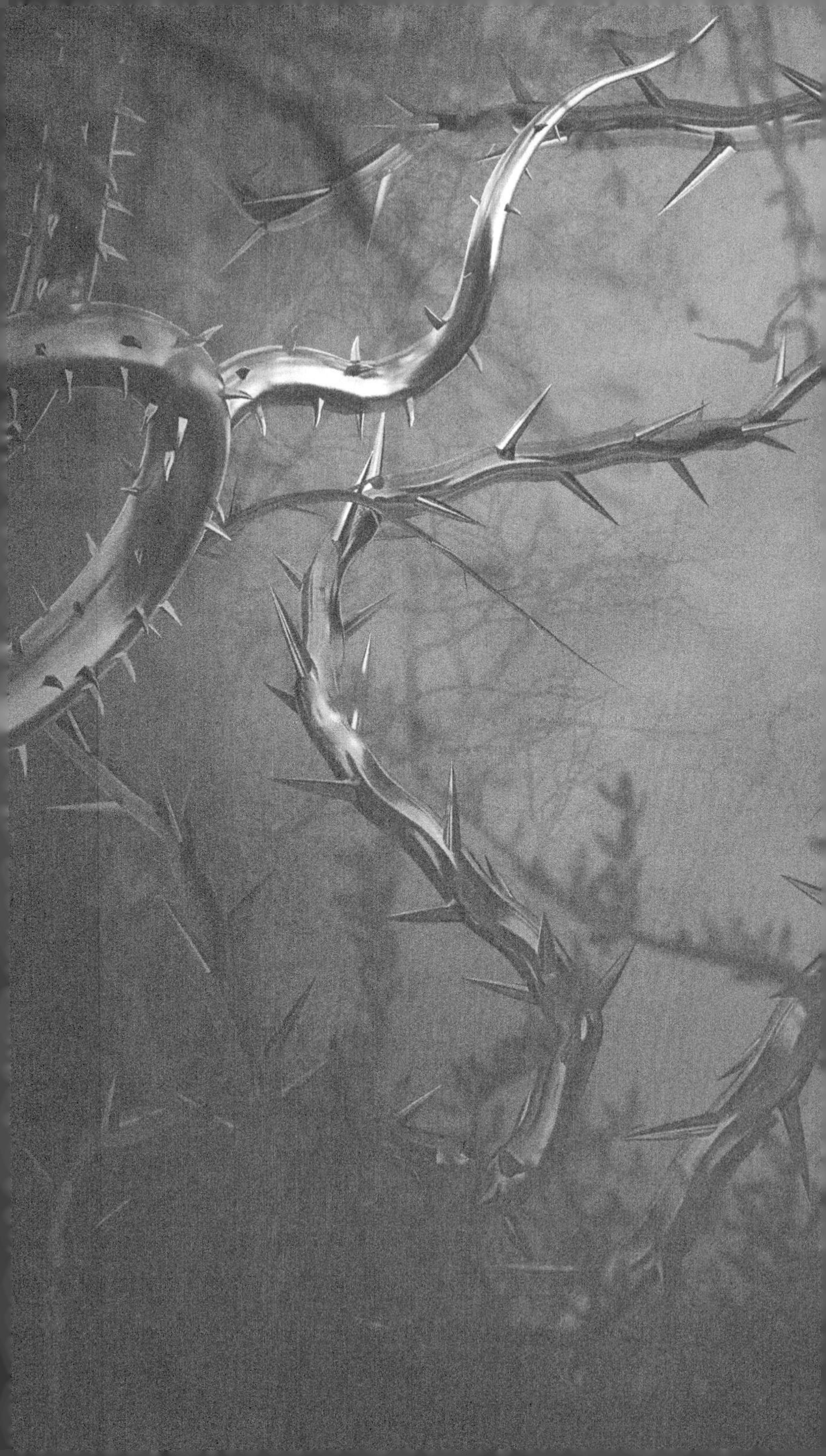

3
DEVYN

For a moment, there's nothing but pitch blackness consuming me.
No sky.
No alley.
No up.
No down.

The only way I know I still exist is by the pounding of blood in my ears and the fact that I'm blinking. I'm weightless, floating between Earth and somewhere.

At least, I think I'm floating.

My limbs are numb, and even though I've never been to space, I imagine this is what it would feel like. I just wish I could see.

There's no way of telling how much time passes before I feel a sudden jerk in my stomach, like the first drop of a roller coaster. The darkness spits me headfirst into a world bathed in dim light, and I hit the ground on my stomach.

The air is ripped out of my lungs on impact, and I whimper at the pain searing my skin. Begging my vision to adjust after being in the darkness for so long, I take several painful breaths before I push myself up onto my knees then glance down to assess the damage.

My right pant leg is ripped and my knee is scraped, blood beading on the surface. A sharp pain across my cheek tells me there's something there, too. I touch it gently with my fingertips, and when I move my hand away, I grimace. Yep, blood. My palms are pink and tender, but thankfully not bleeding, and my whole body hurts from meeting the ground.

Blinking frantically as my vision continues to adjust, I scan my surroundings.

A chartreuse orb glows brightly overhead, turning the sky into a swatch of sickly green, like the eerie moment just before a thunderstorm. It makes my skin crawl. It feels off. Unnatural.

I'm in an abandoned city—if you can call it that —surrounded by dilapidated, gnarly-looking buildings. They're situated randomly, no rhyme or reason to the layout, like architecture from a fever dream. Stretched doorways, uneven windows. Some are so distorted, I don't know how they're still standing.

Where the hell am I?

Beyond the clump of houses are trees—lots and lots of mangled, twisted trees—that are just as eerie as the rest of my surroundings. The ground is jet black, from the sparse patches of grass scattered here and there to the jagged gravel digging into my legs.

As I shakily get to my feet and dust myself off, I scan the area for any sign of Azarius or Elio and come up short.

Shit.

Not only am I lost, but I'm also alone.

This isn't good.

"Azarius," I call out, and my voice cracks. I'm afraid to be too loud, not wanting to draw unwanted attention, but right now, they're my only shot at getting out of this mess. They're my only shot at getting home. "Elio!"

Movement near one of the buildings catches my eye, and for the briefest moment, I expect to find one of the men I followed waiting for me, but that isn't the case. A looming figure steps into view, making my blood run cold.

It's at least seven feet tall, with red leathery skin and impossibly long limbs—its clawed hands almost brush the ground, even as it stands. A head protrudes from an intensely humped back, and its six black eyes are fixed on me. Its gaping mouth shows rows of sharp teeth, and twin tongues tease the air as it steps closer.

It's a monster. And it's fucking ugly.

"Human." The sound that hits my ears isn't more than a hiss, and an icy chill rockets through me.

A voice in my head tells me I'm staring death in the face, and I'm inclined to believe it. The taser in my pocket seems like a feeble hope for survival at this point, and even if I can outrun this beast, I have nowhere to run to.

This is definitely not good.

The monster takes a step forward, and I turn on my heel, breaking into a sprint and tearing between two buildings. A roar rips through the air, and a pang of fear hits my chest when loud footsteps pound against the ground behind me. They're getting closer with every second, and a terrifying truth grips me.

I'm not going to get away.

I brace myself for impact just before something collides with my back, and I stumble, skittering across the ground. My exposed skin stings as I'm dragged across the sharp rocks, and I roll onto my back to find the monster towering over me.

"Such a treat," it hisses. "I haven't seen a human in so long—haven't tasted one in even longer."

I grab my taser, then point it at the figure and press the button to bring the electricity to life, but nothing happens.

Frantic, I try again, but the device does nothing.

A massive hand swings above me, knocking the weapon from my hands, ripping into my forearm in the process. I cry out as the monster lunges, and I throw my feet up to plant them against its torso, all while cradling my injured arm. I try to keep some distance between us, despite the massive weight crushing down on me, but its long arms reach for mine and pin them to the ground.

"Stop fighting, and I'll make it quick and painless," it says, lowering its face until it's inches away from mine. A sweet stink, like rotting fruit, pours off the creature, and my stomach turns. "Although, I do enjoy a bit of fun."

His two tongues dance across my injured cheek, leaving a slimy trail down my face, and I fight the bile creeping up my throat.

"GET OFF, YOU NASTY FUCK!" I squirm, trying to get away, but it's useless.

I'm trapped. This is how I'm going to die: at the hands—or claws—of a monster.

All because I couldn't mind my business and followed Azarius and Elio into a mystery hole in a dark alley. Not one of my brightest moments.

A growl rumbles in the monster's chest, and it opens its mouth wide, exposing razor-sharp teeth. Its claws are digging into my wrists, and I flinch away as much as I can, praying it keeps its word and makes my death swift and painless.

Maybe it won't be so bad. I'm sure there are worse things than dying that could happen in this place.

Just as I accept my fate and begin to wonder where spirits go once they've been severed from their bodies, a pale blur swoops in from the left and crashes into the monster, sending it flying. I gasp, shocked by my sudden, unobstructed view of the green sky overhead, and I struggle to hoist myself onto my elbows. My forearm screams in protest, but I ignore the pain as my gaze falls on a brawl unfolding nearby between the red leather-skinned monster and a newcomer—another monster.

The second monster is tall and lean, but only half

the size of his opponent. If it wasn't for his chalk-white skin decorated with fine black markings, or the six-inch blades extending from the ends of his fingers, he could almost pass as human. Almost. Sharp black horns protrude from the blond hair on his head, and a long, slender tail whips along behind him.

What he lacks in size, he makes up for in speed. My eyes can hardly keep up with him as he rushes and tackles the other monster to the ground. He slashes the thing's chest open, creating deep gashes that seep black liquid, and the red figure howls in pain.

I pry my eyes from the fight just as the red monster rakes his claws across the challenger's face, and I struggle to get to my feet. Pain radiates through my limbs, but I have to get away—if these things are fighting over dinner, I don't want to wait around to see who wins.

Knees shaking, I finally stand. I turn to run, but a third monster blocks my way, his black eyes locked on me. He's broad, with copper-colored skin and dark, shoulder-length hair that hangs loosely around his face. His angled eyes and pointed ears make him look like some kind of reptilian elf, with dark wings folded behind him.

His muscles tense as my eyes fall down his form, and when I realize he's completely naked, heat burns my cheeks. Before I can attempt to run, he grabs my shoulders, claws digging into my skin as he holds me in place.

"Let me go." I half-heartedly fight his grip, but I

have no energy left. My eyelids flutter, and I'm overcome with light-headedness. "Please."

"What the fuck are you doing here?" he asks, his words hinted with an accent. The familiarity of it tickles at my memory.

His gaze flicks to the commotion behind us, and I study the line of his jaw. His mouth is hardened into a line, and the seriousness in his eyes flips a switch of recognition in my mind.

"Elio?"

The world goes silent.

He loosens his grip on me, and I slowly turn around to see the monster with a tail walking toward us. The beast that attacked me lies in a heap on the ground. Dead.

"Azarius?" I say before I can stop myself. The edges of my vision darken, but I fight to stay conscious.

Two red slashes stretch the length of his cheek, but even as I watch, they shrink, closing up until his face is unmarred. His mouth slides into a lopsided grin, which brightens his otherwise intimidating features. "The one and only."

My gaze drifts from Azarius to Elio and back again as my brain struggles to catch up. My vision sways, the world tilts, and I stagger before catching my balance.

"You're monsters," I gasp, mostly to myself. Even though my scrapes and scratches are more than proof, saying the words out loud makes everything more real.

"Well spotted." It's Elio who speaks, and when he takes a step toward me, my heart jumps into my throat. Azarius made easy work of the leathery-skinned monster, and I know he could snap me in half if his heart desired. His eyes narrow as he looks me over. "And what are you?"

I chuckle. Is this a joke?

"Human, obviously. Here I thought you were the smart one."

Instead of laughing like I expect, he shakes his head. "You don't understand. If you were a human, you'd be dead right now."

"I mean, I almost was." I jerk my thumb at the dead monster. "Fifteen more seconds and I would have been."

"That's not what he means." Azarius steps closer and lays a hand on my shoulder. His claws have retracted, but his skin is still milky white. Up close, the black designs on his skin look more like tribal tattoos—they dance up his arms and across his chest, stretching across his forehead like a crown. "Humans can't survive the portal between realms."

The portal between realms. So I was right. This isn't Earth, or at least not Earth as I know it. We're in a different realm.

A monster realm.

"Well, one did." I cross my arms over my chest, irritated now. My head is starting to swim again, and I cling by a thread to consciousness as my eyes bounce between them. "I'm a human, plain and simple. I don't have any powers. I can't turn into anything else.

I've been the exact same for my entire, boring-ass existence—sorry to disappoint you both."

Azarius and Elio exchange a glance.

"What if she's telling the truth?" Azarius asks, his voice low. "Maybe something's changed with the portal. It could explain what a Malev was doing this far west."

"I don't think so," Elio says, narrowing his eyes in my direction. He cocks his head to the side as he considers me, and I can almost see the wheels turning. "We won't know for sure unless we try again."

I nod in agreement, the thought of going home filling me with relief. I never thought I'd miss the hectic streets of Atlanta, but I'd choose them over this monster land any day.

"Yes, let's do that," I say. "It's been fun—well, not really. It's been pretty fucking terrible—but I have to get home. Elio, if you'll open the portal thing again, I can find my way, and the next time you two are in town, you can make sure I survived the trip."

Neither of the monsters move.

There's a tense moment of silence, in which I bounce eagerly on the balls of my feet. Elio cocks his head and stares absentmindedly at something in the distance.

"I can't do that."

My stomach plummets to the ground, and I glare at him. "Wh—why not?"

"Because you've seen too much."

I open my mouth to argue, but Azarius steps in. "Come on, Elio. I'm sure she won't go back to the human world screaming from the rooftops about monsters. Besides, we saved her life. She owes us."

He's not wrong. I'm indebted to these men—monsters. If that means harboring a huge secret—like the existence of a monster world—it's the least I can do. Besides, I'm liable to get committed to a psych ward if I go home babbling about an invisible world of monster men.

Not something I'm eager to add to my to-do list.

"I promise," I say, taking a step toward Elio and staring into his dark eyes. "I won't breathe a word to anyone. Just send me home, and we can all pretend this didn't happen."

For a second, I think he might believe me and send me home, and hope flickers to life in my chest. Unfortunately, it's quickly snuffed out when he shakes his head again.

"I'm sorry, but I can't," he says, looking away as his jaw tenses. "If we tell you, they'll kill us. Remember? I'm not willing to die for you."

"Then what am I going to do?" I look frantically between the two of them. "I can't stay here, and I can't go home."

Elio opens his mouth, but Azarius cuts him off. "You'll come with us. We'll take you to Rafe—he'll know what to do."

"Az." Elio groans and rubs his temple. "I don't think that's a good idea."

Azarius shrugs and his tail whips around to point in my direction. "If the plan was to leave her here, why did we save her? We have to do something fast.

She smells like blood, and I wouldn't be surprised if another Malev has already picked up the scent."

"Malev?" I ask.

Elio impatiently points to the red carcass several feet away from us. "A Malevolent—the result of monsters breeding with demons. They have no empathy and kill without remorse. One we can handle, but if there are more, we'll be in trouble."

Azarius crosses his arms over his pale, sculpted chest as he waits for an answer, and I feel myself swaying again. I escaped death once by the skin of my teeth, but if they leave me here, I'm a sitting duck.

"Fine," Elio finally sighs, and the tightness in my chest lessens. "But I can't promise Rafe won't kill her himself."

"Excuse me?" Planting my hands on my hips, I furrow my brow in their direction. "Who says I'm going to go with you?"

"We do," Azarius says.

"Like hell. I want to go home," I snap. Anger flares in my chest, and the darkness surrounding my vision thickens. I stagger, and Azarius grabs my shoulder to keep me upright.

"Devyn," he says, and his voice sounds distant. "Are you alright?"

"I—" My grip on consciousness is slipping.

"She's lost a lot of blood," Elio says, pointing to my injured arm.

I follow his line of sight to my arm, turning it over to get a better look at my injury, only to see a trail of blood dancing down my fingertips before dripping to the blackened soil on the ground. The adrenaline coursing through my veins had masked the pain, but as I look now, my skin burns white hot, making me wince.

"It's not that bad," I say, but even as the words leave my lips, I know it's a lie. Seeing the rips in my skin makes me weak, and my vision fades to black.

Azarius' voice calling my name is the last thing I hear before I go under.

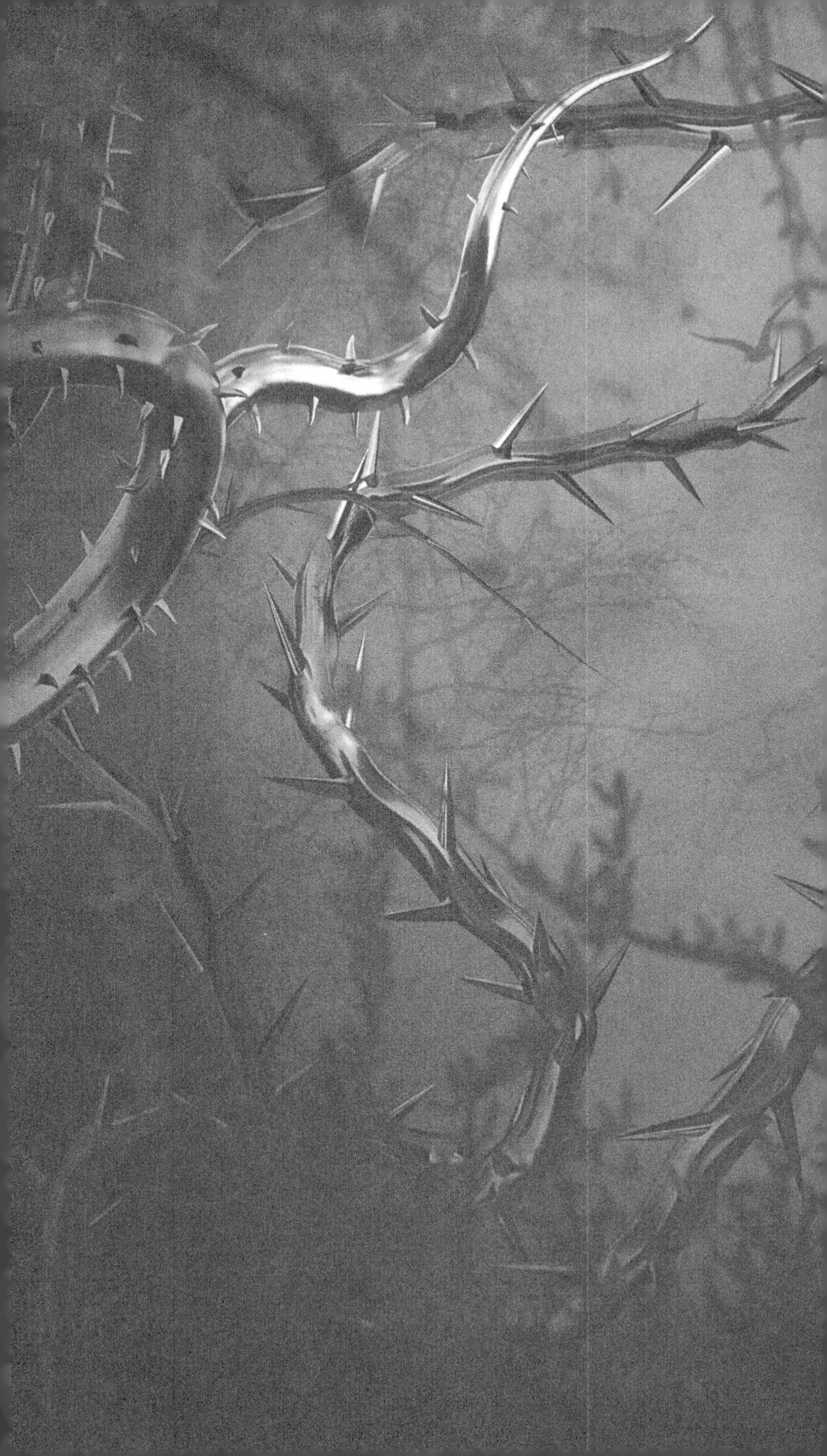

4

AZARIUS

I haven't decided yet if Devyn is brave or stupid, but I know two things for certain.

One, even unconscious in my arms and covered in dirt and blood, the sight of her is enough to make my cock twitch with need. If I keep stealing glances at her, I'm going to be walking back to Rafe's with a raging hard-on, so I keep my gaze focused ahead as much as possible.

Two, the girl has a death wish and an insane amount of luck.

Stepping through the portal separating the monster and human realms could have—and should have—killed her. The fact that she's still breathing is a miracle, and one I'm having a hard time wrapping my brain around. Then, she picked a fight with a Malevolent, one of the nastiest monsters this world has to offer.

If Elio and I had been any farther away, we

wouldn't have heard her screams. I wouldn't have been able to save her.

The harshness of that reality prickles across my skin, and I shake the thought away. I try to tell myself it's just because she's hot as hell, that her dying would be a waste of beauty, but that's not it. There's something mesmerizing about her.

No. Magnetizing.

An invisible cord draws me to her, and the harder I resist, the stronger it pulls.

It's intriguing and extremely annoying.

I shouldn't care if she lives or dies. I shouldn't be worried about whether Rafe will kill her or let her go. But as we approach his mansion, which is hidden in a secluded area of the twisted woods, fear creeps up my back, and I find it harder to breathe. I cradle her body closer to mine unintentionally.

My hopes aren't high.

Rafe's a dick, known for being cruel and callous, but that's what makes him such a threat. To rule the monsters, you have to be the biggest and baddest of them all.

"You know he'll probably kill her anyway," Elio says grimly, making my jaw tense.

He walks a few feet to my right, weaving through the trees as stealthily as he can with his wings, but he isn't very graceful. The trek is normally much easier for me, but with Devyn in my arms, I move with extra caution. The closer we get to the mansion, the closer the trees grow together, making it difficult to navigate. I turn sideways to maneuver between two trunks, careful to avoid hitting Devyn's feet.

"Maybe not," I say through clenched teeth.

There's hardly enough room for us to squeeze through the foliage, so I know we're close. Considering most of the Malevs are huge, lurking fuckers, they don't bother trekking this far into the woods. In all my years working for Rafe, I've never seen a Malev make it to the mansion.

It's possible they're too dumb to figure out where he lives, but my guess is it's not worth the hassle. They'd have to bring an army to take Rafe down, and most Malevs are solitary creatures. They wind up eating one another if they're stuck together for too long.

We finally emerge into the clearing, where the mansion sits in a pool of green light cast from the moon overhead. It's one of the largest buildings for hundreds of miles, aside from a castle past the mountains in the West, and it's by far the most ornate. Rafe gets off on dramatic architecture.

Tall, slate-gray walls engraved with intricate details stretch up the length of its three stories to a spiked black roof, and dark foliage creeps its way up the sides, stopping just below the first set of windows. Black marble steps lead to the entryway—a large set of wooden doors outlined in gleaming black metal.

"If he lets her live, then what?" Elio's sharp voice grips my attention, and I glance in his direction. "Are you just going to send her home? What if she doesn't survive the portal this time?"

His questions grate on my nerves, but I know he's right. I haven't thought about what I'll do if Rafe spares her life. The only thing I can think about right now is keeping her alive.

Elio helped me tie a strip of fabric around her arm to staunch the bleeding, but she's lost a considerable amount of blood. Her breaths are shallow, but at least she's breathing.

I just need her to hang on a little longer so I can properly tend to her wounds.

"I'll figure it out," I say, brushing him off.

Hopefully.

"Take her in through the back," Elio says, dropping his voice. "I doubt Rafe will appreciate us tracking dirt and blood through the foyer."

He's not wrong. We should at least get cleaned up before presenting him with our half-dead human. Increase our odds as much as possible.

"Come on, before he figures out we're back." I turn to follow the tree line, Elio on my heels.

At the back of the mansion, there's a hidden door, mostly obscured by twisted vines, originally built as an emergency escape. Nowadays, the employees—monsters like Elio and me who've signed part, or all, of our lives away to Rafe in exchange for money, power, and protection—use it to get in and out of the mansion.

"Where are you taking her?" Elio wrenches the door open and stands aside to let me in.

"My room. Where the fuck else can I put her?" I step inside and lead the way down the hall, thankful the plush rug running the length of the floor muffles my footsteps.

He doesn't say anything else, so I assume he doesn't have a better idea. Go figure.

My room is on the second floor, down the hall from Elio's. We climb the stairs as quietly as possible, even though there's very little chance of running into Rafe in this half of the mansion. He's many things, but sociable isn't one of them.

I pause outside my room and wait impatiently while Elio skirts around me to open the door before I carry Devyn over the threshold. Unlike the rest of the mansion, which is a blend of sleek blacks, grays, and reds, my room is adorned in navy blue and silver. Nearly everything, from the rich blue comforter draped over the bed to the abstract artwork on the walls, came from Earth—all snuck through the portal a little at a time over the years.

Devyn moans softly as I lay her on the bed, and my eyes dart to her face, searching for any sign of consciousness.

Nothing.

Undeterred, I set to work unbandaging her arm. The wound needs to be cleaned and re-dressed if she has any chance of avoiding infection. I have no idea how her human immune system will react to the filth in this realm, and I'm starting to second-guess saving her. What if all I did was prolong the inevitable? What if I doomed her to a death worse than being mauled by a Malev?

I shake the taunting thoughts from my mind.

"I'm going to check Xia's room for clothes," Elio says from the doorway.

"Check for any first-aid supplies, too," I suggest, even though I know it's a long shot. Monsters hardly need medical supplies, considering how fast we heal, so it's not likely anyone has anything stashed in their room. Still, I plead silently with any deity listening that I'm wrong.

He disappears as I strip the fabric away from Devyn's arm. It's stuck to her skin with dried blood, and I wince as I tug it away, worried I'm hurting her somehow. The reality of the situation crashes onto my shoulders, and I realize with a shaky breath just how fragile she is.

Fragile.

Vulnerable.

Beautiful.

You fucking creep, she's unconscious. Stop staring.

What the hell is wrong with me?

I tear my eyes away from her porcelain face and shake my head sternly, shifting my attention to her injury.

The scratch isn't as deep as I originally thought, which is surprising, considering how much blood she lost. Now that it's crusted over, it doesn't look life-threatening, but I could be fooling myself with optimism.

"Hang in there," I mutter.

Elio returns several minutes later with a stack of folded clothes in one hand and a small white box in the other. The corners of his mouth are downturned as his gaze falls to Devyn's body, and he quickly looks away.

"Xia's clothes are going to swallow her," he says, handing me the garments.

Most of the women who visit Rafe's mansion come as escorts or personal conquests, but Xia is a force to be reckoned with.

She's fucking terrifying.

I don't know her history with Rafe, nor do I want to. All I know is he hired her shortly before Elio and I came to work for him, and I avoid her when I can. Six feet of pure muscle and a poisonous personality—she would probably kill us both if she knew we'd gone through her things.

Thankfully, she spends most of her time in the human world.

"It's only temporary," I say.

He hands me the box, his frown deepening. "All I found was frex oil and some gauze. I don't know how she'll react to the oil, though."

I nod numbly. Using frex oil or any of our other remedies could end up causing more harm than good at this point, but a weight in my gut tells me it's worth trying. If she can survive portal travel, which up until now was impossible for humans, she can hopefully handle frex oil.

"I'll try a little to be on the safe side." I set the clothes and box aside. "What do you think the chances are of sneaking one of your warlock friends in to heal her?"

Elio laughs forcefully and shakes his head. "You've lost your fucking mind, Az."

Our eyes lock and my jaw hardens. "I'm serious."

"No, you're fucking nuts is what you are." He shakes his head again. "You're going out of your way, risking pissing Rafe off, for what? To save a fucking human?"

"There's no way she's just a human, Elio, and I think you know that." I point to Devyn for emphasis. "There's nothing wrong with the portal. There wasn't a mistake. I think she has some monster blood in her. I just have to prove it."

Typically, Elio and I are thick as thieves. We've been friends for so long, he's practically a brother to me—much more so than my ten biological siblings, anyway. So, when he presses his lips into a line and slowly shakes his head, I'm genuinely surprised.

"Az, you know I'm normally in your corner," he says, dropping his gaze to the floor. "But this is a bit much. You're a monster, for fuck's sake, not a bleeding heart destined to save the world."

Silence creeps through the room, and a flicker of anger springs to life in my chest. Elio's reluctance to help irritates me, and even though I'd fight a Malev army for him, I just want to punch him. He can be so fucking dense sometimes.

"Thanks for your help," I snap, desperately trying to diffuse the tension. Fighting isn't going to get us anywhere or help Devyn. My energy is best spent focusing on her right now. "Let me know if you change your mind."

We stare each other down for a long moment before Elio's shoulders sag, and he turns on his heel, heading into the hallway. He closes the door behind him, leaving me alone with Devyn and my thoughts, and a sliver of doubt creeps through my mind.

Maybe he's right, and I'm the one being dense. After all, I'm risking a lot trying to save a girl I barely know, who might end up dead anyway.

Goddamn it.

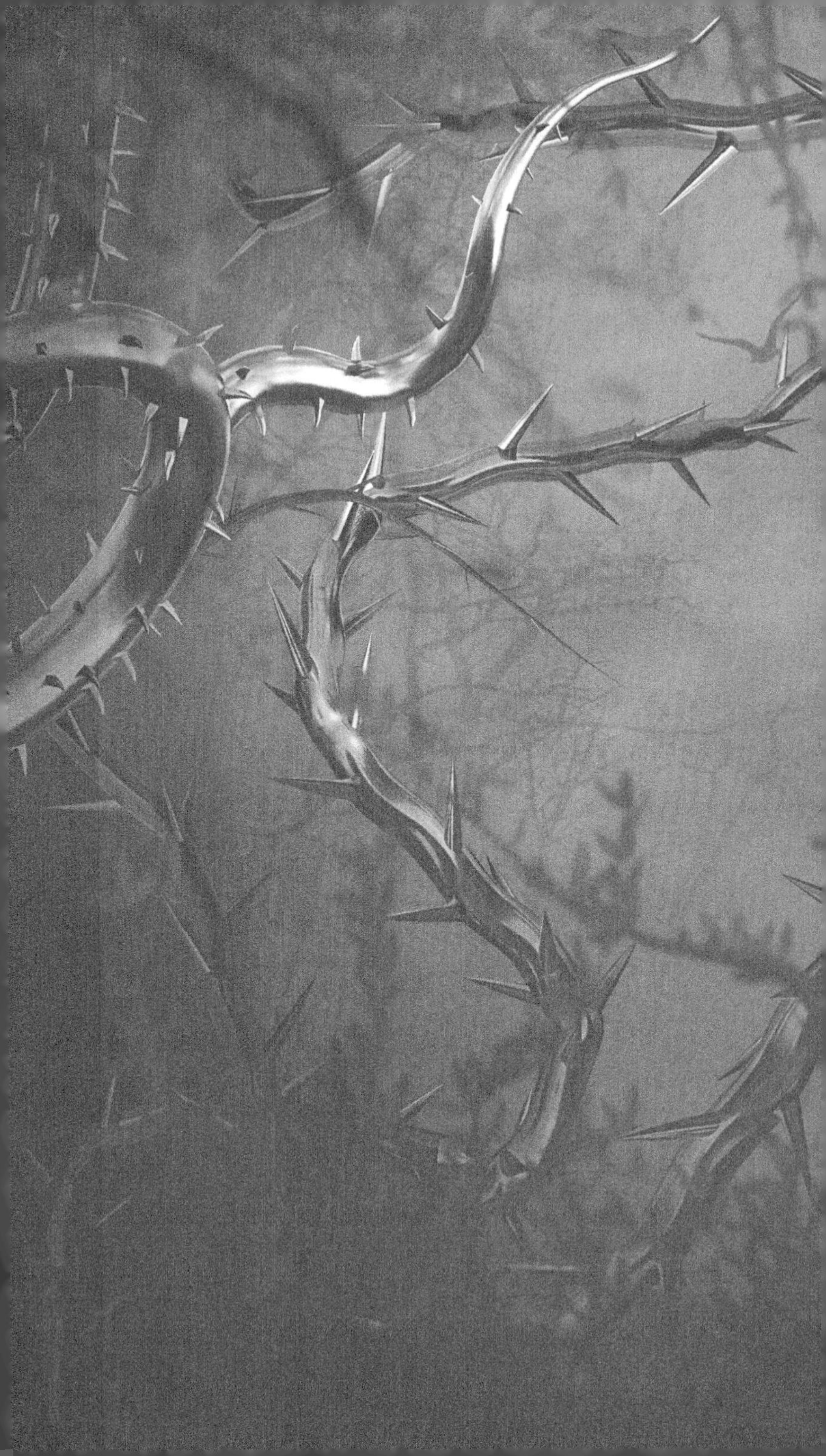

5
DEVYN

I don't remember falling asleep, but despite trying to claw my way to consciousness, exhaustion continually drags me under. My limbs each weigh what feels like a hundred pounds, and moving is nearly impossible, but I can wiggle my fingers across my comforter.

I don't remember it ever being so soft.

Fevered images haunt my thoughts as I try to fight sleep, and I can't distinguish between dreams and memories. Maybe they're all dreams, and Azarius and Elio were merely my imagination.

Their handsome faces fade in and out of view. A giant red monster chases me, and I move my legs as fast as I can, but it doesn't seem to get me anywhere. Cara is hanging up missing person signs on every storefront in Atlanta, and they all have my face on them.

After what feels like a lifetime of dreams, I wake in a cold sweat and pry my eyes open painfully. I expect to find myself staring up at the popcorn ceiling of my bedroom, but instead, I'm greeted by a sleek black ceiling with a silver chandelier, and my heart plummets.

Where am I?

I try to sit up, but my limbs are restrained.

No, not restrained. Drained of any strength, and I'm unable to move.

Fucking fantastic.

A door to my left swings open, sending my heart crashing against my ribs, and I look over to see Azarius step inside. The last time I saw him, he was butt naked and covered in blood, but now, he's dressed in black pants and a loose-fitting T-shirt. The black markings on his skin dance up his arms and disappear beneath his sleeves, and his chalk-white tail curls behind him.

Our eyes meet, and the corner of his mouth flicks upward.

How is it possible for a monster to be so attractive?

"You're alive," he says, sounding mildly surprised.

"Yep." My throat is dry, and my voice comes out in a croak. "Barely. Where am I?"

His smirk widens into a grin. "We're at Rafe's place, and you're in my bed." He waits a beat before asking, "Did you know you talk in your sleep?"

My eyes widen as heat singes my cheeks. Considering he and Elio were featured in my dreams, it's probably best not to ask what was said. I can't be embarrassed if I remain blissfully unaware.

"How long was I out?" I ask, eager to change the subject. If they had time to bring me here, it must have been at least an hour or two.

Az cocks his head to the side. "I'd say sixteen hours or so."

"S-sixteen?" I look down at my body frantically, checking how severe my injuries are, and even though the comforter is pulled up to my armpits, I instantly realize I'm naked. My blood boils. "Where the fuck are my clothes?"

Azarius steps closer and drops his voice. "The smell of your human blood was getting to be a bit much, so we burned them."

"You what?" I glare at him in disbelief. If he comes any closer, I'll muster every ounce of strength I have to slap him.

"Don't worry, Devyn, we're not going to make you prance around naked. We have clothes for you to wear," he says, crossing his arms over his chest. "When you're feeling up to it, you can bathe and get dressed."

"I feel fine," I assure him as I throw back the blanket. The cool air prickles my skin, making my nipples hard, but I push away my embarrassment. After all, they had to see me naked to get my clothes off. What's the point in worrying now?

When I attempt to sit up, my head swims, and I blow out a frustrated breath. Why am I so weak? I know the portal and being attacked were draining, but I can barely function. In a flash, Azarius is there, gently helping me to sit, guiding my legs off the side of the bed.

"I don't need your help," I grumble.

He chuckles softly. "Sure you don't. Here, eat this."

He pulls a wadded-up paper towel from his pocket, and when he unfolds it, there is a lumpy brown sphere sitting in the palm of his hand. I poke at it and grimace when the surface gives under my touch.

"It's squishy." I scrunch up my nose. "What is that?"

"It's kind of like a fruit," he explains, offering it to me. "It should make you feel better."

I take it reluctantly and roll it between my fingers. "Should?"

He nods. "Eat first, then I'll explain."

With a groan, I roll my eyes and sink my teeth into the fruit, more eager for an explanation than any relief this squishy morsel might offer. It's not the worst thing I've ever tasted—somewhere between a Fruit Roll-Up and a gym sock—but I chew quickly and swallow as fast as possible.

"Alright," I say, sticking my tongue out at him. "Now tell me."

"That was a frex fruit," he says, offering a hand to help me stand. "Pretty rare in this part of the realm, but Rafe has a small plant for emergencies. They have strong healing properties for monsters but they're rumored to be poisonous for humans."

"Poisonous?" I jerk my hand out of his and

stumble back onto the bed. "Are you trying to kill me? I told you I'm human. Just a human."

"I don't think you are," he says, offering me his hand again. "You survived the portal trip, and you are healing faster than any human could. Look at your arm."

Reluctantly, I tear my gaze away from his and observe my injury. Two strips of fresh pink skin run the length of my forearm—they're all that remain of the wound from the red monster. An injury like that would normally take weeks to recuperate from, but here it is, only sixteen hours later, and my arm is almost healed completely.

I run my fingertips along the lines to test them. No pain, barely any tenderness.

"I don't understand." The words come out in a whisper.

"Monsters heal quickly in this realm. I don't know what you are, but there's something in your blood that belongs here."

A knock at the door makes me jump, and I half-heartedly attempt to cover my chest before Elio slips into the room. His eyes lock on me, and heat gathers in my cheeks again.

"Oh," he says, his gaze tracing my exposed skin. "Sorry if I'm interrupting."

Az steps between us, blocking me from Elio's sight. "Not interrupting. Devyn was just about to take a shower."

"Right. Rafe expects us downstairs in an hour to deal with this."

By this, I'm assuming he means me.

Azarius nods once. "Thanks."

After lingering in the doorway for another second, Elio turns and disappears, tugging the door closed behind him. Az turns to face me, his expression harder than it was moments ago, and he jerks his head toward a gaping doorway in the corner.

"We'd better hurry," he says. "Rafe doesn't like to be kept waiting."

I can feel the energy from the frex fruit coursing through my veins, replacing the weakness that'd been swallowing me since I woke up. I feel almost normal, except for a sinking feeling in my stomach at the thought of meeting Rafe, plus the tingling of an existential crisis plaguing my brain. If Az is right and I am part monster, what does that mean for me?

I don't have much time to consider which one of my parents might be at fault before I'm stumbling into the bathroom, and Azarius is showing me how to work the shower knobs. Surprisingly, it's a lot like showers back home, only with a few more levers and knobs for soaps and water functions.

"Whatever you do, don't press this one," he says, pointing to a black button under the shower head. "Unless you want to feel like you've been run through a cheese grater."

I shake my head. "No, thanks."

Even though I want nothing more than to relax under the spray of hot water until I melt to the floor, I hurriedly scrub my body and step out onto the plush bath rug. If Rafe is as bad as Azarius and Elio make him out to be, I don't want to piss him off by being late.

There's a neatly folded stack of clothes waiting for me on the end of the marble counter, but one look at them tells me they're far from my size. I hold the pants up to my waist and groan when the ends roll past my feet.

I wish I had my damn jeans.

Whoever they stole these from is huge. I look like a child wearing her mother's clothes when I'm finally dressed, and I have to roll the pants several times so I can walk without tripping. The shirt is a lost cause, and the collar sags between my breasts.

What an unattractive way to meet Rafe. Maybe he'll spare my life due to the sheer humor I'll bring.

One can hope.

"Devyn." Azarius's voice sounds outside the bathroom door. "Are you decent?"

I chuckle, but it quickly escalates to a full-on belly laugh. "Considering you've seen every part of me but my asshole, I think it's a little late for manners."

I wrench the door open and find him staring down at me, his sapphire eyes raking over my face, and uneasiness washes over me. I suddenly feel small, and the reality of how easy it would be for him to overpower me slaps me in the face.

I can't say I'd stop him.

Knowing the sheer power he can conjure at any moment—enough to single-handedly take down a Malev—while conducting himself like a gentleman makes me weak in the knees.

It would also make my panties wet, if I were wearing any.

"Who says I haven't seen your asshole already?" He cocks a mischievous brow.

I shrug. "You didn't ask about my tattoo, so I was assuming you haven't."

He gapes, a curious glint in his eye, but I shove past him with a laugh.

"What's your tattoo of?" he asks as he follows behind me.

I don't actually have one, but stringing him along is fun, especially because he's so gullible.

"If you're lucky, you'll find out." I flash him a wink and gesture toward the door. "Don't we have somewhere to be?"

For a moment, Az is speechless, but he finally regains his wits and heads for the door, leading us into a long, darkly decorated hallway. Everything but the red rug running the length of the hall is black, and dim lanterns hang at even intervals on the walls. I feel like I've stepped into a gothic fairy tale.

"It's beautiful, huh?" Az whispers at my side.

"It's like a castle. Is the whole place this elaborate?"

I look over in time to see him nod, but his eyes stay transfixed ahead. "You haven't seen anything yet. The main floor is way better."

He pauses outside a sleek black door and raps his knuckles against the wood. A few moments later, it pops open, and Elio sticks his head out.

"You coming?" Azarius asks.

He nods, and his eyes find their way over to mine. Dressed in a white shirt and navy pants, he looks stunning, and after watching him for a moment, I realize something looks different.

"Where are your wings?" I ask, staring over his shoulders.

I distinctly remember enormous wings folded behind him, but they're nowhere to be found.

"They make wearing clothes difficult," he says, tugging on the hem of his shirt. "If you'd prefer, I can go naked."

My cheeks flame.

Damn it.

"That's not what I said." I shake my head. "But I won't complain either way."

He grins. "I can use them when I need them, and I put them away when I don't."

Of course. Wings that appear and disappear whenever he wants. That makes perfect sense. About as much sense as any of the rest of this monster realm.

We fall into step together, making our way to the end of the hallway, where the mouth of a staircase awaits us. Azarius takes the lead, the wood creaking under his weight as he goes, and I follow behind, while Elio brings up the rear.

The staircase ends in a wide foyer with a black floor so polished, I can see our reflections, like a giant demonic mirror. Ornate columns run up the walls to the high ceiling, separated by slate-gray walls. A chandelier made of skulls—both with and without horns—

dangles from the ceiling, glimmering like a beacon of imminent doom.

My throat tightens at the sight. It hits me that I'm about to meet the nastiest monster I've faced yet—and that Malev was pretty scary.

I don't think I'm ready for whatever Rafe is.

"Let me do the talking," Elio says as we make our way across the foyer. Silence is wrapped so tightly around us, every footstep, movement, and breath feels offensive.

Can Rafe hear us? Is he watching us?

A chill wiggles up my spine at the thought, and I clamp my mouth shut.

"You?" Az scoffs. "You didn't want to bring her here in the first place."

I glance in Elio's direction—he isn't paying me any attention—and he shrugs. "True, but you're practically famous for letting your mouth get you in trouble. Remember the deal with Pearson?"

Azarius huffs. "Yes, but that wasn't—"

"And last week, when we met with Anderson," Elio continues.

"That's not fair. I was just trying to—"

"And the time before that with Ross? Face it, Az. You suck at negotiating."

We're headed for a set of double doors at the end of the foyer. They're taller and wider than any doors I've seen before, and they almost blend in with the slate-gray wall, save for a pair of huge silver handles.

My heart is racing in my chest, blood pounding in my ears. I don't have to be told Rafe waits on the other side of those doors. It's almost like I can sense his sinister power seeping through the wood, but I know the feeling is just in my head.

Isn't it?

At this point, I wouldn't be surprised if the monster in me was calling to him. I'm not entirely sure it isn't.

"Az," I say, my voice hardly more than a whisper. "Maybe we should trust Elio on this one."

They stop short and turn to stare at me, which only makes my heart beat harder. Azarius narrows his eyes in my direction and opens his mouth to argue, but he snaps it closed again.

Elio's obviously the best shot we've got at convincing Rafe to let me live. We all know it.

"Fine," Az snaps and crosses his arms over his broad chest.

I take a step forward and catch Elio's gaze, pointing a finger sternly at his chest. "If you get me killed, I'm kicking your ass."

The corners of his lips curl into a lopsided smile.

"Of course." He reaches for one of the door handles, his copper-colored skin contrasting starkly against the metal. "Shall we?"

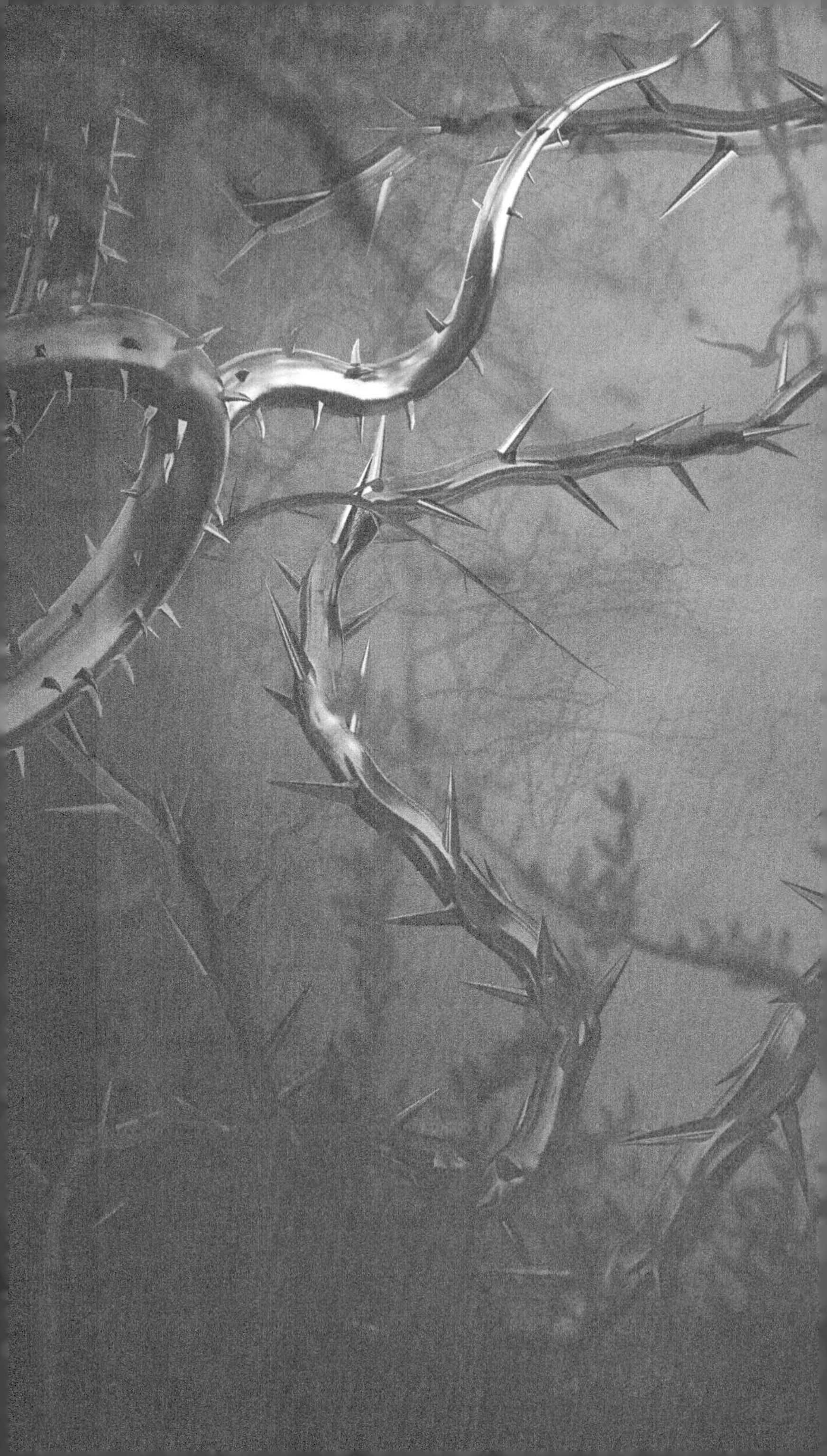

6
DEVYN

Elio tugs on the door, and it swings open slowly, every drawn-out second sending anxious adrenaline pumping through my veins. I've forgotten about my ridiculous outfit and the fact that Az and Elio have already seen me naked. I'm not thinking about how dumb it was for me to follow them through the portal, or how I was almost killed by a Malev. I'm not even thinking about how badly I want to survive so I can go home to the crazy streets of Atlanta and pay my rent on time.

The only thing I can focus on is treading lightly around Rafe, hoping he doesn't kill me.

I haven't come this far just to die at the hands of a man on a power trip.

How anticlimactic that would be.

Azarius steps inside first, and Elio tips his head toward the doorway, gesturing for me to follow. I swallow hard and fall in step behind him, careful to avoid his tail swaying in front of me.

The room we're in is about as large as the foyer, mostly occupied by furniture. An impressive dining table with six, high-backed chairs sits off to the right, made of dark wood and set with red and gold linens. To the left is a set of couches, positioned around a short, black coffee table. A wide fireplace crackles with warmth behind them, creating an inviting space.

At least, it would be inviting if I wasn't scared out of my fucking mind right now.

As my eyes skate across the room, soaking in the beautiful details, I see him…a dark, menacing figure who seems to materialize out of the black wall. For a moment, he's all shadows and smoke, and then he's standing before us in the middle of the room.

I watch him for several minutes before I realize I'm gawking and shift my gaze away. Even though he's the size of a man, he somehow fills every corner of the room with his presence.

The skin that's not hidden beneath his pressed black suit is smoky gray and covered in black tattoos, but they're not like Azarius', which appear more natural and tribal. No, they're hand drawn and perfectly spaced. There's no telling how many hours he spent under a tattoo gun to get them all done, and I can't help but wonder how far the tattoos go. Is his entire body riddled with detailed art?

Dark hair spills past his shoulders, and sharp horns curl around from the back of his head before turning skyward. His vibrant red eyes are locked on me, and I can tell by the look of disapproval on his face that he already hates me.

This isn't going to go well.

The door behind us closes with deafening finality, and we're swallowed in silence again.

For a moment, no one moves.

No one speaks.

Hell, I can barely breathe.

I don't know what to do or say, so I keep my mouth shut. Besides, we agreed to let Elio talk—which I'm all for. Rafe is a menacing-looking bastard. The less interaction I have with him, the better.

He takes two steps forward, and Elio and Azarius tense beside me. He might be their boss, but something tells me they're no safer here than I am. Fear is one hell of a weapon, and Rafe wields it well.

"When you told me you brought someone to the mansion," he says, his deep voice pounding against my eardrums, "you failed to mention she's a human."

"Yes, that piece of information might have been left out, but we wanted to make sure you had all the information available before passing judgment," Elio explains with a curt nod. "We have reason to believe this human isn't completely human."

Rafe's eyes narrow as he watches me. I don't think he's looked anywhere else since I stepped into the room. I take a sharp breath. The weight of his gaze is almost unbearable, and I desperately want to be anywhere but here.

"She reeks of human blood," Rafe says, disgust prevalent in his voice. Icy fear shoots through me. "Why would you bring her through the portal?"

"We didn't." Elio glares in my direction.

Rafe's mouth shifts, and I take a half step behind Azarius. "I'm supposed to believe she just appeared in our realm?"

"Of course not." Elio shakes his head. "She... she followed us, sir."

For a moment, all I can hear is the crackle of the fireplace and the blood throbbing steadily in my ears. Rafe doesn't seem impressed.

"You were careless," he finally says, and my stomach turns.

This isn't going well at all.

"We were as careful as ever," Elio retorts. "We did everything exactly the same."

"Except you didn't." The flatness of Rafe's voice tells me he's unamused. "This time, you brought a human back."

That wasn't their fault. It was my insatiable curiosity that landed me here—it had nothing to do with Azarius or Elio.

I can't let them take the fall for me. They don't deserve that.

They saved my life. The least I can do is defend them.

Before I know it, I'm interrupting Elio—whose explanation probably would have been much more eloquent than mine. "They've never met a human quite like me... uh... Mr. Rafe, sir."

Smooth.

Every eye in the room is on me, and Azarius takes a step to the right to give me the floor. Dammit. It might have been better if he told me to shut the hell up.

Too late for that.

"I followed them," I explain, unable to cut off the word vomit spilling from my mouth. While I'm at it, I might as well throw in some details for good measure. "They didn't make it easy, but I've always been obnoxiously curious, and I wondered what they were up to. Then, when I saw the portal, it kind of called to me."

"What do you mean, called to you?" Azarius asks, his eyes trained on mine.

"It kind of drew me in," I explain, thinking back to the alley in Atlanta. It feels like forever ago. "Like there was an invisible string pulling me from the other side."

"Interesting," Rafe says, rubbing one hand on his chin. "You survived."

I open my mouth to say something sarcastic, but Azarius' challenging look makes me snap my lips together. I'd better not push it—I might wind up making things worse.

"Yes. She had some injuries, so we brought her here to tend to them," Elio says.

"And what exactly do you want me to do?" Rafe asks, looking between Elio and Azarius.

They both hesitate. Seriously, they couldn't have planned out what they were going to say? They had sixteen hours to work on this shit.

"We would like to send her back to the human realm," Azarius answers.

For the first time, I look at Rafe eagerly, desperate

for his approval. My entire future hangs in the balance, dependent on his next words.

I hold my breath. I count the seconds it takes him to answer.

"We can't do that."

His words resonate in my head like a gong, and I open my mouth to challenge him, but Azarius beats me to it. "Why not?"

"She has seen too much." Rafe glances briefly at Azarius. "She is nothing but a liability."

"So, she has to stay here?" Azarius asks, shifting his weight back and forth. He's antsy, but I'm not sure why until Rafe replies.

"You know that's not possible."

"Then what do you suggest we do?" Elio looks back at me, his eyes full of worry.

"She's your problem. Dispose of her."

I can hardly believe the words as they leave his mouth, and I feel like the walls are closing in on me. His words are my official death sentence, and I'm not sure there's anything I can do to change his mind. Beg? Plead? I don't have my next move planned, and it seems like Elio and Azarius are in just as much disbelief as I am. No one seems quite sure what to say.

"Now, if that's everything you needed, you're excused," Rafe says, gesturing toward the door with a sweep of his hand.

Elio shifts toward the door, but Azarius doesn't move. He's staring Rafe down, his hands balled into fists, and I wonder for a moment what's going through his mind.

Luckily for my curiosity, it doesn't take him long to speak up.

"With all due respect, sir, I can't do that," Azarius grits out.

Rafe straightens. His form seems to grow in height, towering over the rest of us and choking the air out of the room, but it could also be my imagination. My mind is running rampant.

"Excuse me?" Rafe's voice is a threat that makes my throat close up.

"I'm claiming her as my mate," Azarius says, and despite his crystal-clear words, they hit my ears in a jumbled mess.

Did he just say mate?

Rafe chuckles once and shakes his head in disbelief. "The rules of monsters do not apply to humans, Azarius. You know this. Now, please, stop wasting our time."

I expect Az to step down or retract his statement, but he doesn't. He's not backing down—which might be one of the sexiest things I've seen him do yet—and he turns to look at me.

"She might be a human, but she has monster blood in her veins. She survived the portal trip, and she was healed by the frex fruit. I don't know her family lineage, but I am confident enough to claim her as my own."

Rafe's red eyes narrow on his employee. "And if you're wrong?"

"I'm not."

The stare down that follows is absolutely terrifying. Rafe's power thrums through the room, and I swear the air is vibrating. If he wanted to, I have no doubt Rafe could kill us all easily. A brute display of power isn't needed to know how threatening Rafe is. I can tell by the way Elio and Azarius carry themselves.

I meet Elio's gaze and find his eyes wide with terror. So much for Azarius letting him take the lead.

It's Rafe who breaks the silence. "Fine. Claim her, then."

Again, no one moves, but the slight sag in Azarius' shoulders conveys his relief. Or defeat. His expression is impossible to read.

"Right now?"

A challenging smile appears on Rafe's face. "Yes. If those are your intentions, claim her, or stop wasting my fucking time."

Azarius turns on his heel and meets my gaze, his jaw slack, like he's going to say something, but I know what Rafe's implying without an explanation.

He expects Azarius to claim me.

As his mate.

In front of him.

I know it wasn't Az's intention, that he was just trying to save my life, but the thought of fucking him with onlookers isn't how I expected things to happen.

Dinner first, maybe, or at least a nice date.

But it looks like we're fast-forwarding through things a bit. He is definitely going to owe me after this.

He steps toward me, his eyes hooded with lust as he meets my gaze. Despite the situation, butterflies erupt in my stomach when he touches his hand to my cheek, and the room around us melts away. He leans in close, his lips brushing my ear.

"You can say no," he says, his voice a low growl. "But I'd prefer if you lived."

Well, good. At least we're both on the same page.

"It's okay." I reach for his hand, and a smile makes its way across my face when his fingers intertwine with mine. If a show for this creep is the only way I make it out of this room alive, so be it. We'll make it a damn good one. "I'm ready."

Az closes the distance between us, pressing his mouth against mine, and my eyes flutter closed. I push thoughts of Rafe and Elio watching out of my mind —worrying isn't going to help the situation—and focus on the task at hand, which is getting railed by Azarius and making it fucking convincing.

I can do this. It's not like I haven't been considering the idea since we met. I just didn't imagine it quite like this.

His hand skates around my waist, pulling me close to his muscular frame, and I can already feel his erection swelling between us. The press of it against my abdomen has my pussy throbbing—it's been way too long since I got laid—and judging by the thickness of his cock through the thin material of his pants, it's either going to be exciting or excruciating.

Maybe both.

"I'll be gentle," Azarius says between kisses as he

reaches for the hem of my shirt and pulls it off over my head in a swift motion.

My exposed skin tingles with goosebumps as Az's hand skates up my torso and grips one of my breasts, and he squeezes tenderly until a moan escapes my lips. I rake my fingernails up his back, making him shudder. He pulls me against him again and grinds his hips, his swollen cock rubbing against me, and my stomach cartwheels.

Normally, I wouldn't rush through the motions, reveling in every second of this foreplay, but we're on a time crunch. Rafe needs his proof, and we need to get out of here.

Maybe we can go through the motions again later, but much slower.

The thought spurs me on, and I slip my fingers beneath the waistband of my pants and nudge them over my hips so they drop to the floor, exposing every bit of my creamy white skin for them to see.

Azarius smiles against my lips, and my hands find their way to the waistband of his pants. I slip my fingertips beneath the material and brush against the head of his throbbing cock, precum trailing along my fingers.

Apparently, all men—monsters and humans—work the same way. Good to know.

"Get on your knees," he demands, sending my libido skyrocketing. Does he have to sound so sexy when he says it?

I wonder if he's always this commanding, or if this is part of his act for Rafe. If he's not acting, if he goes from gentleman to dominating at the flip of a switch, that only makes it hotter.

It should be illegal how turned on I am right now.

As I drop to my knees, I'm tempted to drag Azarius' pants down with me. I'm dying to see what his raging hard-on looks like unsheathed, but I resist the urge. I'm just as eager for him to order me around more.

My core is begging for it.

I stare up at Azarius as he guides his waistband down, exposing his thick, veiny cock, and I try to disguise my surprise at how big he is. At least it looks like a human dick—I'm in familiar territory. The last thing I want right now is to have to learn to navigate some exotic monster peen in front of an audience.

Like the rest of him, it's chalk white, with a single black marking winding its way up the shaft to the head. The base is nearly as thick as my wrist, curving upward slightly as it stands at attention. My fingers are itching to take hold of it, but I wait impatiently for instructions.

As though reading my mind, Azarius nods. "Put me in your mouth."

My pussy throbs at his words, and I reach out and take his shaft in my hand, hardly surprised when my fingers can't wrap all the way around. A mixture of nerves and excitement wells inside me as I slip the tip into my mouth and suck gently. A smile teases my lips when Azarius sucks in a sharp breath through his teeth.

A quick glance at the smug smile on Rafe's face tells me he's enjoying himself.

What a sick bastard.

I take more of Azarius' throbbing cock into my mouth, working my hand in unison with my lips, up and down the base of his shaft, until he's rocking his hips forward to slide deeper down my throat. His erratic breathing hits my ears, and I pick up the pace as he tangles one of his hands in my hair, knotting the strands around his fingers and tugging firmly.

An inferno swells to life between my thighs as I suck him hard and deep, and I nearly jump out of my skin when I feel a gentle caress on the inside of my thigh. I look up nervously and meet Azarius' eyes, which are hooded and dark, but he nods to urge me on as the touch moves higher, creeping dangerously close to my pussy, which is pulsing uncontrollably.

I run my tongue around the head of his cock, eliciting another moan, and half a second before I feel something tease the length of my labia, it registers that what I'm feeling is his tail.

He's about to fuck me with his tail.

A prickle of hesitation starts at the nape of my neck and rolls down my back. I'm not sure how I feel about being fucked by an appendage, but I don't have much time to contemplate before the tip of his tail slips inside me and slowly thrusts upward.

I moan, despite my mouth being full, and a wave of bizarre pleasure rushes through me. It's a curious feeling—the tail is flexible and gentle, but also hard enough to massage the most sensitive parts of me. It's thinner than his meaty dick, but still thick enough to be pleasurable. Honestly, I'm so turned on that all I want right now is for him to slam his tail into me until I come on it.

He doesn't disappoint.

He thrusts into me slow and deep, withdrawing just far enough to stroke my clit before plunging back inside. He settles on a steady rhythm that has me grinding my hips in response.

He tugs harder on my hair—not hard enough to hurt, but firm enough to make my pussy clench down. I work my mouth faster on his cock, taking in as much as I can without gagging and stroking the rest. His tail thrusts into me repeatedly, mimicking the pace of my mouth on his dick, and warmth pools in my center, swelling more with every passing second.

The fire between my thighs builds to a nearly unbearable peak until I'm bouncing on my knees to speed up his thrusts. I want more, need more, of him inside me. As though sensing my desperation, Azarius hooks his tail forward, and my orgasm smacks into me full force.

I moan as waves of euphoria tumble through me, racking my body with pleasure. I work my hand faster, eager for Azarius to find his release, and he does a few seconds later. He pants as he fills my mouth with cum, and I swallow it down as the high of my own orgasm dissipates. I release him and wipe my mouth on the back of my hand.

Azarius helps me to my feet, and the reality of what just happened has my cheeks flushing with embarrassment. I look nervously to Rafe, hoping for some sort of approval. He hasn't moved from his spot in front of us. Is he happy now? Will he let me live?

"Very well," he says, looking past me to Azarius.

"Very well?" The question flies out of my mouth before I have time to register it. "What the hell does that mean?"

Rafe's blood-red eyes slowly crawl back to me and lock with mine. His mouth hardens and his eyes narrow as he considers me.

I probably should have kept my fucking mouth shut. When will I learn?

"It means you live for now," Rafe says, his voice sharp as a knife. "Don't get comfortable. This is my house, and should I decide you've overstayed your welcome, I can change my mind."

What a dick.

As much as I want to tell him how much of an ass he is, I keep my mouth shut. Azarius bends to snatch my clothes off the floor and grabs me by the hand.

"We'll see ourselves out."

Then, he's dragging me butt naked toward the door.

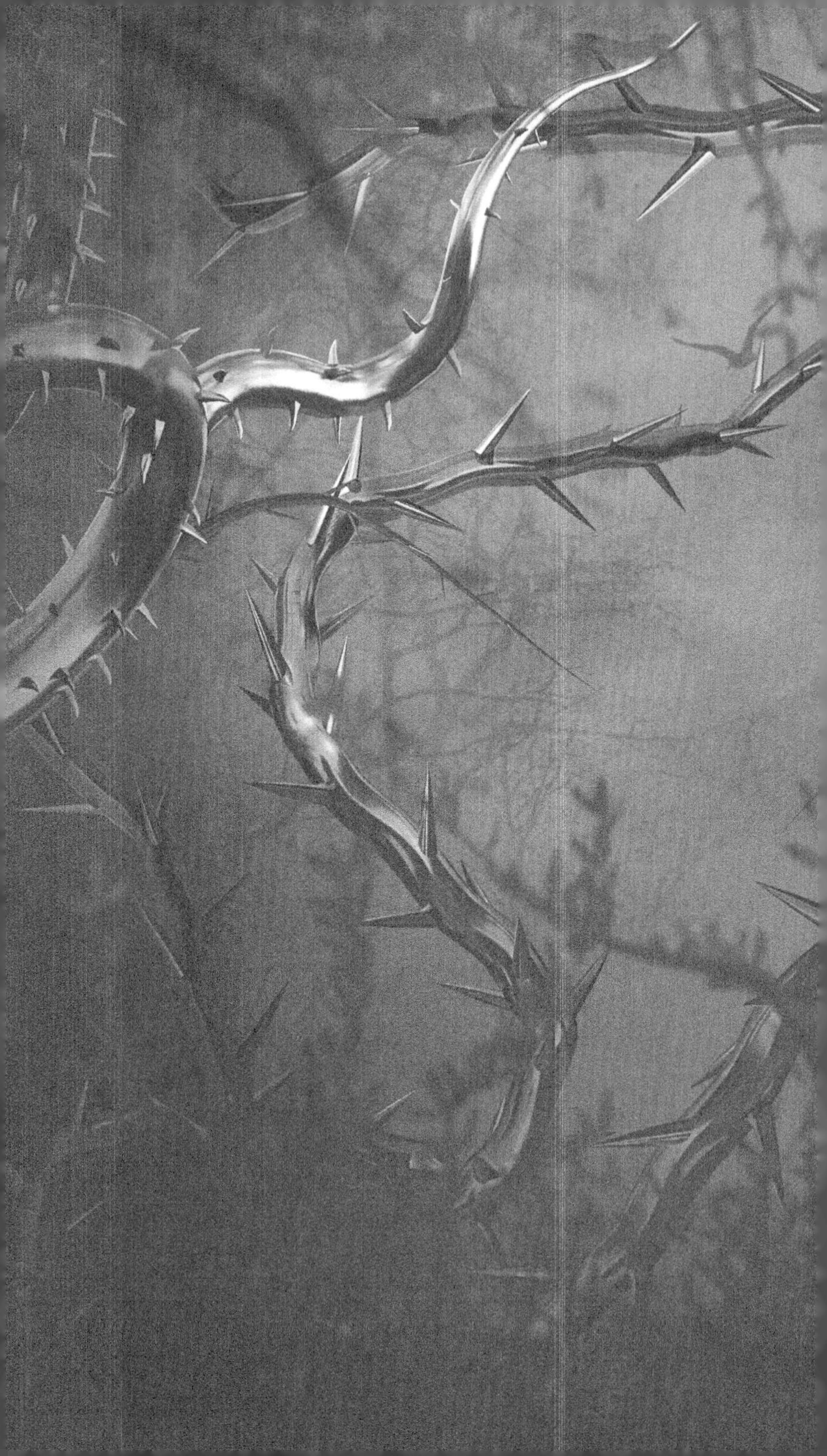

7
ELIO

I bow myself out of the room and the door snaps closed behind me.

That didn't go at all as planned, but at least Rafe was feeling generous. I half expected to be mopping blood off the marble, but Devyn is alive and Azarius' bull-headed ass claimed her as his mate.

Fucking great. Looks like she'll be around for a while.

It wouldn't be an issue, and I wouldn't even care, if the sight of her didn't stir such obnoxious feelings of desire in me. Of all the goddamn Uber drivers, we had to get a hot stalker.

Keeping my distance is useless, because now she'll be living in the mansion with us.

She'll be everywhere.

I almost wish Rafe would have killed her—then, the thought of sharing a mate with my best friend wouldn't be teasing my mind.

Fuck, I need to blow my load so I can get that

ridiculous idea out of my head. As if I'd ever share a mate with him.

There's no sign of Azarius or Devyn as I cross the foyer toward the stairs. They're probably fucking again somewhere, and I don't blame them. It's what I would have done.

The way she stared up at him as she took his cock in her mouth—I wish she was staring that way at me right now.

For fuck's sake, Elio. You're pining for a human.

I've stooped to a new low.

My feet steer me toward the second floor, toward my room, but I know what'll happen when I get back there. I'll be jerking my dick to the thought of Devyn's naked body and the memory of her dropping obediently to her knees.

Nope. Can't do that.

I reluctantly head toward the front door of the mansion. I need to take a walk. I need air, anything to distract me from my stupid thoughts.

The door swings inward, and a relief of cool air slaps me as I step outside. It's the middle of the night, the time when monsters are most active, and the fluorescent green moon shines overhead like a beacon, drowning the landscape in eerie light. The forest, a curtain of black surrounding the perimeter, stretches like a protective wall into the distance. Aside from a bit of grass and a tiny garden at one end of the mansion, nothing else occupies the area between the house and the trees.

There's nowhere to go, nowhere to hide. Into the trees it is.

I can't count the number of times I've found myself wandering these woods, letting my mind unwind between jobs. Living with Rafe is stressful enough when he isn't sending us out to make treaties with monsters. Dealing with him at all works up my nerves.

He's such an asshole.

Unfortunately, he's a rich and powerful asshole, so I don't plan on going anywhere. I've made my allegiance and sold my freedom for protection and employment. I have to ride it out and do as I'm told, even if that means watching my best friend fuck the girl I've been eyeballing.

My cock twitches in my pants, straining against the material, and I curse silently.

Distraction. I need a distraction.

The trees here don't grow like Earth's plants—these are much closer together, with roots that intertwine and strengthen one another just below the surface. They're as tough as their gnarly black exterior looks. I've had to cut down a few before, and it's damn near impossible.

I weave my way through the maze of foliage, noting how easy it is without my wings on display. While there are advantages to having them tucked away, like navigating the tight avenues between these trees, I never feel quite whole without them in my monster form. It always feels like something is missing, like something's bothering me just beyond reach, with no way to scratch the itch unless I unleash them. If I make it to a wider space, I'll take a moment to stretch them, but I don't have a particular destination in mind.

My only goal right now is to get the fuck away from the mansion.

To get Devyn off my mind.

There she is again—an itch that just won't go away. Every time I try to get her out of my head, she's there, making a mockery of my failed attempts to erase her from my mind. I warned Azarius after our last meeting that she would be nothing but trouble, that we should keep our distance.

Now look where we are.

Azarius is bonded to a human—or mostly human—female, and we can't send her back to Earth, just in case she decides to reveal our existence to the world.

The whole situation is fucked. Royally so.

With a huff, I keep walking farther from the mansion as I let my mind spin out of control. Everything's taking a toll on me. Devyn. Azarius. Rafe. My boner.

There's also the mystery of how Devyn is even in our realm, able to screw Az and troll my thoughts. She has some kind of monster blood in her, that's for sure. It's just that I have no idea what kind of monster blood she has, and that irks me.

Typically, we can sense other monsters, but in her case, the amount of monster blood running through her veins must be small. Minuscule. I didn't have an inkling about her in the car or after she arrived in our realm. If the Malev Azarius killed had sensed the monster in her, he might have spared her.

Maybe.

Then again, Malevs are dumb sons of bitches, so he may have lost control when he smelled her human blood. Since Malevs can't create portals and humans can't come here, their experience with them is very limited. They're always trying to figure out ways to cross the threshold, but thankfully for everyone they haven't figured it out. Hopefully they never do.

Their lust for human blood is so strong, they can smell it through the portals, which is why we don't portal anywhere near the mansion. We don't want to risk drawing any uninvited visitors into the woods. We have to be as careful as possible until Rafe secures control of the east end of the realm.

A few more contracts with powerful monsters should do it. Then, we'll be able to mobilize and force the Malevs back into the mountains. We've been working hard on these alliances for years, and we're finally seeing headway.

I can't wait.

I can't wait to be able to move freely without worrying about being attacked, to portal whenever and wherever we want, to exist without constantly covering our tracks or checking over our shoulders.

It feels like some sort of dream, even though it was that way once upon a time.

Back when I was just getting my bearings and figuring out where I belonged in Orlyitha, the realm that monsters and Malevolent demons share, we didn't have to worry about them. They mainly stayed hidden, like wild animals in the human world. They minded their business, and the regular monsters like me—the ones without demon blood—minded theirs.

What happened to draw the Malevs out of the mountains, made them hunt us down, I don't know, but the only way to fix the problem is to fight back.

I pause by a particularly fat tree trunk and lean against it, letting my thoughts flow freely. My mind is racing, and my cock is still aching for some kind of release.

The walk hasn't helped, nor have the distractions.

I groan, knowing there's only one thing that'll alleviate my discomfort and get my head right.

I just wish Devyn was here to handle it for me.

Reluctantly, I rest my head back against the tree trunk and close my eyes, the thought of her standing before me overtaking my senses. I see her poised there, her clothes abandoned on the ground behind her, her delicious curves on full display. She's beautiful, and judging by the coy look in her eyes, she knows it.

Even though I've never seen her look at me that way, I know she's capable of it. The half-cocked smile. The curious tilt to one brow. I guarantee before everything is said and done, I'll have her looking at me that way in real life.

I run my tongue slowly over my lips as my eyes fall down her body. They pause on her perky breasts, which I unintentionally memorized as I watched her earlier, and I wish she was here so I could reach out and caress them. No such luck. It's just me, my painfully throbbing cock, and my hand for this round.

My eyes pop open, and I glance around cautiously, making sure I'm alone, even though I already know I am. No one ever ventures into these woods. No animals live here because the trees can't sustain life. It's just me and my phantom image of Devyn.

Reassured, I close my eyes again and slip my hand down the front of my pants as I focus on my dirty daydream. She steps toward me, hips swaying gracefully as she moves, and my eyes travel lower—down the smooth skin of her stomach, past her hips, to the hairless V between her thighs.

My mouth waters. I want nothing more than to taste her.

As much as I would love for her to get on her knees and suck my dick, I want to kneel before her, have her grind her pussy on my face, lap at her with my tongue until she's trembling. I grip my shaft, tugging upward slowly before bringing my fist back down, imagining how her juices would drip down my face and roll off my chin.

Fuck, that would be so hot.

As my hand picks up the pace, I thrust my fingers inside Devyn's dripping pussy in my mind.

God, how I want to feel her. Touch her. Fuck her.

Azarius may have beaten me to it, but that means nothing. I'd have her screaming my name, begging me to fuck her. I'd have her bent over every flat surface, slamming into her hard and deep from behind.

I lower my pants enough to free my straining cock and work my hand over the head where precum has collected. With my eyes closed and my thoughts firmly trained on Devyn, I pretend it's the sweet arousal from her pussy on my hand, and a fiery wave overtakes my body.

I want to be buried balls deep inside her, my hands and mouth working their way over every inch of available skin.

Devyn spins around and drops to her knees before me, and my balls tingle as I imagine staring down into her eyes filled with lust.

I want to fuck her mouth with no restraint until I come deep down her throat.

"Do it," her voice sounds in my ear, and I pump my hand faster. "Have your way with me."

I groan unintentionally as my climax nears, and I imagine her running her tongue down the length of me. She takes me into her mouth, sucking on my head in sync with my hand, and a rush of warmth rolls through me.

So close.

"Take it all, princess." This time, it's my voice I hear, but it wasn't out loud. "Swallow it for me."

She continues to work her mouth down until I'm balls deep in her throat, and she looks up at me with innocent, wide eyes. That's enough to send me over the edge. My balls clench and my body convulses as I come all over my hand. The waves keep coming, crashing into me, and when they finally stop, I'm spent.

I adjust my pants and wipe off my hand. It takes several deep breaths to get my pulse back to a reasonable pace, and I finally push myself off the tree trunk. I can hardly believe what I've just done, but I shrug it off. It was here or in my room, and at least there's no chance of being bothered out here.

My edge is gone, as are the lustful thoughts that plagued my mind minutes ago.

Maybe it was worth all that trouble.

Hell, maybe now, I won't find myself thinking of Devyn at all. Perhaps it's out of my system.

Probably not, but it can't hurt to be optimistic.

I glance in the direction of the mansion, not ready to go back yet. Despite everything looking the same and not having a compass to guide me, I somehow always know which direction the mansion is. I'd like to think of it as uncanny intuition, but it's probably just luck.

Instead of heading that way, I turn and walk in the other direction.

I have more time to kill. Rafe won't have another job for us until tomorrow at the earliest, and Azarius and Devyn need their alone time. Even if they don't, I'm giving it to them anyway.

I've made up my mind that I'll walk to the edge of the woods and maybe hang out at the tree line for a little bit before turning to head back. That should be plenty of time.

Unfortunately, I don't get that far.

I only get a few dozen feet away when something unusual catches my eye. There, spread out and running perpendicular to the path I'm walking, are footprints.

Big ones.

I freeze and look around for a third time. I'm certain I'm alone—there hasn't been a whisper of life since I came out here—but something has obviously been through here recently. Judging by the size of the prints, my guess is a Malev.

Cautiously, I bend to examine the footprints, and the distinctly rotting smell of a Malev hits me. The fact that I can still smell it means it wasn't too long ago that it came through here.

They're maybe a couple of hours old?

This isn't good.

There's a chance it's nothing more than a lost beast trying to find its way out of the woods, but it seems unlikely. In all my years working for Rafe, I've never seen a Malev step foot in these woods, much less wander this deep into the trees.

It's strange, and a twisted feeling in the pit of my stomach tells me something is wrong.

I don't like it.

With nothing but time—and possibly a Malev—to kill, I follow the footprints.

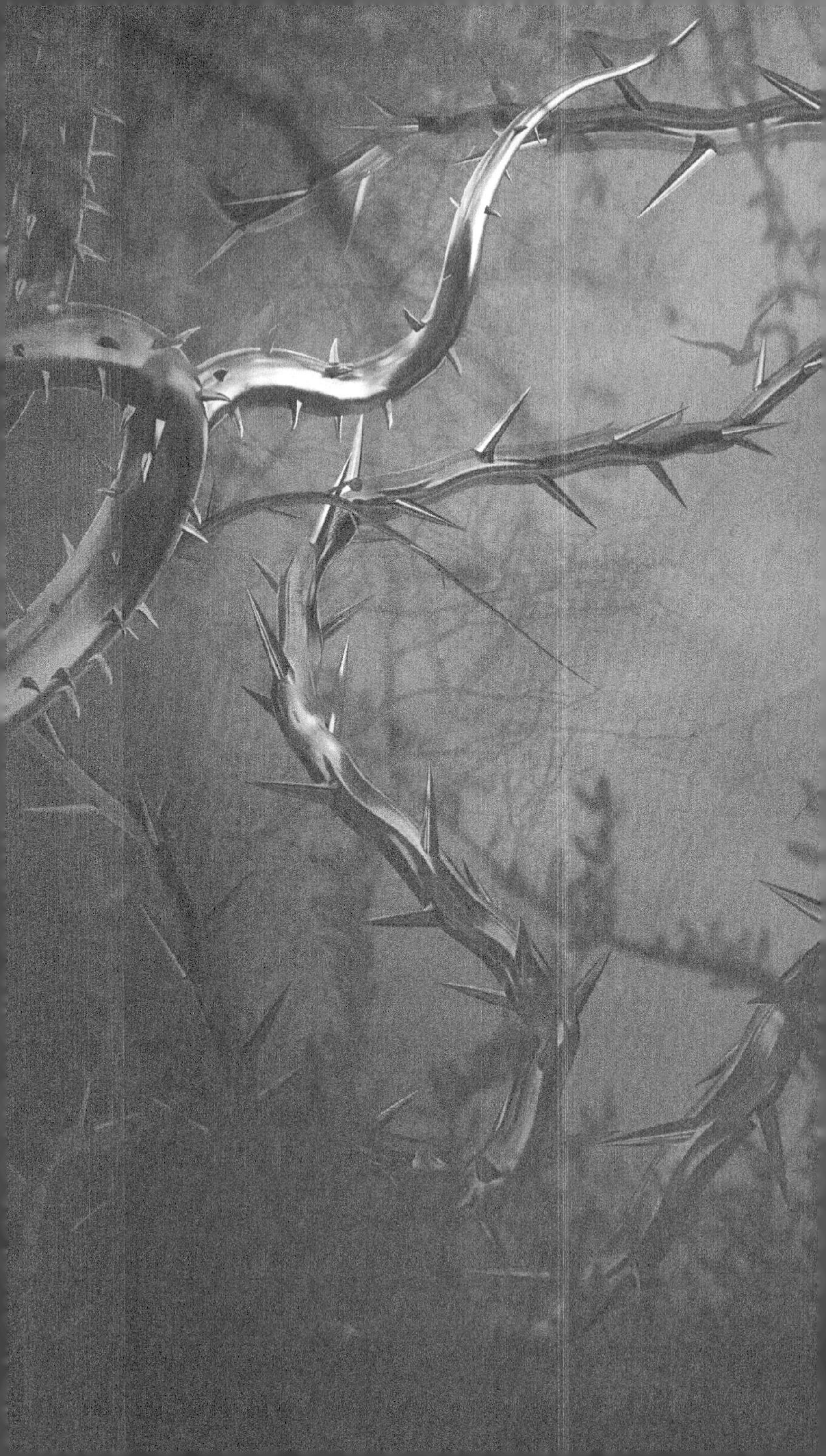

8
DEVYN

Did I imagine going back to Azarius' bedroom with him after he all but dragged my naked ass out of the dining room? Definitely.

Did I also foresee him leaving me alone for several hours while he disappeared to collect his thoughts? Absolutely not.

I probably should have seen it coming. After all, he already made me wait for two hours outside a club. Testing my patience is obviously one of his new favorite pastimes.

Why should now be any different?

With absolutely nothing to entertain me but a torrent of thoughts—a jumble of blurred confusion that only gets more complicated the longer I think—I wind up lying in the middle of the bed, fully dressed in my baggy clothes, blanket pulled up to my chin as I stare at the ceiling.

How in the world did my life get this fucked up?

I mean, I know how. I just can't believe it.

One minute, I'm working in Atlanta trying to scrape together enough money to pay rent, and the next, I'm in the middle of a monster world, fighting for my life. This is like some fucked-up Netflix original series, and I'm just watching it play out, wondering if my character lives to the next episode.

My character better make it through to the finale, or I'm going to be pissed.

I deserve it after deep throating Azarius in front of two other monsters.

A groan passes my lips, and I squeeze my eyes shut. I'm not any closer to making it home, but at least I've avoided a death sentence. Rafe doesn't seem to like me—I'm not entirely sure he likes anyone, honestly—but he's letting me live.

For now.

All I have to do is not screw anything up.

Easy.

Not.

I'm doomed.

After way too long, Azarius returns. He slips into the room with a silver platter in one hand, a goblet in the other, before he takes a seat next to me on the bed. My gaze remains trained on the ceiling until a delicious savory smell hits my nose and I look over.

"I figured you'd be hungry," he says, offering me the plate.

I consider telling him to shove the food up his ass for ditching me, but my stomach groans in protest. I push myself up and take it from him, my mouth watering as I look it over. None of it is familiar, but I couldn't care less at this point.

"Yeah, the sex helped me work up an appetite."

I smile at the joke, but Azarius is unfazed. Obviously, he's still irritable. I briefly wonder if he's upset with me, but I can't fathom why he would be. After all, I did everything he asked.

I played the part. I kept my mouth shut… mostly.

Maybe he's just mad at me for being here in the first place, making him feel obligated to save me.

That's probably it.

Regardless, his cold energy toward me stings.

"Thank you," I say, bringing a piece of meat to my nose to sniff before taking a tiny bite. It's warm and buttery and tastes kind of like chicken.

"Do you want me to tell you what you're eating?" he asks, one of his brows cocked as he watches me.

I shake my head. "The less I know, the better."

I'd rather not imagine what kind of creatures they eat here, having seen nothing but grotesque and scary beings since I arrived. I'm probably eating a cyclops-squirrel hybrid.

"Fair enough." He passes me the goblet, filled with an opaque red liquid, and my heart drops into my stomach. It looks eerily like blood. The thought makes my stomach turn, but before I can ask, Azarius quickly reassures me. "It's juice."

I stare for another second, my heart thrumming against my ribs as I try to find comfort in his words, but it's still hard to believe him. This stuff looks like a vampire's smoothie.

"It's sweet. I promise," he urges. "I've scarred you enough today. I wouldn't feed you blood."

He's trying to joke, but his heart still isn't in it. With a deep breath, I take a swig from the goblet, and a wave of relief swallows me when a sweet honey flavor hits my tongue. It may look like blood, but it tastes like candy. I take another swig.

I could get used to this.

It's a fleeting thought, one I never imagined crossing my mind, but it's there. Besides the power-hungry tyrant downstairs, and almost getting eaten by a Malev, this place isn't so bad. There are worse places to be stuck.

There's no way I can stay here, though. I have to figure out a way back home. My entire life is on hold, waiting for me to get back and straighten everything out.

My car is probably getting towed. Cara is probably worried sick, and if we don't make rent on time, we're going to get evicted.

Now that my life has been spared, my worries are back in full force. There are many problems with only one solution, and that solution—me getting the hell out of here—remains just out of reach.

Not to mention, there's palpable tension between Azarius and I now, and I feel like I need to fix that before I can handle anything else. I take a few more bites, chewing slowly as I contemplate what I'm going to say, but he beats me to the punch.

"Devyn, I'm sorry," he starts. I look over, but he's

staring across the room at something invisible on the wall. "I didn't know what else to do, and I panicked."

He isn't telling me anything I don't already know, but I stuff another piece of food in my mouth to avoid interrupting him.

"I never imagined that Rafe would make me…" He shakes his head. "He's a dark son of a bitch, but I didn't know he was that twisted. I just—I just didn't want him to kill you, or me for defying him."

"It's okay," I assure him. "We did what we had to do. I'm alive. Everything is fine."

His gorgeous sapphire eyes slowly slide over to me. "Are you really okay?"

I finish off the goblet before pushing it and my empty plate aside. Head cocked, I look at him and nod sincerely. "I really am. Humans normally do dinner before sex, but this works too."

I expect him to laugh, or at least smile, but he doesn't. I don't know what happened, but he isn't acting at all like he was earlier.

Instead, he huffs and looks away again.

"Are you going to tell me what your problem is?" I ask, leaning forward more to catch his eye. "Or do I have to guess?"

"This entire situation is my problem, Devyn." He pushes himself off the bed swiftly, running a hand through his hair and up one of his horns, pacing across the room before turning and heading back. "You've probably noticed, but I'm not like the others. I might be a beast by your standards, but I'm far from being a true monster. Elio is an asshole—he mainly cares about himself and his money. Rafe... you've seen. He's fucking terrible. The only thing I've tried to do since we met is help you, and I can't even do that."

Before I know it, I'm on my feet and crossing the room. "That's not fair, Azarius." I stop in front of him, blocking his path. "None of this is your fault. If anything, it's mine."

He says nothing, just rocks his head back and stares at the ceiling. The guilt eating at him is almost tangible, and I'm helpless. I never imagined a monster having so many feelings. I have to admit, it's a bit odd—mostly unexpected—but it's also a relief. With Azarius on my side, I know we can figure out a way to get me home.

If he agrees to let me go. After all, I'm his claimed mate now, whatever that means.

"Az, look at me." He doesn't move, just continues to stare upward. I repeat myself, more sternly this time. "Look. At. Me."

After a moment of hesitation, he meets my gaze. His eyes are heavy with a sadness that tugs at my heartstrings—he has more compassion than most humans I've met. I don't know what he needs to hear to believe that I don't blame him, but I have to try.

"Thank you," I say, taking a small step toward him. "For saving my life, more than once."

The corner of his mouth twitches with the hint of a smile before it vanishes. "You don't have to thank me. I was just doing what's right."

"It would have been a lot easier for you to let me die," I remind him, chancing another half step forward. "You didn't have to do any of that, but you did, and I'm very grateful."

He raises a hand to gently brush my hair away from my face, his eyes studying mine like he can't look away. I wish I could read his mind to get a glimpse of the maelstrom in there, but I'll have to settle for the hints he gives me.

"You're welcome." He brushes his fingertips against my shoulder and trails them down my arm. Tiny, electric sparks spring to life beneath his touch and skitter through me, catching me off guard and making heat rise in my cheeks.

Is it possible to still get butterflies for someone after being coerced into fucking them in front of strangers?

The flutter in my stomach says it is.

Slowly, Azarius leans down and takes my lips with his, but unlike downstairs, this kiss isn't greedy or full of lust. It's soft, gentle, and makes me weak in the knees. It's an unspoken promise to keep me safe, and I believe it wholeheartedly.

When he pulls back, his expression is lighter. It seems I've gotten through to him—he's not wallowing in guilt anymore. His shift in attitude eases my mind about the next question forming on my tongue.

"So now what?"

He sucks in a deep breath and blows it out slowly, letting his cheeks puff up. He lifts one shoulder in a shrug. "I don't know."

Dammit. Not the answer I wanted to hear.

I was hoping he had some kind of plan, especially

after all that time he had to brainstorm when he left me alone, but it looks like we're in the same boat. Neither of us knows what the fuck is going on.

"Do you think I'll be able to go home anytime soon?"

That obviously isn't what he wants to hear, either, because the frown returns to his face.

"Devyn, it's not that simple." He steps back and runs a hand through his hair again before crossing his arms over his chest. "Elio is the only one of us who can create portals, and he's going to take Rafe's side on just about everything. If Rafe says it's not safe, Elio will agree. It would be a waste of time to argue with him."

"You don't know any others who can open a portal?" I plead, fighting the desperation from creeping up into my voice. There's a way out of this. I can feel it in my bones. We just have to think outside the box a little.

He shakes his head, and my shoulders sag. "Not any close by; plus, taking you halfway across Orlyitha would be dangerous. You smell like a human, and I can't sense any monster in you. You would attract every Malev within fifty miles."

I shift my weight from foot to foot, my mind reeling. "Then bring your friend here."

"I can't." He shakes his head again. "We're not allowed to portal anywhere near the mansion—the Malevs can smell them. We would lead them straight here."

I groan and massage my temples. "I can't stay

here forever, Az. I have a life. I have responsibilities. I can't just abandon everything."

"I know." He walks past me and takes a seat on the side of the bed, his tail curling beside him. His jaw works like he's chewing his cheek in thought, and he casually looks from me to the floor to the back of his hand.

"I'll figure something out, but you've got to give me time," he says, looking up at me again. "Alright?"

"How much time are we talking?" I ask, my thoughts flashing immediately to Cara. "My roommate is going to get evicted if I don't give her my half of the rent by Thursday."

He grimaces. "Probably longer than that, but don't worry. I'll talk to Elio. We won't let your roommate be homeless."

I breathe a tiny sigh of relief and nod. At the very least, Cara will be taken care of. That's a weight off my shoulders. I don't know what he plans to do, but if he's going by our apartment, he can probably grab me some clothes and check on my car. Maybe even move it if it hasn't been towed yet.

It's a lot to ask—probably too much—but if I'm stuck here, I at least need some of my own things.

Like pants that don't fall off every time I move.

"I'm going to ask you a favor." Azarius' eyes lock on mine, and I step closer until I'm nearly standing between his legs. "Two favors, actually."

"Anything," I say with an eager nod.

Azarius leans forward, shrinking the distance between us, and rests his hands on my thighs. We're the same height with him sitting, and our faces are only a few inches apart.

"While we're trying to sort everything out, I'd like to figure out what kind of monster blood you have," he explains, rubbing his fingers in methodical circles on my pants. "Elio knows several warlocks who might be able to help—that's typically their area of expertise."

The idea is daunting. We can finally find out what's so special about my blood. We can find out why I'm not like other humans, but at what cost?

Will being told I'm part monster change the way I see myself? Will I have a full-blown identity crisis? What if I really am just a human and Azarius is wrong? Then what? Will that mean that something has gone awry with the portals and humans can now cross into their realm?

I nod the questions away. "Sure. That doesn't sound hard. What's the second favor?"

This time, the corners of his mouth curl upward, and he pulls me closer to him until our chests touch. The sudden closeness makes my heart skip a beat, and I exhale shakily.

"Consider staying."

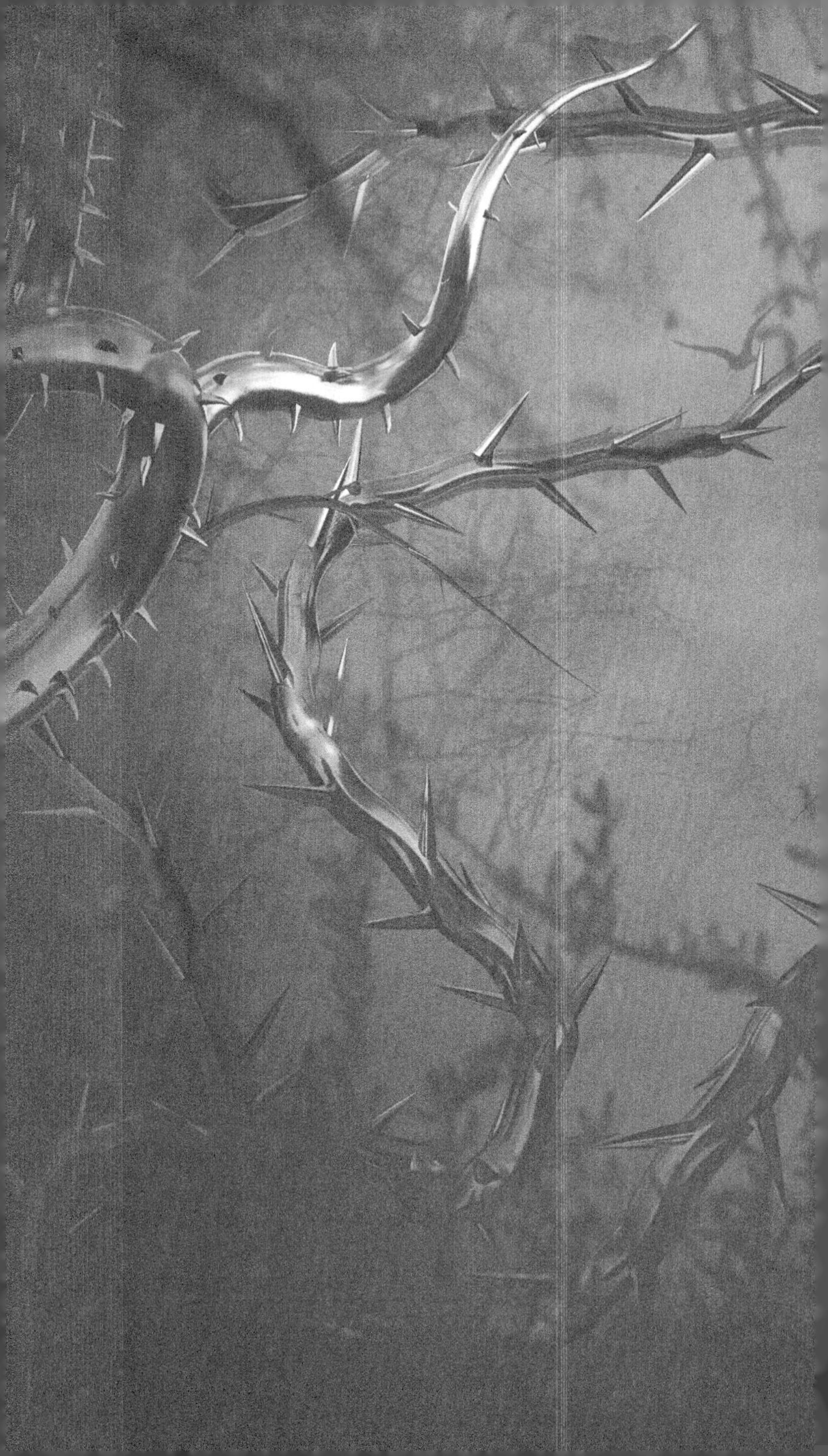

9
DEVYN

Consider staying.

Those two words have replayed in my mind more times than I could count over the last few days, and it doesn't seem like they're going to stop anytime soon. The rest of our conversation was a bit of a blur—my racing heart and the blood pounding in my ears made it hard to focus on anything else. Basically, once a monster claims their mate, it's a lifelong commitment.

Forever.

"Like marriage in the human world," he said, making my stomach turn nervously and my throat close.

It gets worse.

While females are allowed to move on and accept more mates, male monsters typically only have one.

He had one shot, and he wasted it on me.

Wasted wasn't the word he used, but that's how I see it. Even if I wanted to, there's no way I could live here. Unless I stay confined to the mansion, I'll always have a target on my back. I won't be able to go anywhere or do anything. Even with a lover like Azarius, that doesn't seem like a very fulfilling existence.

Now I understand why those princesses in storybooks never wanted to be locked up. It sucks. Yet, here I am, trapped like a damsel, and even my princes can't save me.

Rather than sleeping in Azarius' room, I took over one of the guest rooms down the hall, and while he didn't seem upset by my decision, he's reminded me several times that his door is always open. I was tempted to sneak down once or twice in the middle of the night, if only to avoid staying alone again, but I refrained. I'm trying to behave and take things slow, even though we've already destroyed every typical new relationship boundary. Still, I'm practicing my self-restraint.

We'll see how long that lasts.

I raided Xia's closet again and found a few smaller things that fit me a little better, but they're still not nearly as good as my own clothes. I just want a pair of worn-in jeans and a tank top. None of these clothes come close.

I've subtly reminded Azarius that my rent is due, and he says he's working on it. I can only hope and pray time goes slower in the human world than it does here. Otherwise, Cara is screwed.

As nervous as I am, I trust Azarius. He hasn't let me down yet.

I'm sitting in an oversized, purple lounge chair, flipping through a leatherbound book I found in a drawer, when a knock at the door catches my attention.

"Come in," I call as I toss the book aside.

I look up expecting Azarius, but instead, Elio's copper-colored form slips past the door, wearing a pair of dark slacks with a pale blue button-up, his hair untied and hanging in waves around his face. He's hardly spoken to me since we met with Rafe, which I can totally understand, so I'm even more surprised to see him now.

"Good morning," he says. He looks completely uncomfortable as he hovers near the door, his eyes sweeping the room before landing on me.

"Hey. Is everything okay?"

He nods. "Yes, it's fine."

"Where's Azarius?" I ask, my eyes flitting to the doorway. I'm expecting him to waltz in any second, but he never does.

"He's running an errand before we head to Earth." His tone is flat, but my ears perk up.

"Earth?" I nearly jump out of the lounge chair, excitement tingling over my skin. "You're going today?"

He nods. "We are. We have a meeting this afternoon. Then, as I understand it, we're going to your apartment to pay a debt and collect some of your belongings."

An eager smile teases my lips. "Yes. Lots of blue jeans. My toothpaste would be nice."

I stole an unused toothbrush from one of the many bathrooms on this floor, but the toothpaste the monsters use is disgusting, like sparkling feet juice.

"Sure. Is there anything else you need while we're there?" he asks, shifting his weight uncomfortably.

I purse my lips. "If you could see if my car has been towed, that would be great. I think I lost my keys when I was attacked, though."

Elio reaches into his pocket and retrieves a keychain with several keys and a bottle opener attached to it—my keys—along with my taser.

My jaw drops. "Where did you... Have you had those the whole time?"

"No, I haven't." He chuckles and puts them back in his pocket. "I went for a walk and wound up where the portal dumped you out. I found them and knew they had to be yours."

I close the distance between us and look up to meet his dark eyes. "So, you just decided not to tell me?"

He averts his gaze, suddenly distracted by one of the tasseled throw pillows on the bed, which he runs his fingers over.

"I apologize." His accent makes his apology one or two syllables too long, but it sounds sexy when he says it. "I've been a little... preoccupied."

"And here I thought it was because you hate me."

There's a brief moment of silence before Elio replies. "I don't."

"I don't believe you," I say, mainly under my breath. "Is that all you came to tell me?"

He turns back to face me and tucks both his hands into his pockets, giving him a strikingly poised appearance. If they had male models in the monster realm, Elio would definitely be one. He's fine as hell.

"Yes and no." He shifts again, swaying back and forth on the spot. "Azarius asked me to check on you, to see if you needed anything, and I wanted to warn you. Please refrain from doing anything stupid while we're gone."

Irritation brews in my chest, and my brows knit together over my eyes. "Excuse me?"

"I meant what I said. You have a tendency for rash behavior, and if you get into trouble while we're gone, we can't protect you. You're on your own."

I press my lips into a firm line. While he's not completely wrong—I do have a knack for getting myself into rather…uncomfortable situations—he doesn't have to be such a dick about it.

"I thought Azarius said Malevs don't come this far into the woods."

He steps forward until we're toe to toe and drops his voice to an intimidating whisper. "I'm not just talking about what lurks outside these walls."

Rafe.

That's who he's trying to warn me about.

If I mess around and cross Rafe, they can't save me this time. There's no telling if Azarius' claim will hold any weight without him here.

"So, I'm just supposed to stay in this room while you're gone?" I ask, gesturing around us with a sweep of my hand.

He nods once. "I'm glad we're on the same page. Azarius was worried you might try to argue, but I'll be happy to tell him you enthusiastically agreed."

My jaw drops, and I struggle to string words together. When I don't respond immediately, Elio takes the chance to bow his head slightly and turn for the door.

"See you later, princess."

Princess?

Before I can say anything else, the door snaps closed behind him, and he's gone. I'm left standing with my jaw slack, wondering what the hell I did to make Elio hate me so much. Rafe, I can almost understand; he probably hates Elio and Azarius to some extent. But I've been nothing but nice to Elio. I have no idea what his deal is.

Maybe Azarius knows. They're best friends. Surely, they tell each other everything.

I make a mental note to ask him when they get back.

As I gaze around the room, it suddenly feels small and stuffy, despite being nearly as big as Azarius' quarters. I perch my hands on my hips. He wants me to stay in this room all day and behave like a good girl?

I think not.

If he really wanted me to stay in one spot all day, he would have locked me in or chained me up, which might be kind of hot if I wasn't so pissed right now.

Just to spite him, I'm going to wait until he leaves and take a stroll around the mansion. If I'm stuck here, I might as well get acquainted with the place. Top to bottom. Side to side. I want to know where all the exits are. I want to see all the rooms. I'll just do my best to avoid running into Rafe along the way.

After checking out the window every few minutes for nearly half an hour, I see Elio's form cross the stretch of grass and disappear into the trees. I wait a few more minutes, just to make sure he isn't going to come running back for anything, before turning on my heel and heading for the bedroom door.

The prickle of reality dances at the nape of my neck like a warning as I step into the hallway. I'm alone, and as far as I know, there's only one other person in the entire mansion. I haven't seen anyone else coming or going, other than Elio and Azarius.

No butlers.

No staff.

No one.

After meeting Rafe, I'm not surprised. It would take a very special individual to tolerate being in the same building as him for any extended amount of time.

No wonder everyone else prefers hanging out in the human world. This place seems kind of miserable without Elio and Azarius to keep me company.

Despite the gleaming decorations, grand staircases, and extravagant furniture, the grandeur of the place dissipates in the wake of Rafe lurking somewhere inside. It's more like a haunted castle than a home.

Aside from the guest rooms on the second floor,

there is a long sitting room at the end of the hall that's beautifully decorated with red-velvet couches, small tables, and a crystal chandelier that casts flecks of rainbow light across the room. Several paintings, all framed in thick, black wood, hang on the walls, and knickknacks are scattered across everything. A sand-filled hourglass here. A clawed hand with the palm outstretched there. Candles. A skull. A clock with fourteen numbers and six hands.

It's a beautiful place to spend an afternoon lounging around—I can see why the aesthetic appeals to Rafe.

If he wasn't such an insufferable asshole, he might be able to enjoy this beautiful sanctuary he's created with other people.

Then again, he probably doesn't want to.

From there, I head to the staircase, running my hand along the banister as I make my way downstairs. I walk slowly, looking for any sign of movement in the shadows that might give Rafe away. I haven't decided if I'll say hello or turn and run like hell if I bump into him.

I'll have to wait and see, I guess.

Aside from the foyer and dining room, there are two sitting areas and a gorgeous kitchen. There's no sign of a refrigerator, which I personally find disappointing, but there are tons of marble countertops and cabinets lining every wall, and a huge island in the middle.

I decide to wait for the boys to return before I

explore outside—if what they said is true, a Malev could potentially smell its way to me.

Not a risk I'm willing to take.

Some people would probably rather take their chances with a Malev than Rafe, but not me. Besides, I haven't seen any sign of him since I started exploring. Who's to say he didn't step out too?

Finally, there's only one place I haven't explored—the third floor. I'm assuming that's where Rafe sleeps, but I don't know for sure. Does he even sleep?

He's probably running on pure hatred and his inflated ego at this point. No need for downtime when you're trying to rule the realm.

I climb the stairs to the second floor and pause on the landing, my eyes dancing up the next flight of stairs. A tiny voice at the back of my mind begs me to stop exploring. It tells me to go back to my room and wait for Azarius and Elio. Then my curiosity tells that voice to shut up, and my feet find their way to the bottom stair.

It won't hurt to look.

I don't even have to open any doors. I can sneak up and sneak down without being seen.

A nervous flutter in my stomach erupts when I take the first step, careful to test it for creaky boards first. I wait, nervously anticipating the worst, but nothing happens. As quietly as possible, I try another step, then another. After several excruciating minutes, I reach the top of the stairs and freeze on the landing, afraid any wrong move will draw Rafe out of his hiding place.

Wherever he is. I'm really starting to think he's not home and that I'm completely alone.

I don't know how I feel about that, either. Do I want to be completely alone in a world full of bloodthirsty monsters? Would I rather be trapped with the scariest monster I can imagine, who might be able to protect me should worse come to worst?

If he doesn't toss me into the yard as monster food first.

The third floor of the mansion is the smallest. The hallway is much shorter than the second floor, and there are only three doors: one to my left, one to my right, and one straight ahead.

My heart gallops in my chest, thundering against my ribs, and every tiny noise is suddenly deafening. Every breath I take is like a scream. My pulse, which I can feel in every limb of my body, beats like a war drum.

I want to know what's inside each of these rooms, but I'm also not willing to risk my life for that knowledge. If Rafe is home, he's more than likely in one of them, probably sleeping or participating in some form of debauchery.

I would piss him off by interrupting.

A single knock nearby makes me jump, and I cling to the handrail to steady myself. An uneasy hitch forms in my chest; I feel like someone is watching me, even though there is no one else in sight. Frantically, I glance back over my shoulder toward the stairs. Nothing.

Still, I can't shake the unsettling feeling pumping through me, and it's getting worse by the second.

I glance at the doors ahead of me, making sure they're all closed tight.

Time to go.

I spin on my heel, ready to dart toward the stairs, but my path is blocked by a cloud of black smoke steadily materializing before my eyes. A head with forward-curling horns, followed by a broad set of shoulders. A shirtless, tattoo-covered chest, followed by a pair of black pants. In the few seconds it takes me to register what's happening, Rafe is standing at the top of the stairs, blocking my way.

Shit. Shit. Shit.

"What do you think you're doing?" he asks, his voice sharp. His red eyes zero in on my face, making my blood run cold, and I can't make my tongue work.

"Just… looking…" I choke out. My body is paralyzed with fear, and I can't move. I'm rooted to the spot, arms stiff at my sides.

"Did you find what you were looking for?" He takes a step closer, towering over me.

I stumble backward, my legs finally deciding to cooperate, and smack into the wall. The lantern closest to me rattles, and I place my hands beside me automatically, making myself as flat as possible. Not that it'll help, but it's as far away from Rafe as I can get. He takes a step toward me, and I suck in a sharp breath, curious what his next move will be.

Does he want to play with me before he kills me? Or does he want it over and done with?

He cocks his head and moves closer, all the while my body screams in protest. Being this close to him feels wrong, vile. I know what kind of monster he is. I've heard the stories. I've seen it in action.

"Did you?" His voice comes out as a low, guttural growl that makes my bones quake.

He's so close, I can feel the warmth radiating off his skin, and my eyes are still caught in the web of his gaze, unable to break eye contact. I'm entranced, my body acting of its own accord. Almost indiscernibly, I shake my head.

Faster than I can process, he slams his left hand beside my head on the wall, making me whimper, and leans in so close that our faces almost touch. His right hand slips up to my throat, and he squeezes his fingers against the sides of my neck. Warmth flushes through my body, and the edges of my vision darken a little.

His voice is deep and commanding when he speaks. "Do not come up here again, unless you want to be bound, bruised, and brutally punished. Do you understand?"

I can barely process what he's said, because my entire body is alight with adrenaline, fear, and, for some unexplainable reason, lust. After an extra few seconds, it finally sinks in.

Bound.

Bruised.

Punished.

"Y-yes," I choke. The dark ring around my vision is growing thicker, and my pulse is beating angrily against his hand on my throat.

"That's not a threat," he says, squeezing a little harder as my knees go weak. "I promise, I'll have you begging for mercy."

My eyes flutter closed as he lets me go, and I crumple to my knees. I gently cup my hand around my throat, willing the pain away as I focus on breathing, and Rafe disappears through the door at the end of the hall.

Gasping, I scramble to my feet and take the stairs two at a time before sprinting to the guest room I've decided to call my own. I close the door and lock it in a blur, then take several deep breaths to calm my nerves.

"Holy shit," I whisper, running my fingers carefully over my sore neck.

It would have been nice to know the third floor was off limits before I decided to check it out.

My hands are shaking as I collapse on the bed, the scene replaying over and over in my mind. When he said brutally punished, I immediately thought he meant torture—and to some extent, that still might be true—but the more I consider it, I don't think that's what he was getting at.

He meant he'd punish me sexually.

It could be his terrifying demeanor, or his ruthless personality, but something in my bones tells me he'd do it.

And he'd do it well.

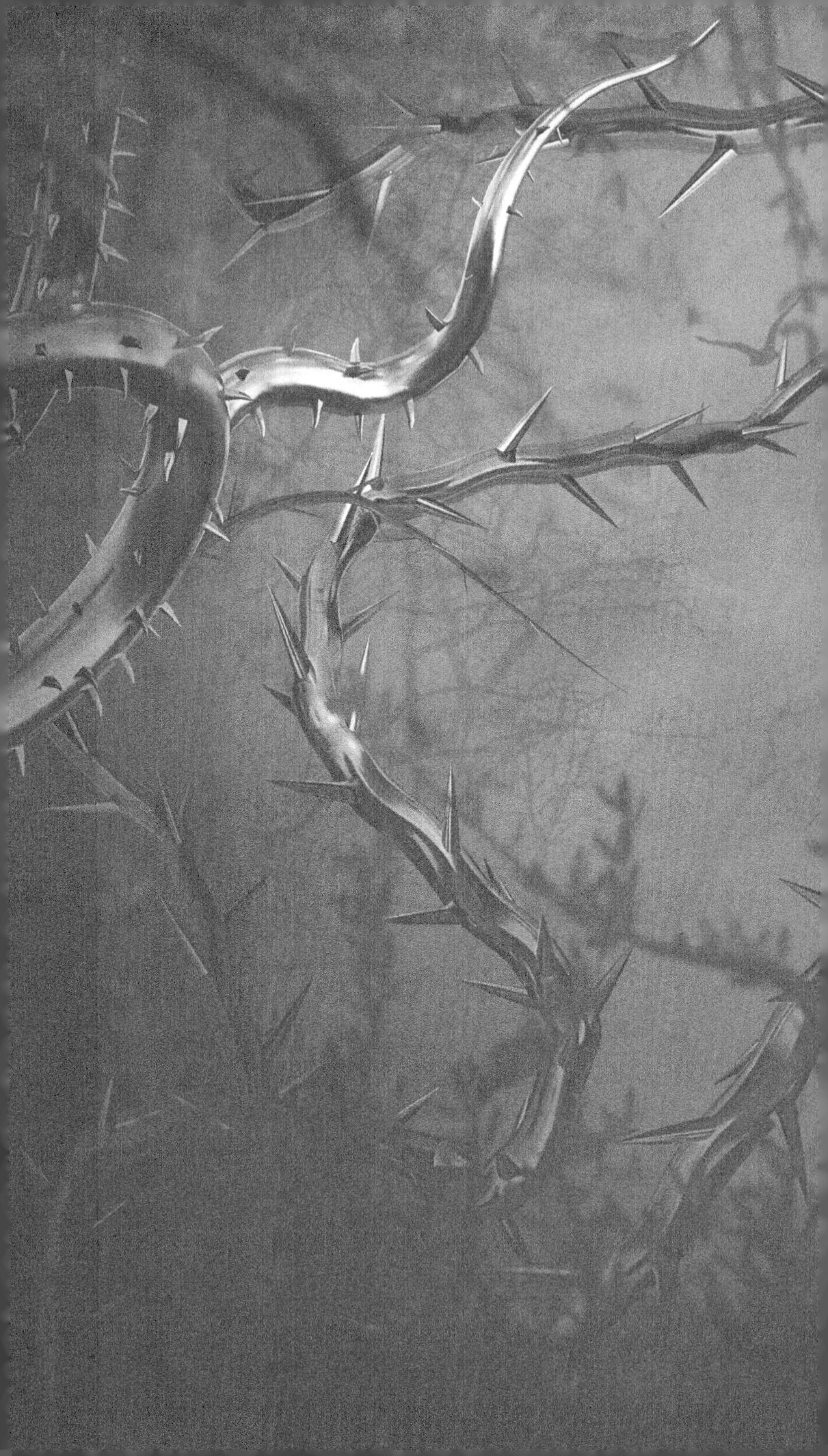

10
AZARIUS

Elio should be out here doing a perimeter check, not me.

It's true, I'm much faster on the ground—I haven't met many monsters who can keep up with me—but making sure there's nothing suspicious near the outer edge of the woods would be even faster from the sky.

Still, what Rafe asks me to do, I do. That was part of the deal when I came to work for him.

I've been running along the edge of the woods for hours, my legs moving as fast as they can, my feet beating against the ground. I'm tired, and we still have a long day ahead.

I stop where Elio and I are supposed to meet up—outside the abandoned village we normally portal from—and scan the area. He's not here yet.

"Where the fuck—" The words come out between heavy breaths.

I did two complete rounds of the woods. That's

plenty of time for him to get his ass here, and he's typically punctual. Maybe Rafe held him up.

Our cell phones aren't an option—human technology doesn't work here—so I can't call him to see where the hell he is and why he's taking so long. That's one thing I love about being on Earth. You can track down anyone anywhere with the click of a few buttons. Here, you have to literally track them down, and sometimes, the person you're looking for doesn't want to be found.

I sling the backpack I'm carrying off my shoulder and unzip it, revealing the business clothes I brought to change into, and I debate changing forms while I wait for Elio. My human form puts me at a severe disadvantage in a fight. While I'm still fast and just as strong, I don't have horns or claws or even a tail to help. All those things come in handy when taking on a Malev.

Still, since I just did a perimeter check and didn't see anything out of the norm, I decide to chance it.

I tap into my ability to change my appearance and let the transformation take hold. A ripple rolls over my body as the black marks staining my skin fade, and my complexion darkens to a peachy flesh color. I lose several inches of height, and the weight of my tail disappears.

It doesn't take long—a minute at most—before I'm in a naked, human body.

I grab the pair of slacks and button up out of my bag and get dressed. Elio emerges from the woods as

I'm finishing with the buttons. He's already transformed and dressed in business attire.

"Took you long enough," I shoot, narrowing my eyes before retrieving my empty bag.

"I got caught up. You ready?"

"No shit. I've been ready."

Elio walks past me looking annoyed, his mouth pressed into a hard line, and heads for the nearest building. It's wide and squat, with a caved-in roof, but it's the most structurally sound of the bunch, which makes it the best place to open a portal.

At least, that's what Elio says.

Like every time he makes the connection between realms, he places one hand on the wall and closes his eyes to focus. Under his breath, he mutters an ancient incantation, one taught to him by his warlock grandfather, and the black hole springs to life a second later. He steps back while the portal swells, swallowing the side of the building.

"Do you ever get tired of doing that?" I ask, pointing to the gaping hole.

He nods, rolling his eyes. "All the time."

When we first met several years ago, I envied Elio's magic. Most monsters descended from warlocks can't harvest enough power to wield it successfully. Others don't bother to try, because having power is dangerous. People like Rafe seek to control those with magic, or destroy them, which is why Elio ended up working for him. Employed is better than dead.

While it would be convenient to open portals and do other cool magic shit, I don't have any warlock blood in me. I don't envy Elio anymore, either—magic is one hell of a burden to bear. Still, I'm glad he's on our side. Having a portal bitch handy whenever I feel like traveling to Earth isn't too bad.

"I thought so," I say before we step into the void.

A few moments later, we emerge into a familiar alleyway. It's the one we always use when we travel to Atlanta, the same one Devyn followed us down.

Not only is it one of the longest, most secluded alleyways I've come across in the city, it's right next to The Château, which is run by monsters. They help keep the alley clear of humans, and they're close by if anything should ever go wrong with the portal.

It works out nicely.

Elio pulls out his cell phone, turning it on with the press of a button, and we make our way down the alley while it powers up. While technology doesn't work in the monster realm, it survives the journey just fine. We figured that out by accident years ago, when we hurriedly jumped through to avoid a nasty fight between rival monster gangs in Florida.

"Where's the meeting?" I ask.

Elio's pulling up his Uber app to arrange a ride. "A restaurant called Parisi's. We're meeting with Ross again."

I snap my head in his direction. "Why?"

He shrugs. "I don't know. He asked to talk to us. Rafe thinks he'll ask for more land, or money."

"Or both." I roll my eyes. I hated dealing with him the last time, so I'm not looking forward to seeing him again. "Are we going to give it to him?"

"It depends on his offer. We'll see, I guess."

The brightly lit sidewalk is a stark difference from the shadow-filled alley, and it takes my eyes a moment to adjust. People bustle around, paying us no mind. Cars streak by on the street ahead. It's all so different from the monster realm, where everything is still and silent most of the time.

"Fucking great," I mutter, staring down the sidewalk as people continue to pass. "You can't meet him by yourself?"

"So you can go to your girlfriend's house and play with her stuff?" Elio's voice is unexpectedly sharp. "Fuck no."

"She's not my girlfriend." I wheel around to face him, and my eyebrows climb my forehead. "And no. It's because he's a fucking assbag. What is your problem?"

"Your mate, then. Whatever. I don't have a problem." He huffs and shoulders past me, heading up the sidewalk.

For a second, I consider letting him go so he can blow off some steam, but I know it's best if we stick together. I groan and hurry after him.

"I claimed her to save her," I explain, keeping my voice low. That should have been fucking obvious. "Rafe was going to kill her."

"Yeah, and you've brought this entire clusterfuck of a situation upon us," he says without glancing my direction. "Way to go."

An argument forms on my tongue, but I swallow it down. I don't know what crawled up his ass, but I'm not fighting him in the middle of downtown Atlanta. I also don't want to waste any more time. We're on a schedule, and if we don't hurry up, we're going to be late.

I'll deal with Elio later.

A familiar blue car catches my attention by the curb. It's a four-door sedan with a Tennessee license plate and a small dent in the back door.

"Hey, isn't this Devyn's car?" I ask, though I'm sure it is. "How has it not been towed yet?"

The meter by the car has half an hour left on it, as does the one next to it. Someone must have come through and put money in all the meters, so the cars left overnight didn't get towed. I don't think I've ever been so relieved by a small act of kindness.

"Yeah, I think so." Elio stops beside me and pulls out a set of keys. "Want to go for a joy ride?"

"Only if I'm driving." I hold out my hand expectantly. "I'm never riding with you again after Douglasville."

I might have only driven a handful of times, but I'm way better at it than Elio, and I've never almost killed us.

He sighs and drops the keys into my palm. "That was two years ago. Let it go already."

I shake my head and make my way around the car, pressing the unlock button on the key fob. "That chicken house will never be the same."

The shift in conversation seems to have improved Elio's mood as we climb into the car. I can hardly fit my legs under the steering wheel, and I have to slide the seat back as far as it will go. After adjusting all the mirrors and familiarizing myself with the levers and knobs on the dash, I crank the engine and we pull away from the curb.

The GPS on Elio's phone says the restaurant is only fifteen minutes away, and judging by the clock on the dash, we'll be right on time for our meeting with Ross. I'm ready to get in and get out as quickly as possible. Elio can do the talking. I'll just be backup if anything goes sideways.

"Sorry about that back there," Elio says suddenly, catching me by surprise. The edge to his voice is gone. "I just have a lot on my mind."

"It's fine," I assure him. "Everything's screwed up right now. I get it."

He's quiet for a moment before clearing his throat. "I do have a question for you."

The stoplight we're approaching turns red. After I tap the brakes a little too hard, we stop abruptly, and I chance a glance at Elio out of the corner of my eye. He's rubbing his beard methodically, staring off into space. For a moment, I wonder if he forgot his question.

"I know you claimed her because Rafe was going to kill her," he says slowly, "but do you actually want Devyn to be your mate?"

Blindsided.

Of all the things I expected him to ask, that definitely wasn't one of them. Is Devyn the reason he's been in such a piss poor mood? It's possible, but it doesn't make any sense. He's been annoyed by her since the beginning, and he probably would have let the Malev eat her if I hadn't intervened.

I consider his question. It doesn't really matter if I want her to be my mate. I claimed her, so she's mine. The connection we have is obvious—sparks fly between us every time she's close—but we haven't spent much time together. Rafe keeps sending us on errands, and I haven't slept with her since our rendezvous in the dining room.

It's complicated. There's no other way to describe it.

I'm confident things could work out between us, though, if she decides to stay in the monster realm. If she'll give it—and me—a chance.

"Yeah," I finally answer. "I do."

"If she decides to claim more mates, monster or not, will you be okay with that?"

I stall. I haven't exactly considered that scenario, but it's not uncommon for female monsters to take multiple mates. The same rules would apply to Devyn, if that's what she wants.

"I'll be fine with whatever makes her happy," I assure him. "She has the right to choose."

He nods but doesn't say anything else, and we spend the rest of the ride in silence.

Parisi's is an elegant Italian restaurant positioned on a busy street, and I have to park a block away in a parking deck. I could have chanced parallel parking, but the last thing I need is to hit someone's car and have the cops called. Explaining that I don't have a license—or any proof I exist—isn't how I want to start the day, though meeting with Ross isn't much better.

We step inside the restaurant, and my eyes automatically sweep across the dining area, searching for any sign of Ross. It's too early for a lunch rush, so the restaurant is still mostly empty, but Ross is sitting in the back corner alone in a booth. He's wearing a vibrant, Hawaiian print shirt, a gold chain hanging around his neck, his gray hair combed over neatly.

Elio and I walk straight past the hostess station and stop beside his table.

"Good morning, Mr. Ross," Elio says as he nods his head in greeting, and I echo him.

"Hello boys." He gestures to the seats across from him, and his face breaks into a wide smile. "Please, have a seat."

The last time we met, I thought his cheery demeanor had been an obnoxious act. Now, I'm less sure. The overly wide grin suits him, even if I know what's hiding under the surface. Like the rest of us, Ross is a monster, a master of disguise. We still have to be cautious.

I slide into the booth first, followed by Elio, and Ross peruses the folding menu.

"The food here is incredible," he says without looking up. "Much better than anything we have back home."

I let Elio take the reins. If I keep quiet, hopefully we can get out of here faster.

"I'm sure," Elio agrees.

"You boys hungry?" Ross asks. "It's on me."

"I'm not really—" I start to say, but Elio kicks me under the table to cut me off. He answers instead.

"Thank you for the offer, sir. It was a long trip and we skipped breakfast."

He reaches for his menu and flips it open before nudging my menu a little closer to me.

Fuck. Looks like I'm stuck here for a bit.

A waitress appears next to our table to take our drink order and disappears a second later. After scanning over the menu, Elio sets it aside and folds his hands together on the table.

"You asked for a meeting with us," Elio starts casually.

Ross nods. "That I did, but it's a shame to talk business on an empty stomach, isn't it?"

Double fuck. This is going to take way longer than I thought.

"I agree." Elio looks over at me. "Don't you, Az?"

I fight the urge to roll my eyes and nod instead.

There is no denying Elio has a way with people, but it's annoying. He says all the right things, compliments them and agrees with them. Everything about his demeanor makes him the perfect man to work for Rafe. There's no telling how many deals Elio has secured—deals that never would have happened otherwise.

I, on the other hand, am not much of a businessman. I overshare, and I don't have the patience for forced pleasantries, especially with people who grate my nerves the way Ross does.

The waitress brings our drinks and jots our orders down before taking our menus away.

"What have you been up to?" Elio asks, dragging out the small talk.

"Oh, you know, a little of this and that." Ross takes a sip of his drink. "I just got back from Mexico."

Losing every shred of patience, I tune them out. I'm already here against my will, and the boring conversation isn't improving my mood. I want to hurry up and get to Devyn's so we can get her things, pay her roommate, and get back to her.

I nod along as they talk, only catching a couple of words here and there, and I occasionally offer a grunt in response. My thoughts are far away from the restaurant, imagining the excitement in Devyn's eyes when I deliver her things, especially her blue jeans. She's most excited about those for some unfathomable reason, and the possibility of repeating what transpired in the dining room has me almost salivating.

Finally, our food comes, and my stomach growls as the rich aromas hit my nose. The pasta plate that's placed in front of me looks incredible, and I don't hesitate to dig in. Elio follows suit, and for a few minutes, the table is silent.

Thank God. If I have to hear about one more hot Latina on the beach feeding Ross grapes, I'm going to lose it.

I expect Ross to make us wait until we're done eating, but he doesn't. I'm about halfway done when he lays his fork down and folds his hands together, elbows propped on the table.

"The reason I wanted to meet with you is that there's a rumor going around." He keeps his voice low as his gaze bounces between Elio and me. "I'm curious to know if it's true."

"A rumor?" I say as I twirl a clump of noodles around my fork, but I quickly shut my mouth. I forgot I'm supposed to be keeping quiet.

He nods slowly, his eyes fixing on Elio. "A Malevolent was killed this week, a few miles from that mansion Rafe keeps hidden in the woods."

Elio shrugs and lays down his utensils to entertain Ross with more conversation, but I keep eating. "Malevs are killed every day. I didn't realize that was hot monster gossip."

The only dead Malev I know of is the one I killed to save Devyn, but even if it was the same one, I don't get why it would matter. We've killed dozens over the last few months that got too close for comfort, and no one batted an eye.

I'm clearly missing something.

"The Malev, no," Ross says, waving a dismissive hand. "They're saying a human weapon was found near the body, as well as traces of human blood."

The blood drains from my face and an icy chill rolls down my spine as his words sink in. I fight to keep my expression blank, but my pulse begins to race.

Who the hell could have possibly found the human blood? How the fuck did Ross find out about it? My mind is spinning, but I'm too stunned to ask the questions burning through me. Luckily, Elio and I are on the same wavelength.

"Interesting," he says, his tone a little drier than normal. I can tell he's caught off guard too. "Who are they?"

Ross leans back in his seat and adjusts his bright floral shirt. "Monsters," he says, keeping it vague. He's obviously not going to drop names. "The thing about rumors is they spread like wildfire. There's no sure way of knowing where they start, or when they will end."

"Or if they're even accurate." Elio's words are sharp. I nudge him with my foot beneath the table, and he quickly picks up his fork. "It's a very bold claim. We all know humans can't pass through the portal."

"That we know of," Ross says as he reaches for his drink. "That doesn't mean they won't start trying."

I pause and meet Ross' gaze across the table. "What are you saying?"

He waits while our waitress stops by to refill his drink and only continues when she's out of earshot.

"I'm saying that people are intrigued. Do you know how many monsters would kill to take their human pets home with them if they could survive the trip?" Ross points his fork at me, his gaze intense. "Loads of them. It would change everything."

I shift uncomfortably in my seat and imagine Devyn. If other monsters already know a human made it through the portal, how long can we keep her completely hidden? How long until monsters start to put more pieces of the puzzle together?

Would they come after her? Would the Malevolents? Suddenly, I've lost my appetite.

"Some people are even saying the human killed the Malev," Ross goes on. "That he's still in the monster realm somewhere. Hiding."

"If he is, he won't last long," I assure him. "If there was blood, that means he's injured, which will only attract more Malevs."

"Naturally."

"Why are you telling us all this?" Elio asks. "Surely, you didn't bring us here to gossip."

"No, I didn't. I wanted to warn you."

My brows knit together, and I stare at him across the table. He set up a meeting with us and bought us breakfast to warn us? Seems a bit much in my opinion.

Then again, Ross clearly enjoys theatrics.

"Warn us?" After holding my tongue all morning, I'm finding it harder and harder to keep quiet, but Elio doesn't make any effort to shut me up. I guess I'm in the right this time.

Ross nods. "If the monsters know about it, I guarantee you the Malevs do. They're stupid, yes, but they're ruthless when it comes to something they want. The blood wasn't found far from Rafe's. If the human went into the woods, it's only a matter of time before the Malevs come looking."

Anxiety hits me, making my chest seize. Normally, I wouldn't worry about Malevolents trekking too close to the mansion, but Devyn being there has me on high alert.

The footprints Elio found in the woods suddenly make sense. A Malev was more than likely tracking her scent.

"We appreciate your concern, Mr. Ross." Elio tosses his napkin on his plate and pushes it away. "If you hear anything else, please keep us informed. We'll be on the lookout for any signs of a human."

"Anytime." Ross grins, looking thoroughly pleased with himself. "What are allies for?"

The waitress brings the check in a little black book, standing it up on the end of the table. Elio shifts to get out of the booth, but Ross catches our attention one more time.

"Could you pass along a message to Rafe for me?" he asks, but he doesn't wait for us to respond. "Can you let him know I would pay an exceptional amount for a human who could survive getting in and out of the monster realm? In case he runs across the one who killed the Malev."

Fire flares behind my eyes, and I open my mouth, not quite set on what I'm going to say, but Elio grips my arm.

"Of course," he says, dipping his head before climbing out of the booth and dragging me with him. "We'll pass the word along."

I wave a hasty goodbye and follow Elio, nearly running him over to get to the door. With everything we've just learned, I'm more eager than ever to get back to the mansion. If the Malevs—or monsters—are hunting Devyn, I need to be there to protect her.

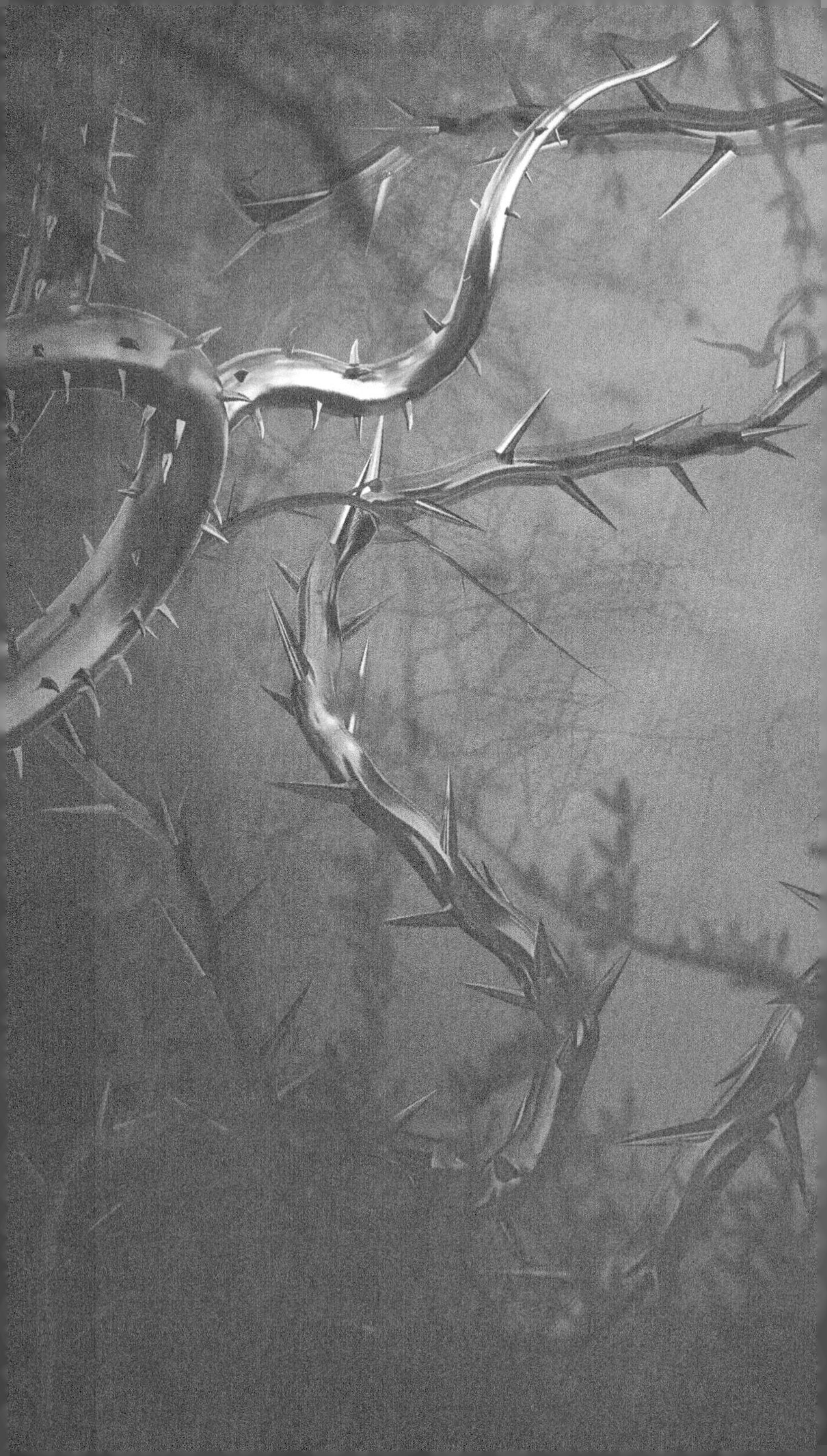

11

DEVYN

Time drags by as I sit in my room, waiting for Elio and Azarius to return.

I'm tempted to make my way through the mansion again, but I'm not eager for another run-in with Rafe, so I stay put. Images of our encounter replay in my mind; the way he stared daggers through me, the feel of his hand squeezing my throat.

Just the thought is enough to spike my pulse, and I can't tell if it's from fear or curiosity.

My imagination runs rampant with what could be hidden on the third floor, every idea crazier than the last, until I'm imagining a sex dungeon with whips and chains and unfamiliar monster devices.

There's still the chance he meant punished as in being tortured, but I'm unconvinced. The way he lustfully watched Azarius and me in the dining room. The way he pinned me to the wall and knew exactly how to choke me without crushing my windpipe. My gut tells me he meant something painfully pleasurable.

Or pleasurably painful.

Either way, I don't know if I intend to find out.

After several hours staring at the four walls of my room and wishing desperately for an escape from my boredom, a knock at the door makes me jump. My eyes nervously travel across the room and my heart slams hard in my chest.

Is Azarius bringing me my things? Is Rafe coming to hunt me down? That thought alone makes the hair on the back of my neck stand on end. I don't think I can face him again, especially so soon. I swallow down my nerves.

"Come in," I call, bracing myself for whoever is about to enter.

The door swings open slowly, and I catch my breath. To my relief, it's Azarius. A teal duffel bag I recognize as my own hangs on his shoulder, and upon seeing me, a smile spreads across his face.

"Thank God you're back." I hurry across the room to his side, and, instinctively, I wrap my arms around his middle. I'm instantly overcome by a flutter of nerves; I realize this is the closest we've been since I gave him a blowjob in the dining room. His muscles tense, and I chance a glance up to find him staring at me.

His eyes glint with curiosity. "Happy to see me?"

I fight the tinge of heat prickling my cheeks and put on a smirk to cover my embarrassment.

"Of course," I assure him. "You brought me presents."

I take my duffel bag and carry it to the bed, unzipping it excitedly. I can't wait to strip out of Xia's clothes and slip into something that fits. "Lots of jeans, I hope."

"As requested." He chuckles and crosses to my side as I pull things out.

There are shirts and pants, but absolutely no bras. I can't tell if that was an accident or intentional neglect, but I'm not upset about it.

Bras are overrated.

At the bottom of the bag, I find nearly every thong I own and a strappy lingerie piece that I bought one year around Valentine's Day. Of course, they were buried—those were the first things he grabbed. I fight the urge to shake my head and flash him a smile.

"Thank you so much, Az. Did you give Cara the rent money?"

"She wasn't home, so I left it on the kitchen counter." He takes a seat beside me on the bed, a smile teasing the corners of his mouth. "You don't have to thank me. It's the least I can do for now. Maybe soon, I'll be able to do more for you."

"Well, I'm going to thank you anyway, because I appreciate it."

I turn the duffel bag upside down and dump all the underwear out on the bed.

"If she wasn't home, how did you know which bedroom was mine?" I ask, raising a brow before I start organizing my clothes.

With my house keys and the address, they wouldn't have had any issue finding where I live or getting inside, but Cara's room is right across the hall from mine. I'm curious if they rummaged through both rooms first. I wish I could have been there to watch their confusion.

"Oh, that was easy. You'd never pick the horrendous curtains in her room."

I pause mid-fold and laugh, recalling Cara's sheer pink curtains with colorful lace flowers cascading down from the top. She told me she got them from a thrift store downtown, but I secretly think she made them herself. They have personality, but they're repulsive.

"Touché." I finish folding the pair of jeans in my hands and lay them aside.

After a beat, Azarius laughs. "I'm kidding."

"Then what gave it away?" I fold two more pairs of jeans and stack them on top of the first.

He leans closer, shrinking the distance between us, and his voice drops an octave. "I could smell you."

My stomach does a funny flip. "You could smell me?"

He dips his head in a nod. "On your clothes. On your bed." The last word rolls sensually off his tongue.

I look over, and his gaze locks with mine, tangible tension settling between us. The longer we stare at one another, heat rises in my cheeks, and a distinct flutter erupts in my stomach. I shouldn't turn into a blubbering schoolgirl with a crush every time he's near, but I do.

"H-how did your meeting go?" I fumble over my words as I hurriedly try to change the subject.

The smugness in his expression wanes. His jaw tenses, and his eyes flash briefly with worry, but he breaks our eye contact and looks at the stack of clothes to cover it up.

"It went."

His words are followed by an uneasy silence, one my undying curiosity doesn't let live long.

"That doesn't sound good," I say, leaning into Azarius' line of sight and raising my brows. "Do you want to talk about it?"

He massages the bridge of his nose between two fingers, as though the mere thought of the meeting gives him a headache. He sighs. "I'm sure I'll get in trouble for telling you, but since it concerns you, you should probably know."

I freeze, trying to discern if I heard him correctly. How did their meeting concern me? He hesitates, and I wonder if he's debating how much he should tell me. I don't want him to get in trouble with Rafe, but he doesn't have to worry. My lips are sealed.

"We didn't know what the meeting would be about when we got there. I thought Ross was going to ask for more money or more land in exchange for his support, but that wasn't it," he explains, carefully avoiding my gaze. "Apparently, there's a rumor going around that a human made it into the monster realm."

My eyes grow wide. Someone outside the mansion knows I'm here.

"What? How the hell does anyone even know about that?" I gape.

"It was your blood." His shoulders sag slightly, and the corners of his mouth follow shortly after. "I don't know who found it. I don't even know how wide the rumor has spread, but they seem to think whoever made it through the portal killed the Malev and is hiding somewhere."

"That's not bad, right?" I ask, trying to remain optimistic. "Surely, they know a human wouldn't last long here."

He shrugs slowly and drops his gaze to the floor. "Ross offered a hefty bounty if we're able to track the human down alive. There's no telling how many others will do the same."

Fear zips up my back. I hadn't considered what might happen if other monsters figured out I'm still here, and I doubt Azarius has either.

"So what? I'm a wanted fugitive or something?" I ask, crossing my arms tightly over my chest for some kind of comfort. Another question blossoms to life in my mind, and as much as I don't want to know the answer, I ask it anyway. "Do you think Rafe would hand me over?"

He doesn't say anything at first, but after a long moment, he finally lifts his gaze to meet mine. The uncertainty in his eyes is clear, which only fuels my fear. He offers me a hand, which I take, and he guides me between his legs. His fingers intertwine with mine, making my chest flutter nervously, and his other hand finds my waist.

"Rafe is unpredictable," he says. "But I swear, I'll do everything I can to protect you."

For a moment, I can do nothing more than lose myself in the impossible blueness of his eyes and the sincerity of his promise. The comfort his touch brings staunches my fear and gives me hope. Hope that we'll find a solution to get me out of the monster realm, that we'll figure it out sooner rather than later, hope that Rafe doesn't sell me to whatever monster comes knocking.

Azarius gives me hope.

Even if things were completely different—if I wasn't being held captive in another realm and he hadn't claimed me to save my life—I would still be drawn to Azarius. From the moment we met, I experienced something I hadn't felt in a very long time. We had a connection, a spark.

He's gorgeous in either form, sweet and compassionate. He's always making me smile, even when it's not intentional. He really is a catch. Now, he's vowing to protect me.

How can I not swoon?

Overwhelmed by the sudden urge to close the distance between us, I lean in to kiss him. What starts as a light brush of my lips against his quickly escalates to a deep, yearning kiss that takes my breath away. His lips dance expertly against mine, and his grip on my hip tightens, pulling me slowly toward him.

My knees go weak, and I lean into him for

support. He wraps his arms around me and pulls me close, which intensifies the electricity thrumming through me. Then, his hands slide down my back and over my ass. He hooks his hands around my thighs and uses them to pull me into his lap so I can straddle him.

The change in position and the closeness of his body spark my libido to life, and as his lips continue to dance against mine, the spark swells to a steady burn. I'd almost forgotten how incredible our scene in the dining room had been, and the image comes rushing back in detail.

I can't fight the desire to feel him in me. Fingers, tail, tongue, cock. At this point, it doesn't matter what he does to me, as long as he does it soon.

He breaks our kiss and moves his mouth to my neck, kissing and sucking until my eyelids flutter closed. A moan escapes my lips.

"Do you want me to fuck you?" he whispers against my skin.

I nod, and he kisses his way to the other side of my neck, sucking tenderly as he goes. I grind my hips against him, my swollen clit desperate for attention.

"Say it," he says in my ear, his deep voice sending a wave of pleasure vibrating through me. I can already feel my wetness soaking into my pants at his command.

"Please." I barely recognize the needy whine in my voice.

Both of his hands grip my ass and squeeze, pulling me down onto the bulge in his pants. He's hard and ready, but he's holding back, not rushing anything. If he's trying to make up for the first time, he's succeeding. Immaculately.

"Please, what?"

His hands slip under my shirt, fingers brushing against my stomach before inching their way higher. I knead my bottom lip between my teeth, anticipating his hands on my breasts, but his fingers stop just shy.

"Please, what?" he says with a little more grit.

Every part of me is on fire with need, and I don't know how much longer I can wait before I combust. I pull back and meet his gaze, losing myself in the deep blue of his eyes again. I've become so used to his monster form—from the black markings winding their way across his skin to the dark horns that curl out of his blonde hair—I've almost forgotten what he looks like as a human. I doubt I'd find his human form as sexy as I find him right now.

Who knew my type was tall, pale, and monstrous?

Certainly not me.

"Fuck me," I say, burying my fingers in his hair and tugging playfully. "With your cock this time."

He smirks at my words. "Yes ma'am."

In a flash, my shirt is pulled over my head and discarded on the floor. Azarius dips down to catch one of my nipples in his mouth, sucking and working his tongue around it while taking my other breast in his hand. He teases my nipple until it pebbles beneath his touch, and I grind my hips, pressing myself harder against his restrained erection.

I'm eager, but I can't help it. If he can get me off

with his tail, he obviously knows what he's doing. I want to see how hard he can make me come, how many times.

I won't tell him, but I'm a little curious to see if his cock is going to fit. I've never been with anyone as big as he is.

He pulls his own shirt off, exposing his perfectly chiseled torso, and tosses it aside carelessly before hooking his hands under my ass and standing. I suck in a sharp breath, impressed by how he carries me as though I'm weightless.

He turns around to lay me on the bed, and in a swift motion, he slides between my legs and pins me to the mattress. The weight of him intensifies the heat between my thighs, and I gasp as he rolls his hips, pressing the rock in the front of his pants against me.

I can already imagine his hard length thrusting into me, and damn it, do I want it.

He kisses his way down my chest, sucking at my nipples and running his tongue down my stomach before reaching my pants, which he makes quick work of and tosses to the floor. Suddenly, I'm completely nude, legs spread wide as his warm breath rolls over my swollen clit and sends pulses of electricity through my limbs.

I could almost come from the sheer build-up of desire welling in me, demanding release.

He runs his tongue up the length of my pussy before pressing it flat against my clit. I gasp, my legs trembling from the intense pleasure as he works his tongue against me, and I grip fistfuls of the comforter.

He picks up the pace, licking me hungrily, as though I'm the sweetest thing he's ever tasted, before he takes my clit in his mouth and sucks tenderly.

I moan his name between breaths.

His mouth skills well exceed those of his tail—not that I'm surprised—and I can already feel the hint of my climax teasing me. My grip on the blanket tightens as I rock my hips against his mouth, quickly falling into rhythm with the flick of his tongue. It's been so long since anyone has touched me, and even longer since they've traced every inch of my sex with their mouth, but Azarius puts them all to shame.

He's fucking good at it.

I pry my hands from the comforter and bury one of them in his hair. With the other, I grip one of his horns experimentally, pulling him into me, and he moans against me. The vibrations against my clit draw my climax nearer, and I buck my hips faster.

I need to come, but I'm at Azarius' mercy.

"Harder." The word passes my lips in a whisper before I can stop it.

He obliges, increasing the pressure of his tongue, and I moan his name through gritted teeth. He runs his fingers gently along the length of me before slipping two inside. He pumps steadily while his mouth continues its work on my swollen nub.

Tension mounts in my body, like a rubber band being stretched to its absolute limit before it finally snaps. My climax crashes into me, waves of pulsating pleasure starting beneath Azarius' tongue and rolling outward, racking my body until it trembles. I cry out, overwhelmed by the strength of it as Azarius continues pumping his fingers into me until I come down from the high.

"Fuck," I gasp, finally releasing his horn and untangling my fingers from his hair.

The room is sweltering, and I'm the furnace.

"You're breathtaking," he says with a smile. He climbs back up my body, kissing my exposed skin along the way.

He shirks off his pants, kicking them to the floor, and settles his weight on top of me. The head of his dick presses against me, begging for entry, but again, he doesn't seem to be in a hurry.

He has an insane amount of patience, I'll give him that. Way more than me.

He kisses me and rocks his hips forward, pressing himself harder against me. My legs are trembling, and I can't tell if it's the aftershock from my orgasm or my nerves mounting.

His cock is huge, and there's a chance I won't be able to take it. What then?

I guess I'm about to find out.

"You know," he says, brushing his lips against my neck. I wrap my arms around his shoulders, pulling him into me, longing to feel his tongue against my skin. "You lied to me."

I stop, brow furrowing deep over my eyes. I have no idea what he's talking about, or why he's bringing it up now.

"Lied?" I ask, racking my brain. "About what?"

He pulls back just enough that our noses touch.

His eyes are bright, and I don't have to see his mouth to know he's smiling.

"You don't have a tattoo on your asshole."

I chuckle and open my mouth to say something, but it's cut off by Azarius pushing his cock inside me. He slowly stretches and fills me to the max, until I'm teetering on the brink of discomfort, and my fingernails dig into his shoulders. I'm tempted to apologize, but a growl deep in his chest assures me he's fine. In fact, I think he enjoyed that a little too much.

As he pulls back and thrusts forward again, going slow so I can stretch and take all of him, I reach higher up his back and rake my nails across his skin. His eyes close, the growl in his chest growing louder.

"If you keep that up, I won't be able to control myself," he warns.

He buries his face in the crook of my neck, nibbling at my skin, before biting down on just the right spot to make my body turn to mush. I cling to him reflexively, every fiber of my being teeming with anticipation. Now that I've adjusted to his size, I'm ready for him to have his way with me. I belong to him, and I'll do what he wants.

Whatever he wants, however he wants it.

"Are you worried about hurting me?" My words are breathy as he buries himself in me again, his pace slow and steady. When he brushes his lips against mine, I realize how intimate he is. For a monster, he's incredibly docile. I think that's what makes him so damn sexy. He's holding back.

If I gave him permission, he would probably fuck me in half.

"A little." He thrusts harder, burying himself as deep as he can until my pussy tightens around his girth.

"I'm tougher than you think." I grin cockily and roll my hips up to meet his. "Try me."

I reach for his back again and slice my fingernails across his skin. I'm certain I've drawn blood this time. The growl in Azarius' chest peaks as he picks up his pace, slamming his full length into me, eliciting a whimper from my lips. My swollen clit is throbbing, and I reach between us to rub it, but Azarius grabs my hand and pins it beside my head.

"You come when I say." He increases his pace to a blinding speed, slamming into me with such force, we rock the heavy bed, the headboard knocking steadily against the wall.

"Please," I beg, desperate for release. Every thrust sends a jolt of pleasure bursting through me, but it's not enough to make me finish. It would only take a few seconds of clit stimulation for me to come. He could press it like a button and set me off.

Instead, he says, "Not yet."

He releases my wrist and reaches for my thigh, hiking my leg up until it's propped on his shoulder. From this position, he's able to go deeper, and his length is almost too much for me, but I won't tap out, not after I told him I could handle it. Instead, I bite my bottom lip to stifle the cry fighting its way up my throat as he pounds into me mercilessly.

I'll be lucky if I can walk after this.

After a few more thrusts, he slips his cock out of me and sits back on his heels. I wonder momentarily if I've done something wrong, but he affectionately slaps a hand against my thigh and makes a jerking motion with his head.

"Roll over so I can fuck you from behind."

My stomach somersaults, the way it does every time he orders me to do something, and I flip over onto my stomach. I get on my knees, arching my back and positioning myself for him as I feel the pressure of his cock against my opening. He pushes his way inside, letting me stretch and adjust once more before quickly picking up his pace.

I bury my face in the pillow as he strokes fast and deep, every thrust drawing a moan from my lips. He slaps a flat hand against my ass without interrupting his pace, and after the shock of the pain wears off, it's replaced by an enjoyable heat. He slaps the other side, evening them out, and I'm swallowed by another rush of warmth.

"Fuck," I groan into the pillow.

My clit is so swollen, I'm surprised it hasn't burst at this point, and just as I'm considering touching it again, Azarius' hand winds its way around my waist and finds it. It's slick with wetness, and as he rubs in time with his thrusts, the climax swelling inside me is finally unleashed.

My orgasm engulfs me, and I scream into the pillow as he continues to slam into me, his fingers working mercilessly against my clit. He rides me through it, almost to the end, before his own release claims him.

"Shit," he grinds out as he slams into me a final time.

I can feel every inch of his cock contract as he fills me to the brim with cum, and as soon as he withdraws himself, I collapse to the bed.

I'm entirely spent. Thoroughly fucked.

His breaths are heavy as he flops down onto the bed beside me—apparently, he wore himself out too. I drag myself over, curling myself up against him, and lay my head on his chest. I instantly hear his wild heartbeat galloping beneath me.

"Can we pretend that was our first time?" he asks jokingly, resting his chin on top of my head. "We can just pretend the first one never happened."

I completely understand why he feels that way, and if I'm honest, I agree. This is how it should have been, not forced the way it was in the dining room, not in front of an audience.

Still, I can't let him off that easily. He's too fun to mess with. Besides, if I stop using comedy when things get too serious, I'll be forced to admit that I'm falling for Azarius.

I'm not ready for that truth.

"I don't know. I really liked you telling me to get on my knees," I say flippantly and begin to trace one of the markings on his chest with my finger.

He laughs. "I'll keep that in mind for next time."

After cleaning ourselves up and sliding adjusting the bed, which we managed to scoot a few inches away from the wall, Azarius crawls under the comforter and motions for me to join him. As I settle into him again, I put my head on his chest, and his arm curls around my back.

I don't know what to say when he pulls me close and runs his fingers up and down my arm, but I can't deny that I enjoy the fuzzy feeling it gives me. He presses his lips to the top of my head, and I close my eyes, reveling in the moment.

"Do you want me to stay with you tonight?" he asks into my hair, his voice barely more than a whisper.

The truth is, I do. Still, I'm hesitant to say yes.

Spending time with him will only intensify the feelings I have for him, which are already too strong to ignore. On the other hand, the thought of sleeping alone leaves a hollow ache in my chest. It's probably best to tell him no, so I can process my thoughts alone, but I'm so comfortable.

It would be a pity to have to move.

"You can stay." Making it his decision makes me feel better. That way, I'm not having to confront my feelings and decide.

"I know you'll let me," he says. "I want to know if you want me to."

I swallow hard, fighting the urge to say yes. Falling in love with a monster isn't going to get me any closer to home. Honestly, it might end up doing more harm than good in the long run.

I'm scared; admitting it out loud would make me seem weak. I don't want that. I'm already vastly outpowered by the monsters here. The Malev proved that. Adding emotional weakness to my lack of physical strength makes me feel useless, and that's not how I see myself.

But Azarius is my mate. If he's willing to protect me and stand up to Rafe, why shouldn't I be honest with him?

The shadow of an answer flashes in my brain, crawling its way out of my 'emotional bullshit' filing cabinet. Being raw and vulnerable with someone is hard after you've had your heart ripped out and stepped on. It fucking sucks, but the only way to trust again is to give someone else the opportunity to be trusted.

"Yes," I say, tucking my thoughts back into my mental filing cabinet.

With his free hand, he reaches over and tilts my chin up to look at him. A sense of calm melts through me as I stare into his sapphire eyes, and I know instantly that I could get used to this.

"Then I'll stay."

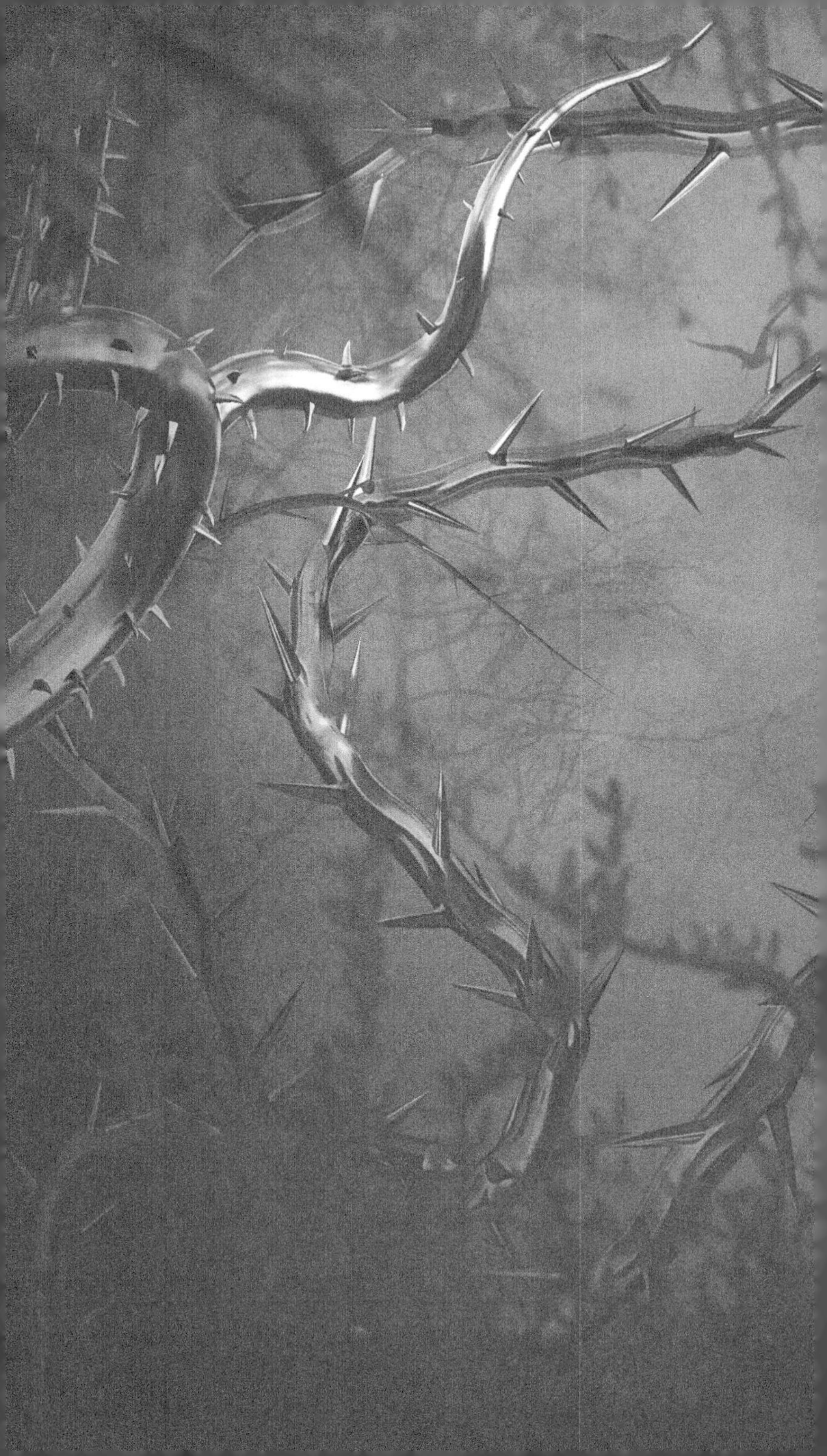

12
DEVYN

The schedule at the mansion is sporadic, and most of the time, Elio or Azarius are sent on errands at the drop of a hat. Still, over the next week, I'm able to somewhat adjust to a routine. Every morning, everyone except Rafe meets in the dining room for breakfast, which is normally prepared by Elio. I tried helping once, but I wound up asking questions the whole time while he cooked. After that, I decided to stay out of the kitchen.

"We had several maids that handled the cooking and the cleaning," Azarius explains to my left as Elio serves a pile of beige and green slop with mashed potato consistency. "But once the Malevs started migrating this way, they got nervous and disappeared. Probably went farther West to the closest city."

"But what about the woods?" I ask, poking my food with a spoon. "I thought you said no Malevs have ever made it through."

"That's right. They haven't," he says, bobbing his

head up and down. "But fear makes people irrational. It distorts truths, can implant a false reality in your head if you aren't careful. They feared the Malevs more than they feared Rafe, and they acted on it."

"Have they met Rafe?" I force a laugh and mumble under my breath. "I'd take Malevs over him any day."

Elio snickers, but his serious expression quickly returns. His metallic skin glistens in the light of the chandelier as he moves around the room, his wings nowhere in sight. "You're right to fear him, but the Malevs should not be taken lightly. You've only seen one. If you saw thousands creeping toward you from the horizon, you would understand their fear."

Thousands.

Up until now, I've never considered how many Malevs exist, or even how many monsters live here. My limited knowledge of the realm had me convinced the entire place was a barren wasteland, home to a few monsters scattered here and there.

Now, I know I'm wrong.

"That sounds terrifying." A chill slips down my spine at the thought.

I have no doubt Azarius, Elio, and especially Rafe can hold their own in a fight, but there's no way the three of them could take on an army. Anxiety kills my appetite—not that the mushy appearance was helping any—and I push my plate away.

"Don't worry about it," Azarius says. He reaches over and plants a reassuring hand on my thigh beneath the table. "Rafe is putting together a legion of monsters to fight them. By the time we get everyone involved, it'll be a breeze."

I know he's only saying the words for my benefit, and I try to cling to them, but the unsettling feeling in my stomach remains.

"How soon do you think that'll happen?"

"It could be today," Elio interrupts, taking a seat across the table. "It could be three months from now. We don't know for sure, but we do know it's coming."

He takes a bite of his slop, making my stomach turn, and kisses the tips of his fingers. "Perfection. I definitely outdid myself this time."

"Are you part Italian, by chance?" I ask, curious about his accent and the hand gesture.

He shakes his head. "No, not at all, but I would like to go there someday. I was born on the opposite side of the realm in a place called Theev. Think of it like another country."

"Wow." I nod, my mind spinning with this new information.

There are multiple countries and countless cities that make up the monster realm, yet the only glimpses I've seen of it are the abandoned buildings where the portal dumped me out, and the inside of this mansion. I still haven't ventured outside because I'm terrified of leading Malevs or monsters—or both—straight to Rafe's front door.

"I feel like I need a whole history lesson to catch up."

"It's not that different from Earth," Elio assures me between bites. "Different races inhabit this realm:

monsters, Malevs, demons, warlocks, and lots of hybrids in between. We've experienced war, famine, and plagues. The main difference is that here, most of the time, you know who the bad guys are."

"The Malevs and the demons are the bad guys," I guess. "Right?"

"Right," Azarius says as he nudges my leg gently with his knee.

"Then what are the—" I don't finish my sentence, because the door behind us opens suddenly, and panic floods me. There's only one person absent from the table, and unless someone broke in, I know who's behind me.

"Azarius," Rafe's voice fills the room and gives me chill bumps.

Az stands beside me and turns on his heel, his tail falling into my lap. "Yes sir."

"Come with me. I need you to run an errand, and we don't have much time."

"Yes, boss."

His gaze meets mine, and he offers me a half-smile before following Rafe out of the dining room. The door settles closed behind me, and I stare awkwardly at Elio, who's finishing his plate.

"Things would be way easier here with cell phones, don't you think?" I ask, trying to drum up conversation.

Normally, Elio would offer a short answer and leave me alone, but this time, he doesn't. Something—or someone—must have put him in a good mood last night, because he was not this friendly at dinner.

"Definitely," he agrees. "Convenience is one thing I miss about Earth. You have everything you need right at your fingertips. Here, you're hours or even days away."

A long pause stretches between us, and the sound of the fireplace crackling is the only thing breaking up the silence. I'm tempted to take my food back to my room so I can try to eat it later, but Elio speaks before I can move.

"What were you going to say?"

I tilt my head to the side. I've already forgotten what we were talking about. "When?"

"When Rafe came in. You said, 'then what are the' and then you stopped."

I rack my brain, backpedaling through our conversation. "I asked if the Malevs and demons are the bad guys." Then my memory jogs. "Oh yeah. Then what are the hybrids?"

"A hybrid is any entity with mixed blood from two or more of the four races. Malevs are technically hybrids, but there are so many of them, we classify them as their own race," he explains, his accent playing in my ears like a song.

If he wasn't so short with me all the time, I might ask him to talk all day, just so I could listen.

"I, for example, am a hybrid," he adds.

My eyebrows shoot up, and I'm unable to mask my confusion. "You're not just a monster?"

He shakes his head and pushes his empty plate away. "My grandfather was a warlock. I'm mostly monster, but warlock blood runs in my veins, too. That's how I'm able to open the portals."

"What about Azarius?"

Elio shrugs. "He's a dumbass."

A smile tries to cross my lips, but not because of the insult. For the first time since I came through the portal, Elio is acting like the snarky guy I met in the Uber. It's a relief.

"He's a monster," he answers, getting serious again.

"What about Rafe?"

To wield so much power, he must have something other than monster blood. The way he can materialize out of the shadows is unlike anything I've seen Elio or Azarius do.

Elio nods, confirming my suspicions. "Rafe is a hybrid, one of the most powerful kinds. He's half demon, part monster, and part warlock."

"Everything but the kitchen sink, huh?"

"Pretty much." Elio pushes his chair back and collects his dishes, finishing off the rest of his drink before making his way around the table. I stay seated, intent on waiting until Elio disappears before I take my plate upstairs, but he stops next to my chair and stares down at me.

"Do you want to go for a walk?" he asks, gesturing to the double doors with a jerk of his head. "We can't go far, but it might be nice to get outside for a bit."

"Sure." I answer too quickly, but I don't care. I'm just glad he isn't being an asshole.

After helping him wash the dishes and store my

food, which I promised to eat later, I slip upstairs to get my shoes and meet him by the front door.

He's dressed in a pair of blue jeans and a tight-fitting, navy shirt, which makes his coppery skin stand out. He redid his man bun, tying it slickly behind his head. My gaze tumbles down his form and stops at the pair of work boots on his feet.

"Not a fan of tennis shoes?" I joke, looking him up and down.

"These are my ass stomping boots." He gestures to them with a smile. "Steel toed, with a blade hidden in the bottom."

I stare shamelessly. "Where can I get some of those?"

"I think I got them in Atlanta," he said, scratching one of his horns. "Or Lexington. Either way, we can find you some. If you're going to be here a while, you might need them."

He pulls open the door, and a column of pale green light spills into the foyer. The twin suns in the wide expanse overhead bathe everything in green light, just like the moon at night. The constant, sickly effect is one thing I won't miss about the monster realm. I can't wait to see sunlight on Earth again.

"After you," Elio says, gesturing to the doorway.

The warm air hugs my skin as I make my way down the stairs, and I pause at the bottom for Elio to catch up. Being outside for the first time in a week is a freeing experience, but the drastic openness leaves me feeling exposed. Vulnerable.

"Are you sure this is safe?" I scan the dark tree

line, but I can't see anything past the closest trunks, all the foliage melting into a smear of thorny blackness.

"Relatively," he says, strolling off to the left. I fall in step beside him, anxiety crawling over my skin.

"Relatively sure, or relatively safe?"

"We're safe, Devyn. These woods are miles thick," he explains, sweeping his hand toward the trees. "We've been running perimeter checks every day, and we haven't seen anything alarming."

"That's a lie." I shake my head adamantly. "You told Azarius you found footprints."

"Okay, yes, I did, but I followed them and checked that entire half of the woods. Whatever it was came in and left. It was probably lost."

I purse my lips, unconvinced, but there's no point in arguing. We're already outside. If something attacks us, he'd better handle it. Otherwise, I'm kicking his ass.

A small garden of different colored plants blooms beside the mansion. It's beautiful, but I wish I could see it under the clear light of Earth's sun to fully enjoy the different hues. The green light here distorts them until I'm not sure what colors they really are.

"Who tends to the garden?" I ask, almost expecting him to say himself, since he handles a lot of the housework.

"Rafe, believe it or not."

I don't believe him.

"That's a good joke." I laugh, and we stop by the rows of plants. "It's Azarius, isn't it? He seems like the tree-hugger type."

Elio shakes his head. "I was being serious. Rafe spends a lot of time out here in the garden. Ironic, I know, but he can grow plants better than anyone I've ever seen."

I stare down at the leaves and flowers, trying to wrap my brain around Rafe the gardener.

"Are these special plants?"

"Some of them are, but the really special ones he keeps in a small greenhouse on the roof." Elio points to a tiny plant near the mansion wall. It has diamond-shaped leaves and small, prickly flowers. "These are poisonous. He hides them throughout the plants, in case something messes with his garden—it'll kill them."

"Ah, you should have led with plants that kill. I see the appeal now." I nudge him playfully with my elbow. "Make it murderous, and Rafe will be all about it."

He looks over, and his eyes lock with mine. "I know you're joking, but that's accurate."

I snicker and Elio joins in, our laughs playing off one another until we're cackling.

We keep walking, curving our way around to the back of the building. I've seen enough of the yard through the windows to know there's nothing out here but the garden, but it's still strange to see such a beautiful, elaborate house in the middle of nothing.

They could have at least put a firepit or something out here to make it a little more inviting, not that Rafe gets a lot of guests. It's just him, Azarius, and Elio now, and he keeps the boys on their toes with assignments and errands. They would never have time to entertain people anyway, all things considered.

"Do you ever get lonely out here?" I ask.

Elio glances over briefly and looks ahead again, avoiding my gaze. "Occasionally. Azarius and I hang out when we have downtime, but it's not often. Rafe has us chasing down monsters most of the time."

"It's good that you have him. He seems really nice."

Elio scoffs. "He's nicer than most monsters, that's for sure. I think spending time with the humans has made him soft. He wasn't always like that. He was fucking scary when we met."

I try to imagine Azarius being a raging asshole like Rafe, or even a decent pain in the ass like Elio, but the image doesn't form. It feels wrong, like two puzzle pieces that don't fit together, and it doesn't sit well with me.

"Being nice isn't a bad thing," I point out. "You should try it sometime."

"I don't know." He rubs his chin dramatically, as though he's considering it carefully. "I have the reputation of being a dickhead to uphold. I wouldn't want anything like manners to go besmirching my good name."

I dissolve to laughter again, and Elio stops walking to let me catch my breath.

"You're right. Leave the good guy act to Az. You're mastered the art of being an ass."

"Besides," he says, raising one of his shoulders in

a shrug. "I've heard some women prefer assholes. Isn't that why they pine for the villains in movies?"

I open my mouth to argue, but I snap it shut again. I can't deny Loki is one of the sexiest cinematic villains I've ever seen, and I've had some very lethal book boyfriends over the years. There's just something about a bad guy who's morally gray and has a way with words that makes you need to change your panties.

"Right again," I say, reluctant to give him the satisfaction of proving his point. I tuck my thumbs into the pockets of my jeans. "I love a good villain too."

"See?" Elio smirks, clearly proud of himself. "If you had to pick between the good guy and the villain, who would you choose?"

I suck in a breath through my teeth, considering heroes and villains I love in movies and literature, but the choice feels impossible. Yes, the good guy will consider your feelings, put you on a pedestal, treat you like a princess, but the villain will challenge you, drag you along on dangerous, riveting adventures.

I don't even know why Elio cares about something so silly.

"Can I have both?" I ask with a grimace. "Settling for just one doesn't seem fair."

"It's a hypothetical. Of course, you can." Elio nods once and moves toward me, his gaze gripping mine like a vice. "It could also be a reality."

My heart jumps into my throat as I stare at him, trying to comprehend what he's implying.

If Azarius is the good guy, is he insinuating he's the bad guy? He's saying I can have both of them if I want.

My stunned silence drags on longer than I intend, and Elio finally smirks and looks away.

"That's not why I brought you out here. I promise," he says, and starts walking again.

I follow along, my mind still reeling. I wonder what he might have done if I'd said yes.

"Was it to warn me about the poisonous flowers?" I attempt a laugh.

"No. I actually wanted to ask your opinion without Azarius interfering."

I shoot him a confused look, my brows knitting together. Why would he possibly want my opinion? Why would it matter if Az was there or not?

"I don't understand. My opinion about what?"

He stops in his tracks again. We're near the back corner of the house now, and I'm starting to wonder if he brought me here to be out of Rafe's earshot. The way he drops his voice only increases my suspicion.

"Azarius is convinced you're not entirely human," he starts, his eyes shifting between me and the trees. "I'm starting to believe it, but we have no way of proving it here at the mansion."

My ears perk up, and my heart skips a funny beat. "Are we going to try the portal again?"

He shakes his head, killing my excitement. "No, we can't use the portal yet. Even if we went against Rafe's orders and sent you back, we can't promise that you'll be safe yet. These rumors are nothing to take lightly."

I nod along, disappointment dragging my shoulders down. "What are we going to do?"

"That depends on your answer," he says. "I didn't want Azarius pressuring you into doing this, because it's dangerous. It could potentially get us all killed, but we would take every precaution possible to avoid that." He shifts his weight from foot to foot and meets my eyes. "A friend of mine, Ignatius, lives in a small city called Havec. He's a warlock—a powerful one. If anyone can tell us what's in your blood, he can, but getting to him won't be easy."

"Because all the monsters will be able to smell me?"

He nods slowly and crosses his arms over his chest. "That's the biggest concern."

The idea of walking into a monster city with a metaphorical target on my back is daunting, terrifying, even. I've seen what monsters can do, and it could easily turn ugly fast.

"Why can't he just come here?" I ask. "That seems way easier."

"You're not wrong. I considered it, but the more I think, the more complicated it seems," he explains. "If we bring Ignatius here, Rafe will know something's up. There's no disguising that kind of magic, and I haven't exactly told him our plans. I'm hoping I won't have to."

"Are you serious?" I drop my voice to a whisper

and glare at him, suddenly worried the walls have ears and that Rafe is listening in.

Elio doesn't seem bothered. He must know something I don't, or he's lying about telling Rafe. He presses on, "Also, Rafe doesn't let just anyone come to the mansion. It's well hidden for a reason—he doesn't want random people knowing his secrets, and while I'm friends with Ignatius, Rafe is not."

"Does Rafe have any friends?" I mumble.

Elio smirks. "Debatable."

"Okay, what about meeting halfway or something?" I'm still trying to help problem solve, to avoid walking straight into a metaphorical lion's den.

"I don't think it's wise to be out in the open," he explains. "I'm honestly not sure what he'll need to figure out what's in your blood. I know I'm part warlock, but the only thing I can do is open portals. That's all that was ever taught to me."

My head is spinning. I wish I had more time to think about it—consider all our options and possibly come up with some alternatives—but the sooner we get this figured out, the better. If this warlock proves I'm a monster, it will solve the mystery of the portal and stop the rumors. I might even get to go home.

"Do you have a plan to get us there?" I cock my head to the side. "You said it won't be easy."

"I do," he assures me. "I'm working out the kinks. Masking your scent will be the hardest part, but I think we can do it."

It might be my desperation talking, or it might be

that I've grown way too trusting of Azarius and Elio, but I'm willing to try. Elio is attentive to details and incredibly smart, so I know he'll handle the difficulties of the plan. Azarius has already promised to protect me. He won't let anyone hurt me if he can help it.

"Okay." I nod. "Let's do it."

For a second, Elio looks shocked. I don't think he expected me to agree so easily, or he would have asked while Azarius was present.

"Are you sure?" he asks, but I think he's trying to reassure himself more than anything.

"Yep." I turn and round the corner of the building. Elio quickly catches up and falls in step beside me. "When do you want to do it?"

Not surprisingly, he's already got an answer.

"Rafe will be traveling in a few days," he says. "I don't know how long he'll be gone. Sometimes, he's gone for a few days, other times for weeks. I think we should do it then."

"That's probably a good idea." I nod in agreement. "Where's he going?"

I look over in time to see him shrug. "There's information he doesn't trust us with, and I've learned over the years it's better not to ask. My guess would be he's going to check in with some of his more powerful allies to discuss our next steps, but he could just as easily be going to a brothel."

I snort out a laugh. "A monster brothel?"

"You laugh," he says with a nod. "But I wouldn't be surprised."

"Murderous plants and monster brothels." Not to mention Elio suggesting I could have both him and Azarius if I wanted them. "I don't think anything could surprise me anymore."

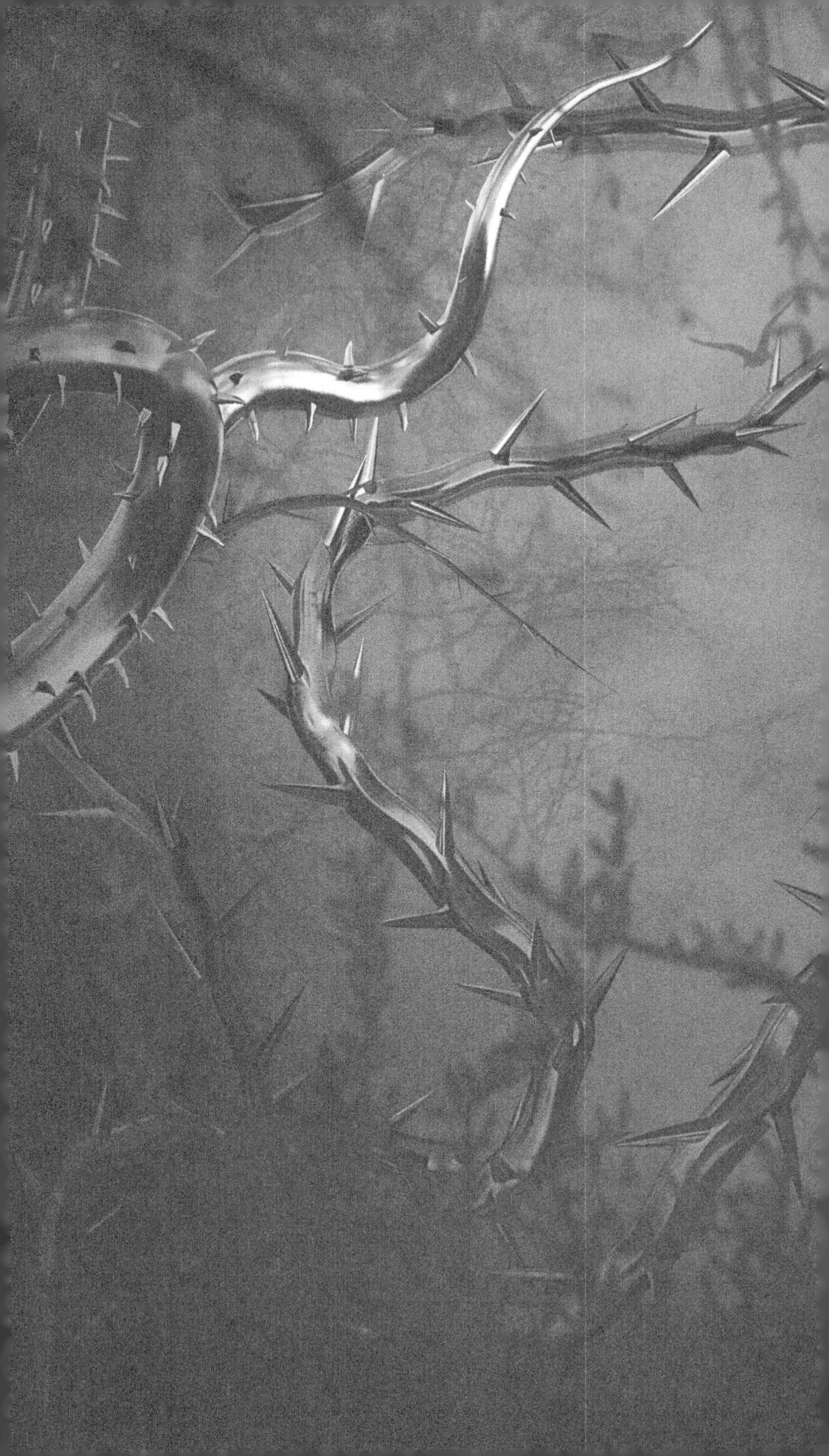

13
DEVYN

I lied.

Despite trying to convince myself that nothing else could surprise me, I am absolutely shocked by what I'm about to do. I'm standing in the middle of Elio's bedroom, which is dripping in maroon and gold from floor to ceiling, covering my nose with the end of my shirt while Azarius sits on the floor, crushing the most rancid-smelling plant in a bowl.

Elio's solution for disguising my scent is the rank sap from these roots. They're going to cover me with it.

"If this doesn't mask you, nothing will," Azarius says, his nose upturned. He's been grinding the roots with a pestle for several minutes, turning it to pulp, and the overwhelming smell has filled the room. "I definitely can't smell you right now."

"Is this guy even going to let me in his house

smelling like ass?" I ask through the material of my shirt.

Elio nods. "He better. Otherwise, we might have to be a little persuasive."

"Agreed." Azarius tests the consistency of the mixture with his fingers, shakes his head, and keeps grinding. "The smell should die down a little when it dries."

"I sure fucking hope so," I say, gagging slightly.

I might be rethinking my decision to see Ignatius just a smidge, but I quickly remind myself what we're doing this for. We have to stop the rumors, figure out if the portal really is broken, and potentially get me home.

It's just one more hurdle.

One more.

"What did you say that thing was called again?"

"Nesda," Elio answers as he crosses to the bed and takes a seat on the edge. "The flowers are an antivenom for Malev bites. The plant itself doesn't smell too bad, but the roots are vile."

I swallow down my disgust and wait patiently until Azarius is done grinding.

"What are we going to paint it on with?" he asks, looking eagerly to Elio for an answer.

Rather than giving a useful suggestion, Elio shrugs. "Your toothbrush."

Az narrows his eyes into slits. "Very funny."

"Can't you just use your hands?" Elio asks.

Az scrunches his nose again. "That's gross, but I

guess if Devyn has to smell like roadkill, I can too." He throws me a wink. "We can stink together."

"Elio's going to smell awful too from carrying me," I point out. "We're going to be The Three Musty-teers."

The boys exchange confused glances, and my mouth falls open behind my shirt. "Are you serious? You've never seen that movie?"

They shake their heads, and I massage one of my temples with my free hand. My comedic gold is obviously going to waste here.

Azarius gets to his feet, careful not to drip the nesda goop on the maroon rug as he steps toward me. "Let's get this over with."

He dips his fingers in the slime, trying to keep a straight face, and pulls them out to examine them. Against his white skin, the nesda root almost looks black; It's probably going to stain his skin.

"Don't hate me," he says as he touches my arm and drags the liquid down to my elbow.

"I could never," I assure him as he does the other arm. "Besides, this is Elio's fault. I can hate him for it."

From the bed, Elio laughs. "You're welcome."

Azarius wipes the nesda on my pants, shirt, and in my hair, which nearly makes me retch.

"I'm going to smell like garbage juice forever," I whine.

"No, you won't," Elio says. "You can have a nice, long shower when we get back. My bathroom even has a tub."

My eyes shift toward the bed. "A tub? Elio, you've been holding out on me. You should know that baths are a girl's best friend."

He smirks. "I thought that was diamonds."

"Close, but no cigar."

"Well, I thought it was dick," Azarius says, wiping his hand clean on my pants. "I was way off."

After a few more minutes, my nose acclimates to the stench, and I finally let go of my shirt. Normally, I'm sad when I can't smell my perfume anymore. Not this time.

"What else do we need to do, boss?" Azarius glances at Elio, who stands up to join us.

"Don't let Rafe hear you say that," he warns. "You know he'll have our heads."

"Yeah, yeah." Azarius waves his stained hand. "I'm not stupid enough to say it when he's here."

Elio crosses the room to an armoire and tugs the two doors open to reveal a row of clothes. He reaches for the shelf below them and withdraws a ball of black fabric, which unfolds into a floor-length, hooded cloak.

"Once we get to the city, it will be best to cover as much of you as possible," he says, meeting my gaze. "The less they see, the less attention you'll draw."

I nod, thankful for how much thought Elio has put into this operation. He obviously cares about my safety more than I gave him credit for. That, or he really likes doing a thorough job.

I'll humor myself and believe the first.

"Can we run through everything one more time?"

I ask, even though I've heard the plan countless times. My nerves are getting to me, and I can feel the prickle of anxiety clinging to my spine.

Elio nods once. "Azarius will make the trip on foot. He's incredibly fast when he wants to be." Az scoffs and rolls his eyes in annoyance, but he doesn't interrupt otherwise. "You and I will still give him a head start, though, because we'll make better time in the air."

"And we'll meet up right outside the city." This part makes me the most nervous. I wish we could just land in front of Ignatius' front door, avoid tromping through the city, but Azarius doesn't know where he's going, and two bodyguards are better than one.

Elio nods again. "It's not a far walk. There shouldn't be many monsters out because it's daytime—most of them move primarily at night—and we've taken every precaution I can think of to avoid drawing attention."

"What if we run into Rafe while we're there?" Azarius pipes up.

Elio narrows his eyes at his best friend. "Then I'm blaming you for jinxing us."

Az throws his hands up. "I'm being serious. How are we possibly going to talk our way out of that one?"

For a moment, Elio is silent, and he runs his fingers over his chin. "We'll tell him we were summoned for a meeting and didn't trust Devyn alone at the mansion."

My jaw drops. I can't believe he would throw me

under the bus like that, but I can't blame him either. It's a better excuse than anything I could come up with on the fly.

"Thanks." I stick my tongue out at him, which only makes him smile, and a warm flutter teases my stomach. I quickly look away.

"Okay, we're burning daylight." Azarius grabs a backpack off the floor, along with the nesda concoction, and heads toward the door. "We need to get a move on."

"Yes, we do," Elio agrees, grabbing a bag off the bedside table and throwing the strap across his body. He gestures for me to follow Azarius, and he falls in line behind me as we step into the hallway.

Monsters carrying backpacks is one of the oddest things I've seen so far—and I've seen some crazy shit—but it makes perfect sense as to why they carry them. Azarius doesn't want to run for miles in his good clothes, so he's already dressed in the pair of shorts he'll be wearing. He'll change when we get to the city. While Elio can wear pants, his wings don't allow for a shirt, so he has to take that with him too, since we'll be flying.

If they were like other monsters, they could just go naked everywhere, but they aren't. They're businessmen through and through.

I also suspect it's out of respect for me too, but I haven't asked.

We head downstairs to the back door, which is all but hidden by vines, and step out into the lime daylight. The twin suns hang far to our left in the sky, signifying that it's early.

How early? I have no idea. I don't understand the concept of time in the monster realm yet, but I know the suns travel across the sky in tandem and the moon rises when they set. All three bodies move in the same direction, chasing one another constantly.

Azarius says there's a moment where you can see a hair of the suns on one horizon and a hair of the moon on the other, if your view is unobstructed. Considering we're constantly surrounded by trees, I haven't had the chance to see it—and probably won't ever be able to—but it sounds cool.

Dumping the rest of the nesda on the ground, Azarius tosses the bowl and pestle near the mansion. The whole house probably would have smelled if he'd left it inside.

"Okay, Az," Elio says, looking toward the forest. "You go ahead; we'll catch up in a bit."

Azarius nods and turns to me. He hesitates briefly—probably deciding if smelling me is worth getting close—before leaning and catching my lips with his. His kiss is quick and deep, leaving me begging for more when he pulls away.

"Be safe. I'll see you soon."

"You be safe, too."

With that, he turns on his heel and sprints toward the tree line. I'm able to see his pale form weaving through the trees for a few seconds before he disappears into the blackness.

I turn to Elio. "How long do we need to wait?"

"Not too long," he says, dropping his messenger bag on the ground. He grabs the hem of his shirt and lifts it over his head, revealing his bulging muscles and chiseled abs.

The first time I saw his monster form, he was shirtless, but I was losing blood and panicking, so I didn't bother to notice how flawless his body is. Now, as my gaze drags up and down, I'm taken aback.

"Az is one fast fucker." He bends to store the shirt in his bag but leaves it on the ground. When he stands, he walks several feet away from me and stops, turning to face me. "He might not be the brightest or the strongest, but I can't fault him. He can outrun anything."

In an instant, Elio's dark wings erupt from his back, stretching at least five feet in either direction. They're thick and leathery, and their shape reminds me of bat wings, with deadly, six-inch claws at the ends of the fingers running through them. I don't know if they're usable in combat, but they look intimidating as hell.

A Batman joke rides my tongue, but I swallow it. Elio probably wouldn't get it anyway.

"Wow," is all I wind up saying. I don't want any flattery to go to his head, but I can't stop staring as he moves his wings, stretching them wide.

"That feels amazing," he groans mid-stretch. "Keeping them put away all the time makes them achy, but they get in the way."

"I think they're awesome," I admire.

He folds them and heads back my way, bending to

snatch his bag from the ground before throwing the strap over his head.

"Have you ever ridden a motorcycle without a helmet before?"

I blink several times. "Umm…no. That's illegal. How is that relevant?"

"That's kind of how it is to fly," he explains. "You're in luck, because you won't be facing straight ahead, but the wind will be wild, and it will be hard to hear. You might want to put your hair up."

I obey, quickly snatching the hair tie off my wrist and pulling my hair into a tight bun before Elio hands me the cloak.

"I thought you said I wouldn't need it until we got to the city?" I ask, letting it unfold and hit the ground.

"Just in case." He nods. "It'll help my nerves a bit."

Again, I follow his instructions, pulling the cloak on and hooking the three silver buttons. It's way too long, the bottom dragging nearly a foot behind me, the arms hanging past my hands comically, but it quickly soothes my nerves a bit, too. Even on the off chance someone looks up at the right time, they won't be able to see me.

"Perfect," he says. "They won't even be able to tell what you are."

"That's all that matters." I push the sleeves up reflexively because I hate not being able to see my hands, but they fall back down. I sigh. "So, how exactly does this work? Do I get on your back? Is there a seatbelt?"

Elio chuckles. "You're funny."

He closes the distance between us, moving slightly to my left, then sweeps me into his arms in a bridal carry. I squeal, throwing my arms around his neck as the ground is ripped away. I take several panicked breaths as he laughs.

"Well, you're not," I snap, still clinging to him. "How about warning a girl next time?"

He chuckles again, spreading his wings wide. "Brace yourself."

The initial ascent is the worst part. Even though I'm not standing, I feel like a rug has just been jerked out from under me, and now I'm falling, only I'm falling up instead of down.

Elio's wings beat aggressively, lifting us past the roof o and over the tops of the trees, but he doesn't break a sweat. I've never been overly afraid of heights, but one glance down at the distant ground makes my blood run cold. The fact that the only thing keeping me from plummeting to my death is Elio's grip doesn't help either.

I instantly feel light-headed, and I worry I might faint in his arms, so I close my eyes and bury my face in the side of his neck. Just as he warned, the air rushes at us in a gust as we move forward and pick up speed over the woods. I barely hear him when he speaks.

"Are you okay?" he asks.

Rather than trying to yell over the wind, I keep my eyes closed and nod against his skin, thankful it's smooth, not leathery like his wings. He squeezes me once, and I take it as a gesture of reassurance. He's got me, and he's not going to let me fall.

I peek at our surroundings occasionally, cracking my eyes open a smidge before snapping them closed when my stomach turns. The wind burns my eyes, and I wonder how Elio remains unaffected. It has to be a monster thing, or tolerance he's built up over time.

I take another chance, turning my head away just enough to do a sweep of what's below us. We've left the woods far behind, and now there's a wide stretch of black land below us. To our right, mountains blossom out of the horizon. They aren't black, but a clash of browns and reds that stick out harshly from the landscape.

"Are those the mountains the Malevs come from?" I yell, hoping he can hear me.

"No. Those are much farther."

To our left, trees dot the flat land sporadically, and a cluster of buildings sit together in the distance. I stare at them, wondering what kind of monsters inhabit that area, and I snap my eyes closed when I start getting light-headed again.

It's been less than ten minutes, and I'm already certain I'm not a fan of flying.

"There's Azarius," Elio calls over the wind, grabbing my attention.

As much as I don't want to look down, I peel my eyes open and look ahead. A white blur streaks across the ground in the distance. We're so high, I can't make out his details, but there's no denying it's him.

Then, my eyes are closed again.

Elio beats his wings slower, and we drop several feet in the air. I know because my stomach temporarily floats, the way it does when I hit a steep hill in my car. My guess is he's trying to keep pace with Azarius, which must be difficult from this height.

Time hardly feels real when you're soaring through the air, traveling huge distances in a matter of minutes, but the suns have shifted noticeably by the time we touch down. Elio's landing is much more graceful than his takeoff, his wings beating in short spurts as we lower, and my eyes pop open as soon as he stops moving.

"I'm alive," I gasp, mostly joking, but also a tiny bit surprised I didn't pass out. Elio sets me down on the ground, keeping a tentative hand on me until I get my bearings. My legs are wobbly, and I still feel like I'm racing forward, even though I'm not.

"See, it wasn't so bad." Elio says, staring down at me.

"For you! I'm already not looking forward to the flight home."

I pull my hood up over my head and turn to observe our surroundings. We're about a football field away from a large cluster of buildings. There must be hundreds of them. Unlike the first ones I saw, these are not dilapidated or abandoned.

Most of the buildings are small and cube-like, with dark walls and roofs, while a couple are several stories tall. One or two have wild architecture—oddly-shaped windows or roofs that stretch up in spikes—

and one enormous building shoots up from the middle like a beacon.

"What's that?" I ask, nodding toward the enormous tower. Its walls are covered in sharp spikes, and there's a single window at the top, just beneath the roof.

"That's where the city leader lives," he says. "Think of it like a governor's house. While they don't control what the monsters do, they keep an eye on things and watch for invasions. Most cities have them, but every city is different, and the power the leaders wield varies. Rafe's in bed with most of them and can call on them at will."

I cock an eyebrow in his direction. "He sleeps with them?"

Elio chuckles. "I don't want to know if he does. That would be terrifying. I just mean that he has ties to many of them. It's part of his plan to overtake the Malevs."

"Oh." My eyes snap back to the tower and climb to the top. "You know, even though he's an asshole, Rafe seems to want to protect the realm. He can't be all bad, right?"

Elio laughs, nudging me playfully with his elbow. "I told you that you were funny. Why would someone as power-hungry as Rafe want to lead a war against evil?"

I hesitate too long, and he answers for me.

"Power. He wants other monsters to revere him, look up to him. He wants to rule them," he explains.

"So why not eliminate the biggest threat to the realm and come out a hero?"

"Damn." I shake my head, scanning the outskirts of the city for any movement. Luckily, there's not any. "That's one way to do it."

I turn back toward the black plain and see Azarius' figure approaching. He slows down as he draws closer and walks the last several meters. He's breathing hard, struggling to catch his breath, and his hair is a wind-tousled mess.

"You almost beat us," Elio says smugly. "Almost."

Azarius takes a big breath in and blows it out slowly. "I see that. I'll try harder on the way home."

"Is running that much safe?" I ask, worried Azarius might fall over dead from a heart attack at any moment.

"Safe? Sure." He blows out a raspberry and takes another deep breath. "Easy? No."

When Az finally recoups, they unzip their bags and get dressed. Elio's wings disappear again before he pulls on his shirt, and Azarius struggles to pull his pants over sweaty skin.

I approach him cautiously, afraid to catch a rogue limb or tail as he fights to get dressed. "Do you need some help?"

He finally wiggles into them before looking up. "No, but you can help me out of them later."

My cheeks burn, and a smile teases my lips. "That can be arranged."

Elio paces as he waits, his eyes darting to the nearby city every few seconds, like he expects someone to come running out to welcome us. Or attack us.

"You're making me nervous," I tell him. "More nervous than I already am."

"Don't be." He stops pacing and puts a comforting hand on my shoulder, squeezing slightly. "Everything's going perfect so far. In a few minutes, we'll be at Ignatius' front door."

I offer a timid smile to appear less worried, but fear is eating at me like acid on the inside. So many things can go wrong from now until we leave the city, and it only takes one of those things to upturn our entire plan. My confidence in our ability to pull this off is decreasing as the seconds tick by.

"Elio," Azarius says, coming over to join us, fully dressed. His backpack is slung over his shoulder, and it looks like he ran his fingers through his hair to make it look decent. When he's close enough, he drops his voice to a whisper. "If things get out of hand, get Devyn out of here."

Elio nods a silent response.

"Devyn," Az says, his eyes flicking to me. "Promise me you'll do what we ask. Run if we tell you to run. Hide if we tell you to hide."

The last thing I want is to be separated from my protectors. I'm completely defenseless without them.

I've always been afraid to walk city streets by myself, but that's nothing compared to the monster realm, where every other entity can kill me with their bare hands.

I nod in agreement anyway, hoping it doesn't come to that.

Elio takes the lead, and I struggle to keep up as I drown in my cloak. I stumble over the fabric a few times before figuring out how to walk with it, and I have to keep pushing the hood back to see where I'm going. Azarius brings up the rear, walking just far enough away to avoid tripping on the cloak.

The three of us are an odd sight: two monsters in sleek business attire, and a kid playing dress up in black fabric. I don't know what monsters deem weird in this realm, but I sincerely hope none of them peer out their windows, wondering what the hell we've got going on.

Or worse, stop to ask us what we're doing.

We move quietly, slipping between two buildings, onto a street that's just wide enough for a few people to walk down, and make our way deeper into the city.

Our next stop: Ignatius' house.

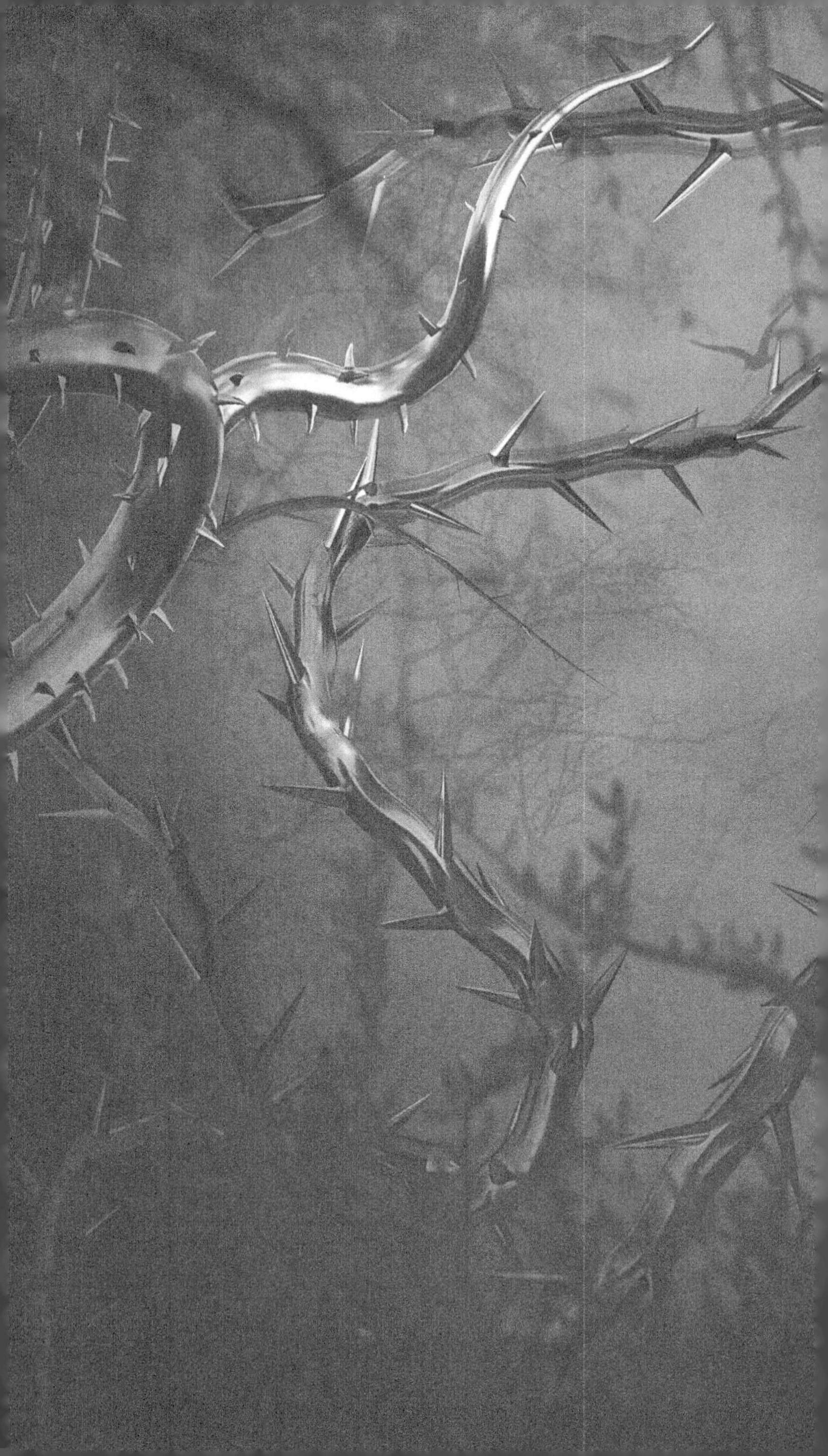

14
ELIO

Getting to the city of Havec was half the battle.

Making it through the city to Ignatius' house unscathed is what I'm most worried about. Unfortunately for us, he lives in the city center, so there is no easy way to get there.

However, we did choose the right time to come, because there are very few monsters wandering about. Fewer monsters means less of a chance we're found out.

Fewer onlookers.

Less eavesdropping.

When the suns are high in the sky, most monsters sleep. We aren't nocturnal by nature, but over time, we've collectively shifted in that direction due to the Malevs. Maybe once we drive them back into the mountains, we can get back to our old sleeping habits.

I glance back over my shoulder after every turn to make sure Devyn and Azarius are still on my tail, and every time I do, I get a fresh whiff of the nesda juice clinging to Devyn's skin. Thankfully, it's still potent.

Even walking slowly, it's hard for her to keep up. I should have sliced the bottom of the cloak off to make it easier, but it's too late now. Besides, she's not complaining, and it keeps her disguised. Honestly, she's been a good sport about this whole excursion, all things considered.

I just hope all of this is worth it in the end.

Ignatius and I go way back, but I wouldn't exactly call him a friend; a close acquaintance at best. He studied under my grandfather when we lived in Theev, back before the city was overrun by demons and their Malevolent offspring.

We've bumped into one another over the years, always keeping tabs on each other. It's good to have people you know nearby, just in case, and there's an unspoken agreement between us: should an emergency arise, we have each other's backs. While I always imagined coming to him eventually for help, this is hardly the emergency I envisioned.

I hope he's still as open-minded as I remember him being.

Ignatius lives in a long, beige house made from clay and stone. It stands out from all the other buildings in Havec, as he had the materials imported from another city. There are various potted plants lining the full length of the building and reflective circular windows that look like mirrors. An enormous emblem is painted on the door, covering most of the dark material, and I recognize it instantly.

The warlock's mark of protection.

I can't use marks, but I have a book that belonged to my grandfather with tons of marks, along with their meanings. Essentially, the mark of protection prevents anyone with negative intentions from entering.

"Could he be any more conspicuous?" Azarius mumbles as he takes it all in.

"Don't give him any ideas," I say.

I approach the door, momentarily nervous that the mark will deem harboring a human as negative intentions, but I still knock three times.

Nothing happens at first, so I hope I'm in the clear. When no one comes to the door, panic flares in my chest. If we came all this way for Ignatius to not be home, Devyn and Azarius will never forgive me. They might kill me and walk back to Rafe's.

Refusing to give up, I knock three more times, a little louder, and wait a full minute.

"Come on, you son of a—" I whisper under my breath before hearing a distinctive click from the other side.

The handle turns, and the door opens a crack before Ignatius' head pokes outside. His skin is bubblegum pink, and he wears his black hair cropped short, the same way he always has. He wears a billowing pair of pants with no shirt, a pendant the size of my fist around his neck on a chain.

"Elio," he gasps, his eyes growing wide. "What are you doing here, my friend?" He glances over my shoulder to observe my companions.

"I need a favor," I say.

His eyes jump back to me, and I can see the skepticism in them. "What kind of favor?"

I look both ways down the street, searching for any sign of monsters. There aren't any in sight, but I don't dare say anything out here.

"If you'll let us come in for a few minutes, I'll explain everything. Trust me on this one."

He hesitates, but he ultimately opens the door to let us in. I motion for Azarius and Devyn to follow before stepping over the threshold, and we are immediately dumped into a kaleidoscope of color.

I've been here before, so I know what to expect, but the look of disbelief on Devyn's face beneath her hood is priceless.

"What a lovely place you've got here," Azarius says, looking around as fast as he can to soak it all in.

We're standing in a living room with three couches, and each one is a different color. Several shelves line the walls, laden with various trinkets. Some are collectibles. Some are art. Some are warlock instruments hiding in plain sight. It's always been a bit of a hazardous mess, but it looks like Ignatius' collection has doubled since the last time I was here.

Marks are painted on all the walls, for strength, clarity, silence, and power. Being a warlock makes you a target for powerful monsters who seek to use them as pawns, but Ignatius does a damn good job protecting himself.

"Come in and have a seat," Ignatius says, gesturing to the cluster of sofas. "I'd offer you something to drink, but I've just gotten back from a six-month hiatus on Earth, and I haven't stocked the kitchen yet."

I wave a dismissive hand. "Don't worry, we're fine."

Devyn and Azarius sit together on the couch to the left, igniting a twinge of jealousy in me that I quickly extinguish, and I sit on the one to the right, covered in twenty too many throw pillows. Ignatius takes the last one and folds his hands in his lap.

"So, what is this favor?" Ignatius asks, his eyes slowly floating between the three of us.

"To be honest, it's a little complicated," I admit, leaning into the mountain of cushions behind me. "Have you heard any rumors floating around?"

He cocks an unnaturally thin eyebrow in my direction. "There are always rumors. Be more specific."

"Sure." I drape one of my arms along the back of the couch. "It involves a Malev being killed several miles south of here, near that patch of dead woods."

Ignatius purses his lips. "I can't say that I have."

Well, that's a pleasant surprise. Maybe Ross overestimated the reach of the rumor.

Or Ignatius is lying, which I hope isn't the case. There aren't many people I trust in this realm, and he's one of the only ones I feel I can count on, aside from Azarius.

"There's a rumor going around that a human came through the portal and killed a Malev," I explain, pushing past the alarm bells ringing in my ears. If I expect his help, I have to be honest, but it feels like I'm directly defying Rafe's orders. He told us not to speak of it, but here I am, speaking of it. "There was human blood and a weapon found at the site."

Ignatius' eyebrows gradually raise until they're nearing his hairline. The genuine surprise in his expression assures me he wasn't lying—he hadn't heard the rumor—but I still have no idea how he's going to take the bombshell I'm about to drop.

"That's absurd," he says with a quick shake of his head. "Impossible. Humans can't survive traveling between realms. Everyone knows that."

"Right. It's common knowledge," I say. "But what if it was a human with very little magic or monster in their blood? That seems more plausible, right?"

Ignatius stares at me for a second before nodding. "Yes, that could be possible, but I still don't understand what you need from me?"

"I'm getting there, I promise." I offer a nervous smirk. It's amazing how, after hours of planning what I'm going to say, my thoughts evaporate when it's finally time to deliver them. I've been spending way too much time with Azarius.

"Would you be able to determine if a human has any sort of magic in them? Or monster?" I ask, fighting to keep my expression cool, despite my nerves.

Ignatius adjusts himself on the couch, unfolding and then refolding his hands. His eyes bounce between me and Azarius before landing briefly on Devyn, who still hasn't lowered her hood.

My throat is tight, and the suspense is killing me.

"There's a chance," he says, sounding skeptical. "This isn't something I have ever had to deal with, so there might be some trial and error. I'd be willing to take a crack at it, though."

A slight sigh of relief escapes from my lungs. "You would?"

"It's an unusual request, but I've been asked to do worse," he explains. His gaze slowly travels back to Devyn, and he gestures to her with an open hand. "I take it this is your human."

At his words, my insides freeze like ice.

Devyn meets my eyes beneath her hood, and I gesture for her to lower it. I can see her hands trembling from where I'm sitting as she reaches up, and I wish desperately there was something I could do to alleviate her fear. If I were in Azarius' place, I'd wrap her in my arms and whisper comforting words in her ear. He's doing a shit job, in my opinion.

As her blonde hair appears and the fabric falls to her shoulders, I look at Ignatius. His jaw is dropped, his eyes round as saucers. For a moment, he's entirely speechless.

"This is Devyn," I introduce her. "Devyn, this is my friend, Ignatius."

She says nothing but offers him a timid wave.

"But…" His voice trails off, and he clears his throat to try again. "I can't smell her. I can't even sense anything magical in her blood."

"She bathed in nesda roots before we left," Azarius says, holding up his fingers, which still cling to the purple color. "That's why you can't smell her."

"Ah, yes, I smell the nesda," he admits. "I just thought it was a rather offensive cologne."

"As for her blood, we can't sense anything," I say, stifling a laugh. "Neither can Rafe."

Ignatius' gaze whips to me. "Rafe knows? And she's still alive?"

"Barely," I admit, pointing a finger at Azarius. "This one claimed her as his mate. That's the only reason Rafe didn't kill her."

Ignatius nods along, seeming unsurprised. "I see. It is complicated."

"But you can help us?" I ask, still clinging to the hope that inspired this mission. "Can you check her blood for any ounce of magic or monster? Everything we do moving forward depends on that information."

"I can try," he says. "I can't promise anything, but you know I'm always willing to help you, Elio."

Ignatius gets to his feet and shuffles across the room to a shelf of books. "It may take a bit to find what I'm looking for. In the meantime, make yourselves at home. Any friend of Elio's is a friend of mine."

A grateful smile curls my lips until I look at Devyn and Azarius. Their hands are intertwined, and he's drawing small circles across the back of her hand. It shouldn't bother me—I've seen them together countless times over the last week—but I can't deny the flare of jealousy in my chest. Despite all my efforts, I can't shake my desire for my best friend's mate.

When we're alone, I can almost swear she wants me too. Still, it's not enough for me to make a move and risk our friendship.

I won't do anything until she tells me to.

Then, all bets are off.

Half an hour later, Ignatius has finally assembled all the tools he needs in the middle of the living room floor. There's a fat spell book opened to the appropriate page, and a tiny altar with a stone bowl on top. A sheathed dagger with a glittering handle lays beside him, along with a collection of ingredients in glass vials.

"This spell was originally intended for magical objects," Ignatius explains as he sets to work sprinkling ingredients into the bowl. "I've modified it some, but it should work just fine."

A smidge of this. A dash of that. I can hardly keep up with what he's doing.

He crushes some dried flower petals before adding them to the mixture and runs his boney index finger down the list of the ingredients to double check everything.

"Yep. Yes. Got it," he mumbles under his breath. "Perfect. Everything is added. Now, we get to have some fun."

He holds one hand a few inches over the bowl, his eyes lasered in on the blend of ingredients.

"Fao."

At his incantation, a red flame sparks to life, incinerating the dry mixture.

"Devyn, I need your finger please."

Her eyes bulge, and she looks a little pale as Ignatius unsheathes his dagger, but she lets go of Azarius' hand and drops to the floor beside him. She offers him her pointer finger and squeezes her eyes shut tight.

The blade of the dagger is so thin, it all but disappears as it barely grazes the tip of her finger. It instantly beads with scarlet liquid, and for the first time since being in my bedroom, I can smell her human essence. Even the nesda can't cover up fresh human blood.

Ignatius instructs her to drip it into the bowl.

"Just a few drops will do it," he says as she holds her hand above the flame. One, two, three drops fall into the fire, and Devyn retreats, instantly placing her finger in her mouth.

I hold my breath, eyes glued to the spell before us as we wait for something to happen. The fire grows smaller but continues to flicker while it incinerates everything in the bowl.

"Come on," Ignatius urges under his breath. "Come on."

After a few more minutes, the fire stops burning, and a ringlet of scarlet smoke curls out of the bowl. This means nothing to me, but Ignatius gasps excitedly and points.

"It worked," he says, bouncing eagerly on the spot. "That's our answer."

Devyn, Azarius, and I all exchange looks.

"Well, what is it?" I ask, losing every bit of my patience.

"The color of smoke determines what properties her blood has. Black smoke means demon. Purple smoke means monster. Red smoke means—"

"Warlock," Devyn interrupts, her mouth hanging open. "I'm descended from warlocks?"

"The spell doesn't lie." Ignatius points to it again. "It might have been several generations ago, but as long as you have one drop of magical blood, it seems the portal is your gateway to use."

"Yes!" Azarius punches the air. "I told you my girl was special. I was right."

I can hardly believe it. In fact, I'm pretty sure I'm in shock, because I can't think of anything to say.

It's a relief to finally have an answer, although I'm slightly annoyed Azarius had it figured out before me. He trusted his gut and risked everything for her on a whim, but it paid off. His mate claim cannot be challenged, since she has magical blood.

He's such a jackass sometimes.

It does bring me a tiny bit of satisfaction knowing Devyn and I have something in common that Azarius will never know. Warlock blood flows through our veins. We're descended from the same ancient race. Somehow, that connection makes me feel closer to her. We're more alike than I could have ever imagined.

I don't realize I'm staring at her as I mull over my thoughts until she locks eyes with me. Her expression is mixed with relief and excitement, and as I watch, the widest smile spreads across her beautiful face. I fight to return the gesture, but a realization quickly wipes it away.

Now that we know the truth, she might actually be going home. It's what she's wanted since the beginning, but the thought of her leaving makes my chest seize. I know it's always been our goal to get her home, but now that our doubts have been eradicated, I'm struggling.

I don't know if I can let her go.

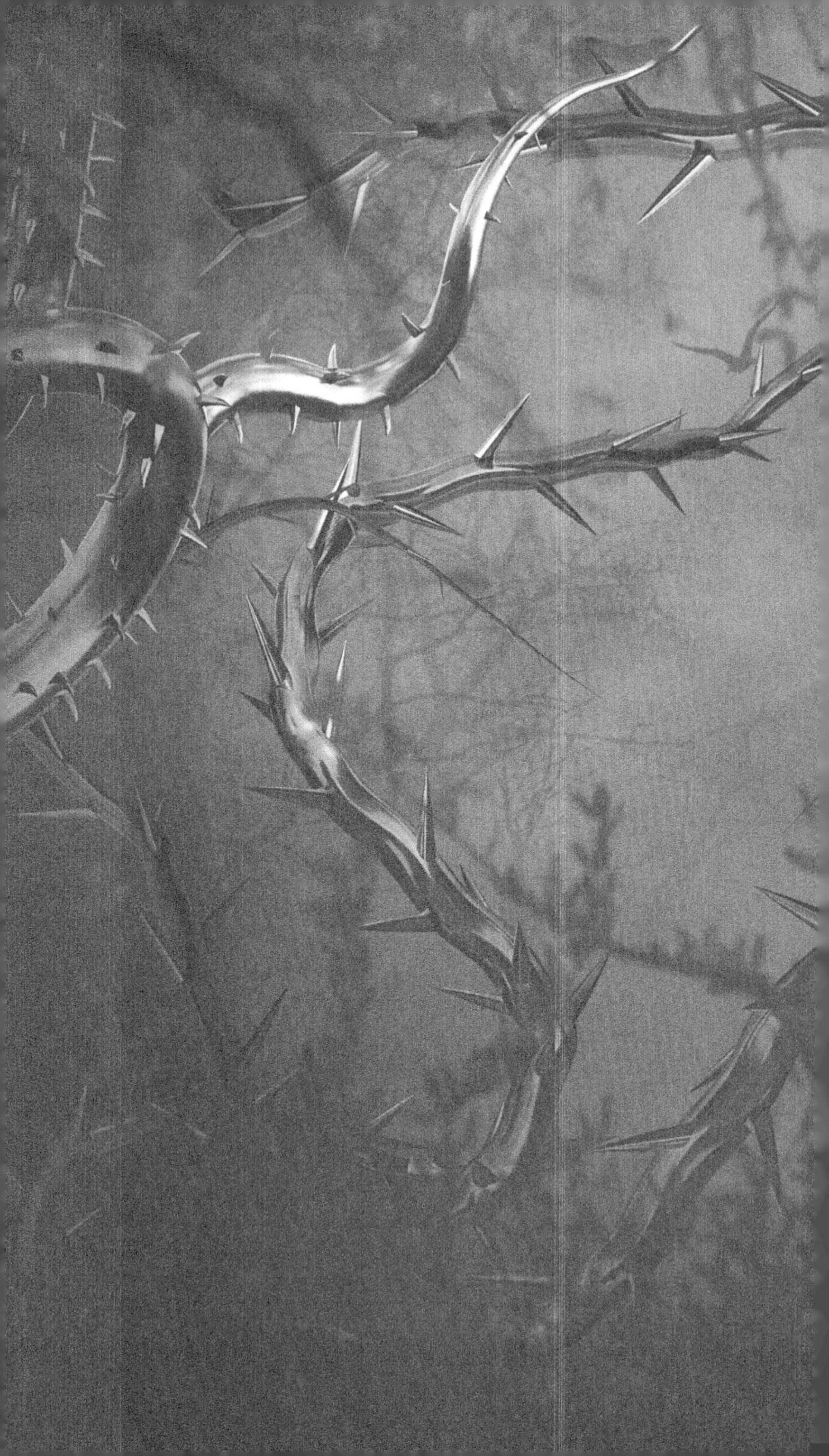

15
DEVYN

When we leave Ignatius' house, Elio decides it's best if I keep wearing the cloak, at least until we're out of the city. While I'm technically part warlock, I still look very much human, and if the nesda wears off anytime soon, I'll be smelling like one, too. Not how I want to end the day, especially considering how difficult it was to get here.

We retrace our steps through the city, passing a couple of monsters who stare curiously in our direction, and I keep the hood low over my face. No one says anything, but Elio keeps looking back over his shoulder. Does he think I'm going to run now that I figured out the truth?

Because the only place I want to go to is Rafe's mansion to take a bath in Elio's tub. I'll worry about everything else after that.

We stop about a hundred yards past the border of the city, and everyone gets ready for our journey back.

Azarius strips to his shorts and stuffs his clothes into his bag. Elio takes his shirt off and whips out his wings, stretching them wide.

"Are we racing?" Elio asks, wagging his eyebrows at Azarius.

"You bet your ass." He waves with two fingers and spins on the spot, darting away from the city and booking it across the plain. I look to Elio, whose smug expression says he knows something I don't.

"Are we giving him a head start again?" I ask.

He shakes his head. "Definitely not."

I brace myself as he approaches, and he swings me up into his arms. I'm less afraid this time, but I'm still not excited about being so high off the ground. As he leaps into the air and pumps his wings, I close my eyes and bury my face into the side of his neck.

I might not enjoy flying, but being held like this by Elio isn't so bad. Maybe we can try it on the ground later.

After my bath. Nothing comes before my bath when we get back.

With Elio flying as high as he is and beating his wings like he's getting paid for it, we make it back to the mansion well before Azarius has a chance to catch up.

"That was so unfair," I joke, bumping into Elio gently as we make our way down the hall to his room.

He shakes his head. "He knew he couldn't win." He pushes open the door to his bedroom, revealing the beautiful décor as he leads the way to the bathroom.

A monster-sized, white clawfoot tub sits against the wall to our left. It's situated by the shower, which is done in red and black tile, and I watch as he turns on the water before plugging the drain. He checks the temperature several times to get it perfect, then grabs a bottle from a shelf, dumping a glob of blue liquid into the water. Instantly, bubbles erupt to life.

"You're a dirty girl," he says, tsking his tongue at me. "Make sure you use extra soap and soak for a while. I don't know how easy that nesda root will come off your skin."

He hands me a washcloth to bathe with, and I stare up at him for a long second, studying the details of his face and wishing he'd lean down and kiss me. He doesn't.

The nesda smell must be super unappealing. That, or he's changed his mind about me having him.

I half-hope he'll linger in the bathroom and talk to me while I bathe—after all, he's seen me naked more than once already—but he slips out to give me privacy, leaving me a little disappointed. I peel off my clothes, drop them in a pile by the door, and step into the tub.

Relaxing into the hot water, I blow a mound of bubbles away from my face and close my eyes while the tub fills, inch by inch. When there's enough water and more than enough bubbles, I twist all the knobs until the water stops running.

Suddenly, the room is silent, aside from the waves I make getting comfortable again. I listen hard for Elio in his bedroom, but I don't hear anything.

Maybe he went downstairs for something to eat, or maybe Azarius arrived and they're chatting somewhere.

I set to work scrubbing every inch of my skin. I wash my hair, eager to get rid of the putrid smell I've been wearing all day. I wash my body a second time for good measure.

My mind begins to wander while I scrub, reflecting on everything that's happened, from waking up next to Azarius in his bed to soaring across the realm in Elio's arms.

It all seems like a fever dream, but I'd happily relive it over and over.

Elio's plan had worked out flawlessly. Almost a little too perfectly, but I attribute that to his careful planning and cautionary steps. I can't thank him enough for everything he did for me, including risking his life and going behind Rafe's back.

On that thought, I don't think I've thanked him directly at all. Damn it.

I decide to call for him. "Elio?" My voice reverberates off the marble.

"Yes?" he replies, his voice muffled through the wall.

"What are you doing?"

"Waiting on you to finish bathing."

"Can you come here, please?" I listen expectantly, waiting for an answer that doesn't come. Surely, he didn't disappear that quickly. "Elio?"

The bathroom door pops open, making me jump,

and Elio leans inside. He's shirtless and wearing the pants he's been in all day.

"You called?" He doesn't budge from the doorway but stands there watching me.

"Come closer," I urge, waving him over with a hand covered in bubbles.

He stares at me for a beat longer before slipping into the room, letting the door fall closed behind him. With slow steps, he crosses to the side of the tub and looks down at me.

"What do you need?" he asks, his expression unreadable. Is he mad? Annoyed? Hopefully neither, but I can't tell.

"I wanted to thank you," I say, my stomach turning nervously. "You did so much for me today, and it truly means the world to me. So, thank you."

The corner of his mouth lifts, but I can tell it's forced. My heart drops a little, worried he's already reverted to the asshole content to ignore me. This isn't how I imagined things would be when we got back, now that we know the truth. Shouldn't he be happy, like the rest of us?

I decide to switch tactics.

"You know," I start, summoning every ounce of gall I possess. "You've had me all over you today, and you probably smell like ass too. Why don't you join me?"

At least if he declines, I tried. His jaw clenches and his eyes fall to the bubbles hiding me from view.

"Are you sure about that?"

"Yes." I'm more than sure.

Our relationship has been rife with tension since the beginning, and I'm curious to know if it was all sexual frustration or something else. He went from hating me, to telling me I could have both him and Azarius, to being cold and distant again. I want to know the truth, and the only way to do that is by us getting closer.

How much closer can you get than a bubble bath? Not very.

He holds my gaze as he undoes his pants and nudges them down past his thighs to the floor. I scoot up, giving him room to slide in behind me, and my heart rate spikes as he steps into the water. It's a snug fit with the two of us, but the feel of my back pressed firmly against him is worth it.

"Is this what you wanted?" he asks as he circles his arms around me beneath the water.

"Yes." I lean my head back against his chest. "That's much better."

I breathe in time with the rise and fall off his chest as I tease his thigh with my fingertips under the water. I don't know what I expected, but nothing happens. We sit in still silence for several minutes, and I'm beginning to think I've mistaken his kindness as flirting.

He's so confusing. I wish I could just read his mind. Things would be so much easier.

"Is this not what you want?" I ask, prying for an answer.

He exhales a deep breath. "This is exactly what I want."

There's a hint of hesitation in his voice. Something is wrong.

"But?"

When he doesn't answer immediately, I turn my head as far as I can to see his face. To my surprise, he's just staring at me.

"But?" I urge again.

He attempts a smirk, but it's gone as quickly as it comes, and he sighs. "I've thought of little else this week apart from getting you alone again and doing what I didn't do on our walk: kiss you until I took your breath away and fuck you until you begged me to stop."

I stare in stunned silence. My stomach somersaults at his words, and the tingle between my thighs evolves to a steady throb.

"But now that I have the opportunity," he says, "I'm hesitant. There aren't many things that could come between Azarius and I, but I'm worried you might be one of them."

The flutter in my stomach turns into a knot. "Didn't you say the other day I could have you both? If he was the good guy and you were the bad guy, I wouldn't have to choose." My neck aches from looking back at him, but I don't turn away.

"I did say that, and I meant it. I even asked him, and he said if you chose multiple mates, he'd understand."

"If he said he'd understand, then he's not going to care," I point out.

He nods, his arms tightening around me just

enough that I notice. "I know, but I'm not going to try for my sake. What I want doesn't matter. If it's what you want, that's different."

"Elio, this is what I want. You're what I want," I assure him, desperation clinging to my voice. "Both of you are. I don't want to choose."

I struggle to breathe through the heavy silence that follows. I've drug up my intimate, raw feelings yet again, and it's like Elio can see straight through to my heart. I feel more exposed than I ever could naked.

"Claim me then," he says, his voice gruff. He brushes his fingers against my neck and traces my jawline with his fingertips, making my skin tingle. "Say it, and I'll belong to you."

"You want me to claim you in a bathtub?" I raise my brows at him. I've never been romantic, but this is pushing the limits of acceptability even by my standards.

Elio's chest shakes with laughter. "Where we are is irrelevant, as long as I'm with you."

I swoon. Okay, maybe I'm a little romantic.

"Alright. Elio, I claim you as my mate."

I expect a magical feeling to come over me, or for soft music to suddenly play in the background like in the movies, but nothing happens. I feel a twinge of disappointment until Elio comes to life behind me and presses his mouth against the side of my neck. He runs his tongue over my skin, kissing his way up my jaw before catching my lips with his. They move against mine eagerly, and his tongue sweeps in and out of my mouth with fervor.

"I'd offer to rinse these bubbles off with my tongue, but I think the shower will be way faster." He jokes, nipping at my earlobe. "What do you think?"

He cups my breasts and squeezes, massaging my hardened nipples between his fingers. I gasp, arching my back in response, and feel his semi-hard cock press against me.

"The shower sounds great," I moan, throwing my head back as Elio pinches my nipples harder.

"Does it?" he growls in my ear, sending chills vibrating down my spine, despite the hot water we're in. "Maybe I'll fuck you in there first."

We climb out of the tub covered in bubbles, and I watch a cloud of them slowly slide down Elio's torso as he turns the knobs in the shower. They slip their way down, settling at the base of his erect cock, and my eyes swell at the sight. His dick is massive, and I don't just mean in length. The throbbing girth is intimidating, and I swallow hard at the thought of him inside me.

I'm in trouble.

Elio drags me by the hand into the shower and lets me rinse off under the cascade of water before pinning me to the wall with a kiss. The spray from the showerhead is hitting half of me, but I'm hardly paying attention. His hands are on my body, eagerly memorizing every inch of my skin, and I'm unable to restrain myself anymore.

I reach for his cock between us with one hand and start to stroke, but quickly realize it's more suited for two, and I wrap my other hand around it. He groans against my mouth as I pump my hands over his shaft, slowly and firmly massaging his full length.

"That feels so good," he hisses between his teeth. He slips his hand up the side of my neck and pulls me into a deep kiss that fuels the desire burning in my belly.

Unlike Azarius, who is slow kisses and unyielding passion, Elio is fast and hot. He doesn't hold back when he grabs me or squeezes me. He's firm, but not careless.

I want him to devour me. All of me.

I roll my thumbs over the head of his cock, carefully teasing the slit at the top, and a thick liquid coats my fingers. I know it's precum, but my brain wants to argue because of the consistency. It feels like lube, and it doesn't wash away immediately in the water. Instead, it clings to my fingers, which makes stroking his cock much easier.

Elio's free hand slips down my body, sliding slowly over my hip before diving for my throbbing pussy. I spread my legs to grant him access, and my knees go weak when he rubs two fingers over my clit.

"You're so wet," he groans as his fingers dance in tiny circles.

"That happens when you take a shower," I try to joke, but my words come out in erratic breaths as jolts of pleasure rocket through me at his touch.

With a smirk, he slips two fingers inside me and pumps them slowly. Judging by how easily they slide, he was right.

I'm soaked.

"I bet you taste so good," he whispers in my ear as he continues to finger fuck me.

My libido skyrockets, hitting an all-time high. Is everything this monster does sexy? He proves me right a few seconds later when he withdraws his fingers and brings them to his mouth, sucking my juices off them.

Goddamn.

He lifts me up, his hands hooked under my thighs, and pins me against the wall. I throw my arms around his neck and crush my lips against his. Every inch of my body is on fire, my pussy aching to feel him.

Letting go of me with one hand, but still easily able to hold me up, he reaches for his cock. He guides the head back and forth along the length of my pussy, coating me in his precum before pushing into me.

He goes slowly at first, his mouth pressed firmly against mine as he inches his way inside. It takes a few minutes for me to stretch and adjust to his impressive size, but he's careful and patient. When he's finally buried to the hilt, he breaks our kiss.

"You're so tight, princess," he groans against my neck, both hands now gripping my ass. He kisses his way from my earlobe to my collarbone, then pulls his dick back before burying himself inside again. Every time he fills me, a stroke of pleasure rolls through my abdomen. Whatever he's hitting, he's doing just right. Judging by the look in his eyes, he knows it, too.

"Do you like that?"

"Mm-hmm," I moan, though he already knows the answer.

It doesn't take him long to pick up the pace,

pumping faster until he's slamming into me. The wall against my back is unforgiving, allowing every thrust to hit hard and deep, and I can't control the moan that escapes my lips. He slows down and reaches for the shower knobs, turning them off without looking as he kisses me deeply.

"I want to fuck you on my bed," he says.

I nod, expecting him to take his cock out and put me down, but that's not part of the plan. Still connected, he carries me to the bedroom, laying me on the bed while he remains standing.

He thrusts slowly a few times before withdrawing and running his cock along the length of my slit again, making sure to tease my clit with every stroke. The feeling of his slippery head against me sends a fresh wave of tingles through my body, and I cry out when he slams himself inside me again.

As he pounds into me, his fingers find my clit and draw tight circles around it, pushing me closer toward my orgasm. I buck my hips, meeting each thrust as he speeds up his fingers.

"You're so fucking gorgeous, princess," he groans out. "And you're mine."

I don't know if it's coincidence, or I have a new kink that involves being owned, but his words send me over the edge. My climax tears through me, crashing into me like a wave, and I squeeze my eyes closed to ride it out. Elio slams into me harder, nearly taking my breath away, crying out a second later when his own climax claims him.

He pumps slower and more deliberately as he

finishes inside me, filling me with more cum than I've ever seen at one time as it spills out and drenches the bed. I gasp, my nervous gaze finding Elio's, but he seems hardly surprised.

Insane amounts of jizz must be normal for some monsters.

"You'll probably need another shower," he says, leaning down to kiss me.

Agreed. Definitely agreed.

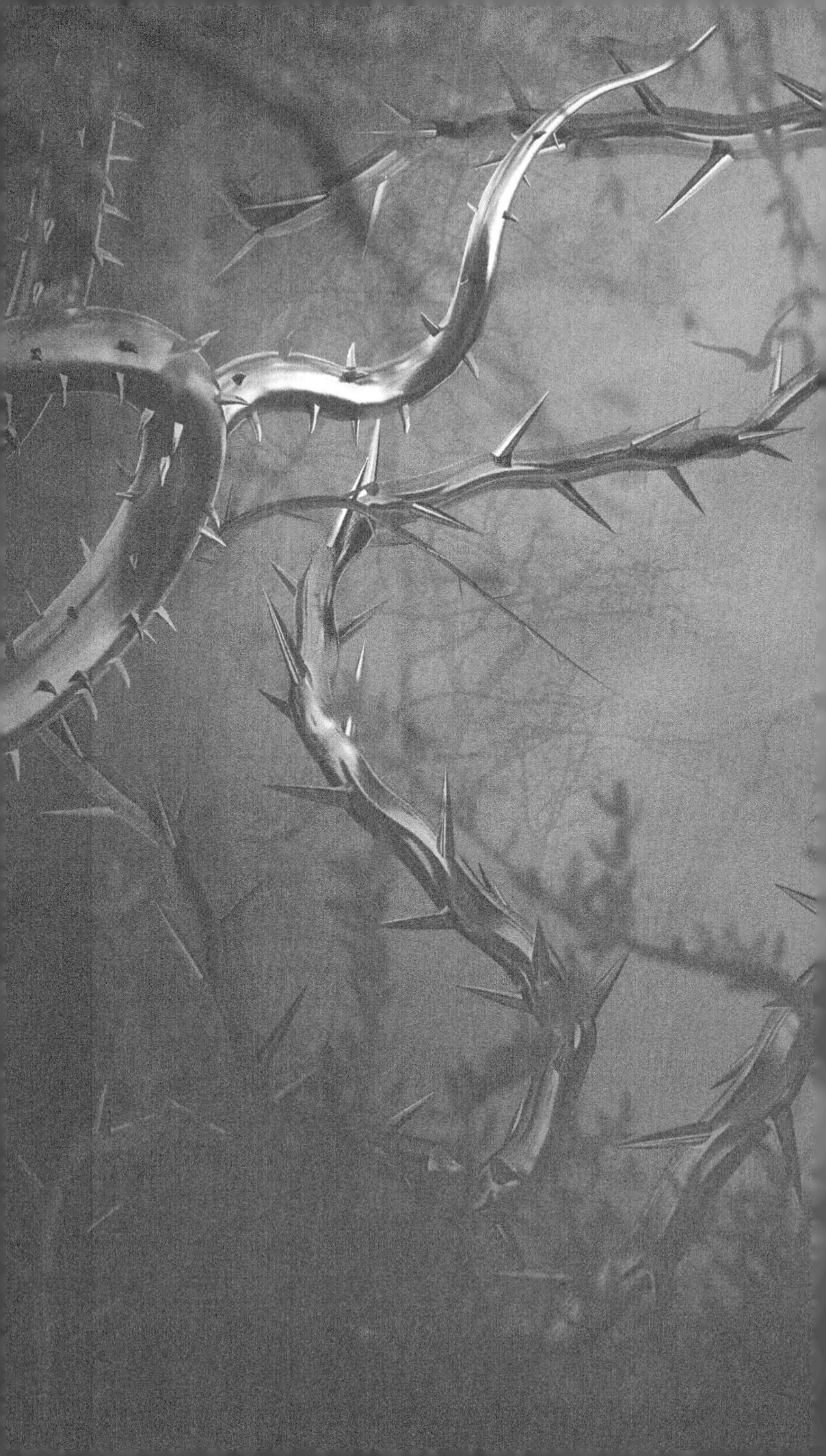

16
DEVYN

After a second shower and lots of kisses, Elio and I head downstairs to find something to eat. I haven't eaten since breakfast, and after all that energy we just burned, I'm starving.

Elio forages through the kitchen before throwing something together, and we head to the dining room to eat. Azarius is there, sitting alone at the table with a half-eaten plate of food in front of him, his eyes snapping to us when we open the door.

"Hey, when did you get back?" I ask, taking a seat across from him. Elio sits next to me.

"A while ago," he replies, his voice dry. He takes a bite of the food on his plate, which looks like meatloaf, but I know is some unusual monster concoction. "You two were fucking in the shower, so I didn't expect you to notice."

The blood drains from my face before I quickly remind myself of Elio's words. Azarius said he wouldn't mind if I decided to claim other mates. He shouldn't be upset.

Clearly, that's not the case.

"Az, I—" Elio starts, but Azarius holds up a hand to cut him off.

"I don't want to hear it from you," he says before locking eyes with me. "I want to hear it from her."

I swallow hard. Everyone's eyes are on me, waiting for my answer.

Azarius looks dejected, soft lines forming between his brows. Elio's eyes are flitting between us, his mouth hardened into a line. I decide not to beat around the bush. After all, drawing it out isn't going to change anything.

"I claimed Elio as my mate."

The silence in the dining hall is deafening, and tendrils of panic crawl their way through me. My heart is racing, and my appetite has been replaced by nervous knots in my stomach.

"He said you were okay with me choosing other mates, if it came to that," I explain without breaking eye contact. "If that's not the case, then I'm sorry."

"I didn't think he was talking about himself," Az snaps.

"Yeah, well, I wasn't trying to—" Elio starts, but Azarius glares at him to shut him up.

Fuck. Elio might have been right. What if being my mates tears their friendship apart?

"In his defense, Elio didn't want me to claim him, as he was worried it might upset you," I point out quickly, words spilling from my mouth like word vomit. "All of this is my fault, but I don't want to choose between you. I want you both."

Azarius' gaze falls to the table, and I can almost see the wheels turning in his head. I probably should have told him differently—maybe alone, when I'd had more time to plan exactly what to say—but what's done is done. I can only hope he'll forgive me and not resent Elio.

"It's your decision," he finally says, briefly meeting my gaze before shoving his chair away from the table. "If that's what makes you happy, so be it."

"Azarius—" I say as he walks around the end of the table toward the door, but Elio places a hand on my arm.

I turn to look at him as the door closes behind us, and he shakes his head.

"Let him go," he says. "He'll be fine."

"How do you know?" The corners of my eyes are beginning to sting, and I blink hard to fight off tears. I know I technically haven't done anything wrong, but the idea of hurting Azarius makes me feel terrible. He's the reason I'm alive, and I owe him for saving me, but this hardly seems like fair payback.

My heart aches.

"Because I know him better than I know myself," he assures me, leaning over to press his lips against my forehead. "He just needs to blow off some steam. You'll see."

My chest throbs painfully as my eyes land on the door, and I wish I could run after Azarius. I'm not sure what I would even say when I caught up with him. Would I apologize for following my heart? For not telling him my plan first?

My mind spins as I chew my bottom lip. It might be best to give him time like Elio suggested, despite how badly I want to ignore his warning.

Hopefully, Elio knows what he's talking about.

After I unsuccessfully attempt to eat and excuse myself from the table, I head to my room to be alone for a while. An hour later, Azarius comes knocking. He slips through the door with a plate of fruit and a goblet in his hands, taking a seat by me on the bed.

"Elio said you didn't eat earlier." He offers me the food with a half-smile, and I take it. The hurt in his eyes is gone, and so is the sharpness in his voice. "Starving yourself won't help anything, you know." I take the goblet from him and bring it to my lips.

"I lost my appetite," I say, trying hard not to imagine the conversation from earlier. I just want to forget it ever happened.

"Devyn, that was my fault, and I'm sorry." He reaches over and tucks a loose strand of hair behind my ear. "It was just a lot to process."

"I would have told you, but it all happened so fast. I didn't want to hurt you."

"I'm not hurt." He shakes his head. "In fact, there's no one I trust more to take care of you than Elio. So, I'm kind of glad it's him."

I breathe a tiny sigh, suddenly feeling lighter. Knowing I won't be the cause of any brawls between them is a relief.

Azarius is quiet for a few minutes while he

watches me eat. Now that the anxious knots have disappeared from my stomach, I'm hungry. After downing the fruit, I sip on the juice, wishing it would last forever. It's quickly become my favorite drink, and I'll miss not having it when I go home.

Maybe Azarius or Elio will bring me some when they visit. The thought of not seeing them every day and having to wait for them to come see me sits uncomfortably in my chest.

"What's wrong?" he asks.

I shove the thought from my mind and glance up. "Nothing. Why?"

"You had this sad look in your eyes, like you were going to cry." He tilts his head to the side. "I know I can't fix everything, but you can talk to me."

Before I know it, I'm nodding with a reply. "I know, but it doesn't help if I can't put my thoughts into words."

He takes my dishes and sets them on the bedside table before scooting closer to me and cupping my cheek in his hand. "Try."

I groan internally, reluctant to share any more feelings today, but getting them off my chest might help. It's not like I have Cara to vent to, and I don't even have a diary I can spill my guts into. Everything is harbored inside me, festering and begging to be released.

"Fine." I lean back against the headboard, unsure of where to begin. I open my mouth, hoping something will naturally come out. "What do we do now?"

Not where I wanted to go, but it's something.

"About?"

"Everything." I throw up my hands. "Now that we have an answer, do you think Rafe will let me go home?"

"Potentially." He scoots closer, so our thighs are touching. "We have to break it to him that we took you to see Ignatius—hopefully, Elio has a decent plan worked out—and see what he says. At this point, I don't see why not."

"Will I be safe if I go home?"

He lifts his shoulder in a shrug. "While I want to say yes, I can't promise you that. If monsters are hunting you, there's always a small chance they could find you, but your scent would be harder to trace among other humans. It wouldn't stand out so much."

I cross my arms over my chest, mind reeling. "If I go home, would I get to see you?"

He exhales a deep breath and shrugs again. "I don't know. I would visit as often as I could. I can promise you that."

"I hope so." I smile weakly. "It wouldn't be nearly as often as if I stayed."

Az offers me his hand, and I let him pull me into his lap. He holds me against his chest, his chin resting on top of my head, and I'm instantly comforted. My worries melt away. My problems seem miniscule. Everything pales in comparison to the safety I feel with him.

"I won't pretend I don't want you to stay here," he says, running his fingers up and down my thigh. "But I also want you to be happy. Being torn away from your entire life is hard. If that's where you want to be, I'm going to do everything I can to get you there, but there's nothing wrong with staying. People embark on new adventures every day without looking back."

"That's the problem." I pull away to look at him. His face is only a few inches from mine, and I'm instantly lost in his eyes. I doubt I could ever tire of looking at them. "I don't know what to do. Choosing both you and Elio was such an easy choice. I can't imagine not having one or the other, but bouncing back and forth between realms would be nearly impossible. We would always be in danger."

"If that's what it takes to make things work, I'd do it. You know I would," he says, running his fingers along my jaw. "If you're not ready to decide, don't. No one is rushing you."

Instead of letting me answer, he closes the distance and catches my lips with his. I pull him against me, snaking a hand behind his neck to deepen our kiss. I try to convey all the emotions churning through me as our lips move together. All the fear, excitement, love, lust, worry; I pour all of it into that kiss and pray he understands everything I'm not able to say.

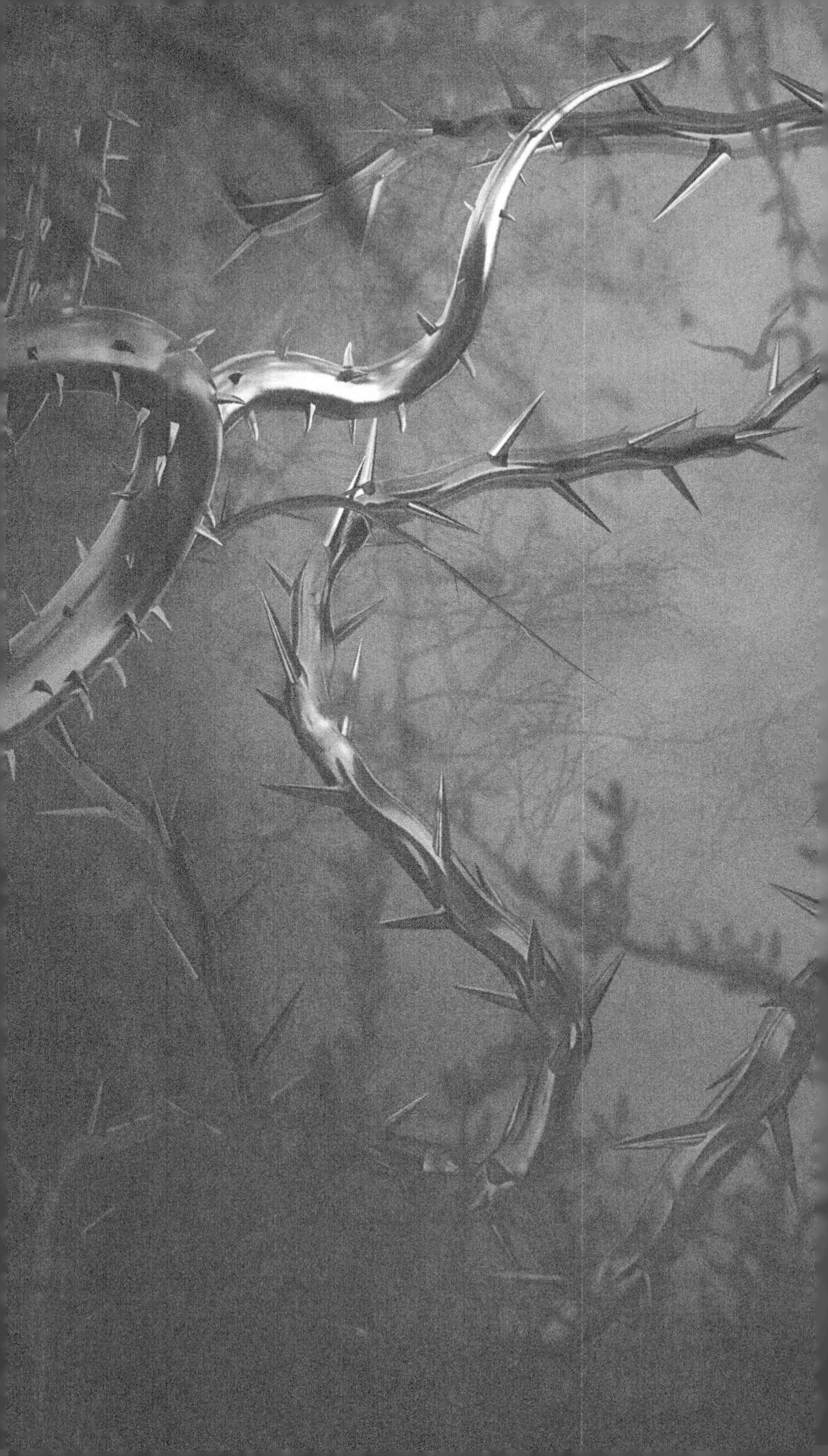

17

DEVYN

Rafe is gone for three days, and every one of them is glorious.

Being able to walk around the mansion without his hungry eyes following me wherever I go is such a relief, I've started prancing around the place naked. What's the point in wearing clothes if either one of your mates might drag you into an unoccupied room and strip them off at any moment?

There's not much of one, in my opinion.

We're hanging out in Elio's room, looking over the warlock's book of marks, when Elio and Azarius' heads snap up. They exchange nervous glances, and Azarius hurries to the window overlooking the front yard.

"What is it?" I ask, looking between them, but I already know the answer. I've only seen them that anxious a few times.

"Rafe's back," he says. "There goes the fun."

"How do you know?" I didn't hear any noises or

anything to indicate someone arriving, so I'm mildly confused. Maybe their hearing is way better than mine, which makes me nervous. If they can hear a door close on the first floor, everyone in the mansion has surely heard me crying out while getting railed.

Oops.

"Well, for one, I'm looking at him," Azarius says, his eyes still trained out the window. "And, for two, we can sense when monsters are nearby. It's like our blood calls to other monsters."

"The more powerful the monster, the stronger the call," Elio adds. "Rafe is very powerful, so we can sense him from a longer distance than most."

"That's... terrifying," I say. "Sneaking up on anyone is out of the question, then."

Azarius nods. "Just another reason why Rafe sends us to do his bidding. Everyone can tell when he moves. It's easier for us to get in and out."

"Speaking of in and out, we'd better greet him and see if he needs anything," Elio says, hopping to his feet. "We'll come right back, if you want to stay here."

"Sure," I say, my eyes falling back to the book. "It's not like I have anything else to do."

The boys sweep out of the room, closing the door behind them, and I'm left alone. Being away from them at the same time feels strange, and a tug in my stomach urges me to follow, but I have no interest in seeing Rafe. I'm sure he doesn't want to see me either.

It's best if I wait here.

I flip through the pages, my eyes glazing over at all

the different marks. There are tiny notes written in the margins, but only part of the scrawl is in English. The rest is written in the ancient, symbolic language of warlocks.

The language of my ancestors.

It's strange to think about, and if I had any connection with my birth parents, I might be inclined to find out more. I might want to know which side passed on the magic, and if either of them knew about monsters. Unfortunately, I never knew either of them—the earliest memories I have are from my first foster family. I'll never know where I came from.

I close the book, resentful of the painful memories it brings up.

The minutes slip by, and I try to find ways to entertain myself, but boredom takes hold and I pace the room. Elio said they would be right back, which was clearly a lie, but I try not to panic. Hopefully, Rafe is filling them in on every dull second of his three-day journey, not sending them out on assignments.

When I reach one end of the room, I turn and head back across it. I'm halfway across the floor when the door springs open, and Elio hurries inside. His expression is serious, lips drawn tightly together.

"Is everything okay?" I ask.

"Rafe said he saw a group of Malevs hanging out uncomfortably close to the woods," he explains, quickly making his way over to me. He takes both my hands in his and squeezes. "He's sending us to check it out."

I peer around him toward the door, expecting Azarius to follow. "Where's Az?"

"Already gone. Don't worry. This isn't the first time they've gotten too close for comfort," he tries to reassure me. "We'll be back soon."

I want to believe him, but my intuition argues. Something isn't right, but I can't put my finger on it. Before I can voice my concerns, Elio pulls me into a heart-stopping kiss.

"Stay inside," he says when he pulls away. "Just in case."

I nod. "Be safe."

He turns and heads toward the hallway, closing the door behind him, and I'm left alone again. This time, I'm overwhelmed by a nagging, intuitive feeling that something dark is coming.

As my anxiety skyrockets, I'm unable to sit still or even continue pacing. Elio told me not to go outside, but I need air. The next best option is the foyer, so I leave his room and head downstairs, hoping the change of scenery calms my nerves.

By the time I hit the bottom of the stairs, my breaths are coming faster. I close my eyes, trying to slow my racing heart, but panic has me firmly in its clutches. I bury my face in my hands, desperate for relief as I choke back a sob.

This is it. All the stress and anxiety from the last few weeks have finally caught up with me, and I'm losing it, having a full-on panic attack. The worst part is, there's no one here to calm me down or make me feel better—Rafe sent them both off to check for the threat of invasion.

I take several deep breaths and wring my hands to make them stop shaking.

"Are you alright?"

I freeze. Rafe's deep voice pierces straight through my chest, making my heart jump into my throat. He's standing in the doorway to the dining room, watching me sternly. Today, he's wearing a light gray suit with a white button-up and black polished shoes. All the gray makes him look like a gargoyle.

"I'm fine," I say, but my labored breathing reveals my lie.

He steps forward, his shoes clicking against the floor as he stops a few feet away. "You don't look fine."

"It's not like you care," I snap, turning away from him. "You're probably disappointed I'm not dead yet."

A tense moment passes, in which I expect him to turn around and return to the dining room, but he doesn't. "Your beliefs are only the words you've put in my mouth. Don't pretend you know what I'm thinking."

Fuck. On top of my panic attack, I now have this arrogant asshole to deal with.

"How silly of me," I say, rolling my eyes while simultaneously feeling lightheaded. "The way you act couldn't possibly convey your feelings."

He steps forward and places a hand on my shoulder, whipping me around to face him.

"Do tell," he says, keeping his voice low. "How exactly should I treat an uninvited guest who does nothing more than breathe my air, eat my food, and pose a constant threat to the safety of my house?"

My jaw drops as I stare into his red eyes, and I'm keenly aware of his hand still on my shoulder.

"I-I didn't—" I stammer, trying to find the words. My mind is a jumbled mess. "Why didn't you just let me go home? You wouldn't even have to deal with me then."

"At the time, you were nothing but a threat," he explains. "A threat to the monster realm, a threat to the security I've established, and a threat to me. Killing you was the easiest option."

"And now? If I'm such a threat, why keep me here?"

He drops his hand from my shoulder but doesn't move. "Mate claims are sacred amongst monsters. I cannot deny my most loyal employees theirs."

Employees. They must have told him about me claiming Elio when he arrived earlier.

"That's almost nice of you," I tease. I'm no longer breathing hard, and my heart rate has returned to a reasonable pace.

A wicked grin breaks across his face, and I don't know whether to smile back or run for the stairs. His normal, unamused glare is way more fitting, more believable.

"Careful. I might have to remind you just how menacing I can be."

A tingle starts at the nape of my neck, and zips

down my back. Was that a joke? A threat? A promise? The lines are blurred at this point, but I'm not taking any chances.

"I said almost. You're still a scary asshole."

He leans forward, and his closeness makes me shiver. I brace myself for a hand around my throat, or something worse, but he whispers in my ear. "Don't forget that."

Brushing past me, he leaves me in the middle of the foyer and heads for the stairs. I'm tempted to follow, hypnotized by his allure, but I root myself to the spot until his footfalls fade to silence.

"Don't poke the bear, Devyn," I whisper under my breath as I make a beeline for the dining room to decompress.

We might have had one decent conversation, but I'm sure he doesn't need a reason to take his frustrations out on me.

I'm still sitting in the dining room when Elio and Azarius return from scouting the area, and I leap off the couch when I hear the front door open. I explode into the foyer, making them both jump, and I hurry across the marble.

"What happened? Did you see anything? How close were they?"

"Slow down," Azarius says, pulling me into his arms. "Everything's fine. It's just a little weird. There's a group of thirty or so Malevs a mile past the woods."

I gaze up at him, my eyes bulging. "A mile? That's close. Were they headed this way?"

"That's the strange part," Elio cuts in. "They

aren't moving, so we have no idea where they're headed or what they're doing."

"It's odd to see so many of them together," Azarius says. "Malevs are stupid and loners most of the time. I've never seen a group that big where they weren't slaughtering each other."

I shiver at the thought of dozens of hulking Malevs fighting in a bloodbath. That's what nightmares are made of.

Azarius lets me go and I slip into Elio's arms, hugging him around the middle.

"What are we going to do?" I ask.

"There's nothing we can do right now." Azarius shrugs. "They aren't quite close enough to assume an attack, and we're severely outnumbered."

"I'm going to update Rafe," Elio says, squeezing me against him. "He'll probably have us check again in a few hours, just to be safe."

I breathe a sigh of relief, but the uncomfortable feeling in my gut doesn't completely go away.

Something still feels off, and I'm pretty sure it has to do with the Malevs.

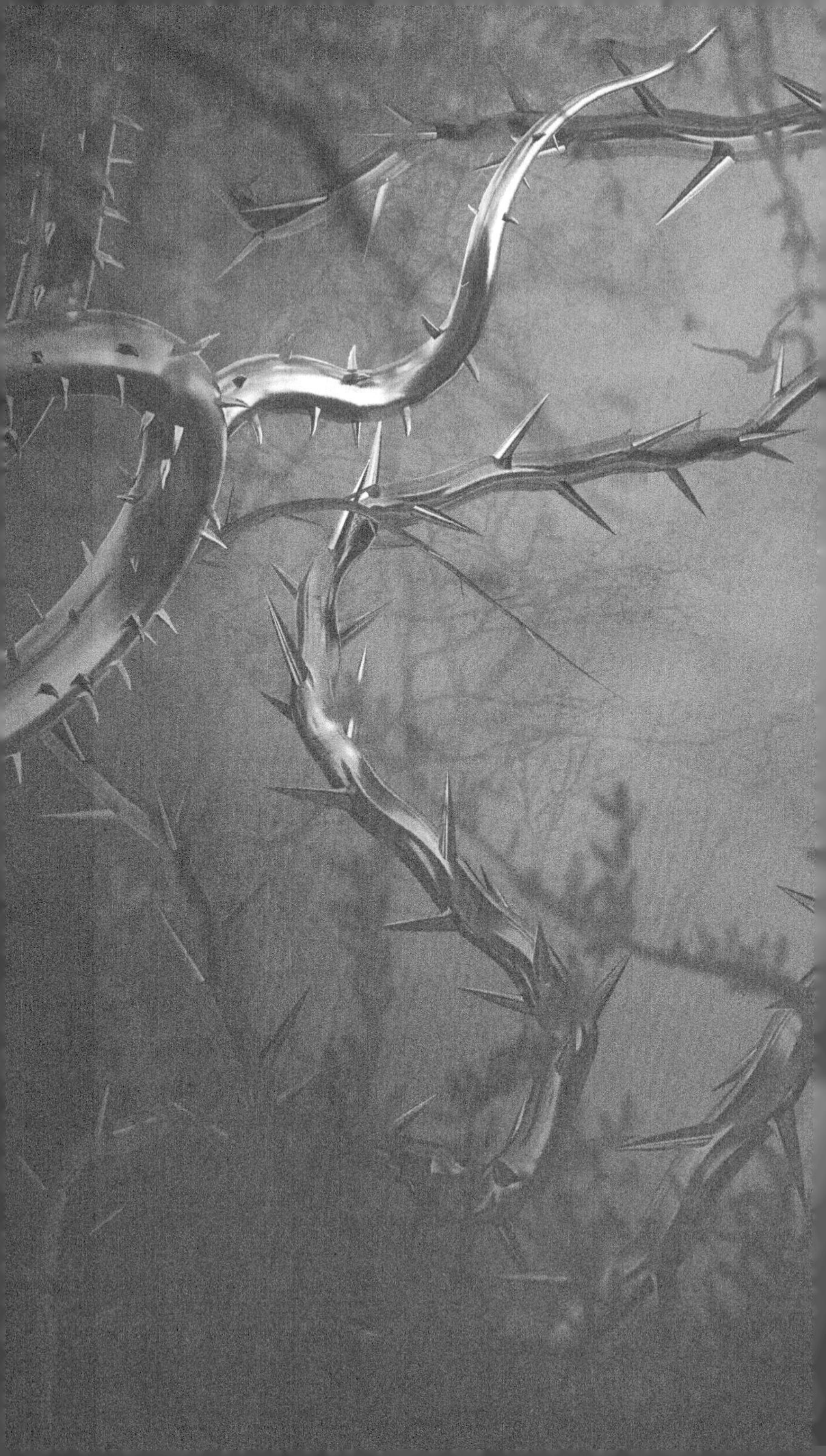

18
DEVYN

Rolling over for the tenth time, I punch my pillow and try to get comfortable, but anxiety sits heavy in my stomach. Everything from the comforter to my clothes is too hot or too heavy, making it impossible to fall asleep. I'm not sure how long I've been laying here, but it has to have been hours.

I should have opted to sleep in Azarius' or Elio's room from the start, but I thought I needed space and time to decompress, to analyze how I felt. I also hate choosing between them, wishing there was a way for the three of us to share a bed but too afraid to ask.

Now, I realize sleeping alone was a stupid idea. Being wrapped in the strong arms of one my lovers would surely settle the nerves setting my insides on fire. Having one of them curled up against me would lull me into peaceful dreams, drowning out any thoughts of Malevs.

With a groan, I toss back the blanket and crawl out of bed, staring at the window as my mind runs wild. Pale green moonlight slips in through the curtains, and the mansion is deathly silent. Everyone is sleeping—everyone except me.

I stand perfectly still for a long moment as I try to decide whose room I want to sneak into. Rafe's is obviously out of the question, but the thought puts a smirk on my face. Would he fuck me or kill me if I wandered up to the third floor in the middle of the night?

Between Elio and Azarius, it's an impossible choice, and I'd almost rather lay here until I can't keep my eyes open any longer, but I'm eager for the relief sleep will provide—a break from the anxiety, the nerves, the worries plaguing my mind.

I head for the door, worried I'll change my mind if I linger in my room any longer, and turn into the dark hallway. It's nearly pitch black, only illuminated by moonlight that spills in through the window at the end of the hall, but I've memorized every inch of this floor. I know exactly where their rooms are, how many doors are in between, how many steps it takes to get there.

I still haven't entirely made up my mind, but I know Azarius was the last to patrol the perimeter, so he must be exhausted from the run. Elio has it a little easier patrolling the sky, though neither job is easy, I'm sure. The woods are miles wide—that's a lot of ground to cover regardless of who does it.

Ultimately, I stop in front of Elio's door, figuring he'll be a little less cranky about being woken up because he's gotten the most rest, and lightly tap my fingers against the wood.

There's no answer at first, so I knock again, a little louder this time.

"Yeah?" a voice grumbles from inside, and I nervously reach for the handle.

I slip into the room and quietly close the door behind me. Elio rubs the sleep from his eyes before propping up on one elbow, concern knitting his brows together.

"What is it, princess?" he asks as I pad across the floor, stopping at the edge of the bed. He must sense my unease, because his mouth dips into a frown a second later. "Is something wrong?"

"I can't sleep," I admit, feeling silly.

Without another word, he scoots over and pats the bed next to him. I slide in, curling up against his side, settling when his arm wraps behind me, pulling me close.

"Can't sleep, huh?" he asks, his voice groggy. He must have been dreaming when I knocked on the door.

"I was too anxious," I admit, keeping my voice low, even though there's no one here to eavesdrop. I'm still anxious, my stomach knotted into a ball, but Elio's presence soothes the worst of my nerves. As he trails his fingers back and forth along my arm, I close my eyes and try to relax.

Try and fail, I should say, because jitters are still

vibrating through me. If I was on Earth, I would be drinking warm milk, bathing in lavender, and looking up all the wives' tales I could find to get to sleep—anything to knock me out for a few hours. Next to me, Elio's breathing is already getting slower, deeper, as he starts to drift off again.

I shift, attempting to get more comfortable, and he stirs.

"Do I need to put you to sleep, princess?" he asks.

I smirk, thinking about all the dirty things he could do to tire me out, but I shake my head. He needs his energy if he's going to get up and patrol in a few hours, and I don't know that a good fuck would be anything other than a temporary distraction.

"No, it's okay," I assure him. "Go back to sleep. I'll drift off in a few minutes."

He leans down to press his lips to the top of my head, mutters something about letting him know if I change my mind, and then he's out again. I can't help but smile as my mind wanders, thinking about everything that led to this moment: the portal, the magic, the Malevs. In moments like these, it still feels surreal, even though it's very much happening, even though we're very much in danger and could go to war at any moment.

My simple life on Earth seems like it was a million years ago. It's amazing how quickly and drastically things can change. I lay there, thinking about all the ways my life has changed forever, for several minutes until I lose track of time. Elio is deep in sleep, his soft snores like a lullaby next to me, but I still can't fall asleep.

A noise outside startles me, and I suck in a sharp breath, freezing stone still.

What the hell was that?

Normally, I wouldn't be spooked by a random noise outside, but nothing ever happens outside the mansion. There are no animals, or anything else for that matter, in the woods surrounding us that could make that sound. It was a sharp, breaking crack—like a twig or a branch snapping off a tree trunk—but that did nothing to ease my panicked mind.

As quietly and gently as I can, I slide out from beneath Elio's arm and tiptoe over to the window in the corner. I peer through the glass without moving the curtain, not wanting anyone or anything to know I'm watching, but I don't see anyone in the clearing below.

Perhaps it's Rafe up at ungodly hours to do his gardening. After all, when else would he do it? I haven't seen him outside at all, much less tending to flowers. Is this when he hides from the others for even more alone time? Does he not want anyone to see him being tender and nurturing, even if it's just to plants? I think about sneaking down to the main floor to get a glimpse of him. If I surprise him in the garden, would he be angry? Annoyed? Would he enjoy the company?

A shadow emerges from the tree line, and my eyes zero in on it. Its details are too dark to make out, but it's large and broad, about Rafe's size. My heart flutters for a moment at the thought of sneaking up on him, wondering if he'd pleasure or punish me in the moonlight, when a second form emerges from the trees.

My heart drops through my ass to the floor, and I watch as they slink across the grass. I'm frozen, unsure what to do, when a third form steps into view.

"Elio!" I hiss, not wanting to scream and alert whoever is outside. I whirl around in time to see him stirring, looking extremely confused. "There are things outside."

In a blink, he's off the bed, sprinting to the window. Unlike me, he rips back the curtain and stares down at the grass below, his eyes trained on the figures.

"Fuck," he grits out. "Those are Malevs."

The blood rushes from my face so fast, it leaves me lightheaded. My eyes bounce between Elio and the scene unfolding below us as several more bodies emerge from the woods.

"Oh shit," I whisper as Elio grabs my hand, pulling me away from the window.

"We have to warn Rafe," he says, dragging me across the room. However, at that moment, his door bursts open, and Azarius' chalk white form races into the room.

"How the fuck are we under attack?" he asks, his gaze bouncing between the two of us. "We checked so many times. There were no signs of them."

"I don't know, but we've got to move," Elio says.

"What are we going to do?" My voice is soft, and I can barely hear it over the blood pounding in my ears.

"You're going to hide," Azarius says with a straight face. "Come with me. You, go get Rafe. I'll meet you downstairs." His eyes bounce to my other mate, who nods in agreement.

Before I can object, Az grabs me by the hand and drags me toward the hall.

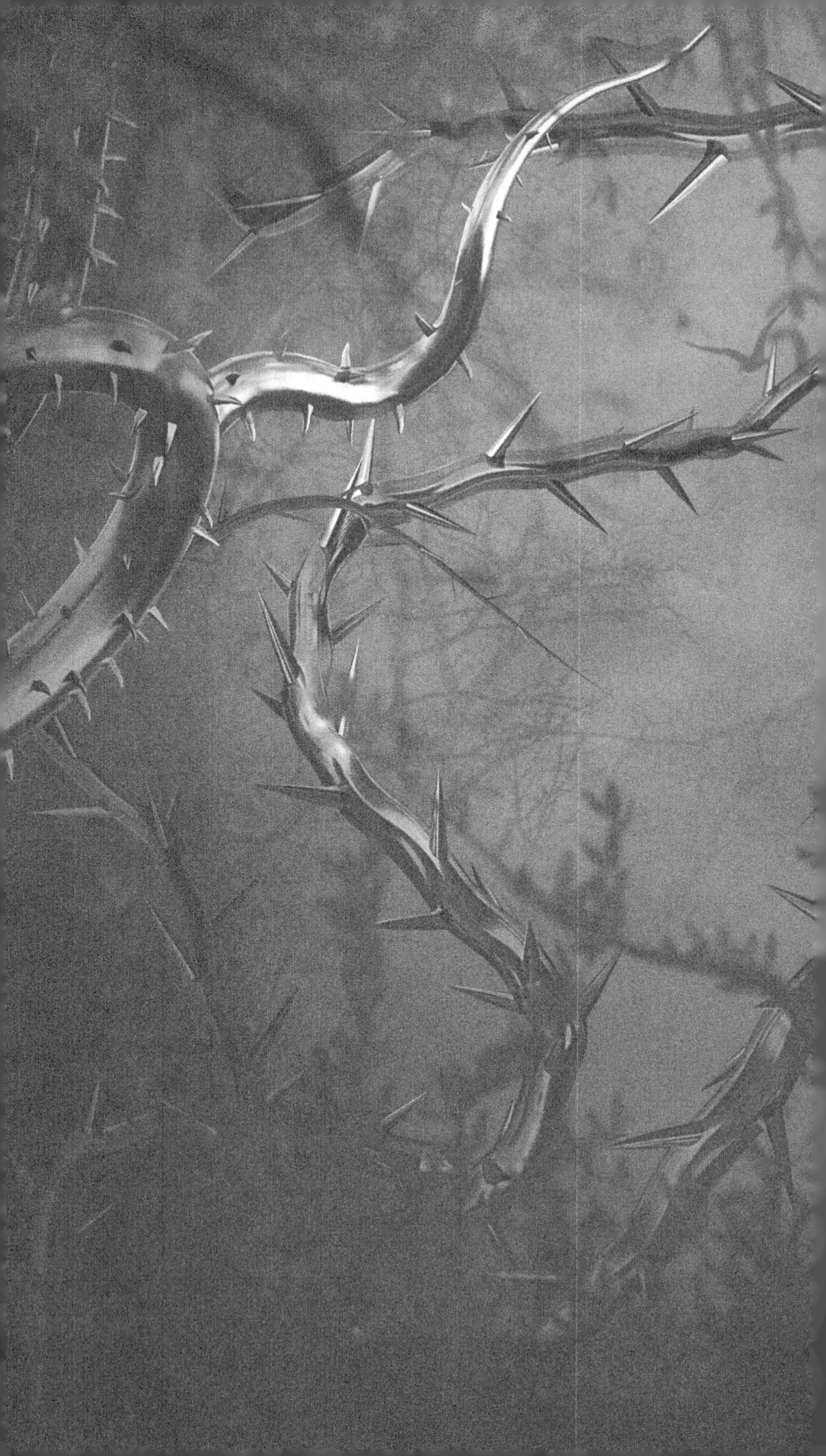

19

AZARIUS

I have no idea how the Malevs found us, or how they made it through the woods without us picking up on their trail, but I do know one thing: I won't let them lay a fucking hand on Devyn. I'll cut down every degenerate demon, rip out their insides and feed them to them, before I let them hurt her.

She's terrified, fear pouring off her in waves as we hurry to my room, and when I let go of her hand, I don't miss the little whimper that leaves her lips.

"You're going to hide in here," I say, whirling around to face her. "Do not leave this room until I come for you. Do you understand?"

"Yes, but—"

I cut her off, the urge to protect her surging through my veins. "No buts. I need you to do this, or I can't promise you'll be safe."

I can tell she wants to argue. She doesn't want to be left alone. Hell, I don't want to leave her alone, but

I can't protect her and slaughter a group of Malevs at the same time. I need her to stay here, away from the fight.

After a long second, she finally nods, and I race to the bedside table. Ripping open the drawer, I withdraw a sheathed silver dagger that glints in the dim light and shove it at her.

"Hopefully you won't need this, but just in case," I say. Adrenaline is slamming through my system, every second that passes giving our enemy more of an advantage, but I don't want to leave her like this. My eyes bounce around the room, searching for anything to help keep her hidden, but there isn't much.

When my gaze lands on the armoire, my heart lurches, and I'm walking across the room before I can think twice. I wrench open the door, shoving the hanging clothes out of the way, and gesture to the bottom of it.

"Get in here," I urge. "Hopefully, my scent will be enough to mask you."

She doesn't budge from the middle of the room, watching me as worry fills her eyes. "They're not going to get up here, though, right?" she asks, a quiver in her voice.

Fuck. I realize I can't promise her that in full confidence, because there's always a chance Rafe, Elio, and I won't be enough to stop them, but I refuse to think like that. I can't think like that.

We're going to fight, and we're going to win.

I'm going to protect my mate, and I'll come retrieve her once the coast is clear.

A few long strides land me right in front of Devyn, and I pull her into my arms, crushing my lips against hers. It's a fast, heated kiss that I hope conveys everything I want to say, and then I'm pulling away way too soon.

"I won't let them hurt you, darling," I say, urging her toward the armoire. "Stay hidden and stay quiet. I'll come back for you."

"Be safe, Az," she says softly, clutching the knife close to her chest.

"I will." There are so many more things I want to say, but the words are jumbled in my brain. Adrenaline won't let me think straight. Instead of wasting more time trying to get my words out, I close the door of the armoire, the image of Devyn's fearful gaze branded onto my mind.

I run, the hallway nothing but a dark blur as I head for the stairs. Glass shatters somewhere in the mansion, and I fly toward the first floor, skipping half the steps along the way. When I skid into the foyer, a rock crashes through one of the windows, and something large slams into the door. It rattles the entire frame, making the wood groan. Thankfully, the door doesn't give out, but it won't keep a swarm of Malevs out for long.

A chaotic mix of sounds spills in through the busted window: grunts, screeches, roars, voices. I want to tear them all limb from limb, bathing in their blood to celebrate their demise, but I can't run out swinging until Elio and Rafe show up.

I have to buy us some time.

My feet move on autopilot to the dining room, and I drag the lounge sofa over to barricade the front door. Unsatisfied, I hurry to grab a heavy lounge chair and add it to the pile blocking the entrance. It won't last forever, but maybe it'll win us a few minutes while we work out a plan, if we even have time to do that.

Somewhere in the mansion, more glass shatters, and my heart drops to the floor. If the Malevs manage to break in somewhere else, if they manage to scale to the second floor and find Devyn hidden away... I feel sick at the thought, and I've never wanted her to be home on Earth more than I do right now, if only to keep her safe.

A loud thud slams against the door again, shaking the floor beneath my feet, and I brace myself. Six-inch razor-sharp claws extend from my fingertips. I can't wait to sink them into Malev flesh, to filet every beast just beyond the walls of the mansion.

I don't care if the odds are against us. I don't care if we're severely outnumbered.

I won't stop until every one of them is dead.

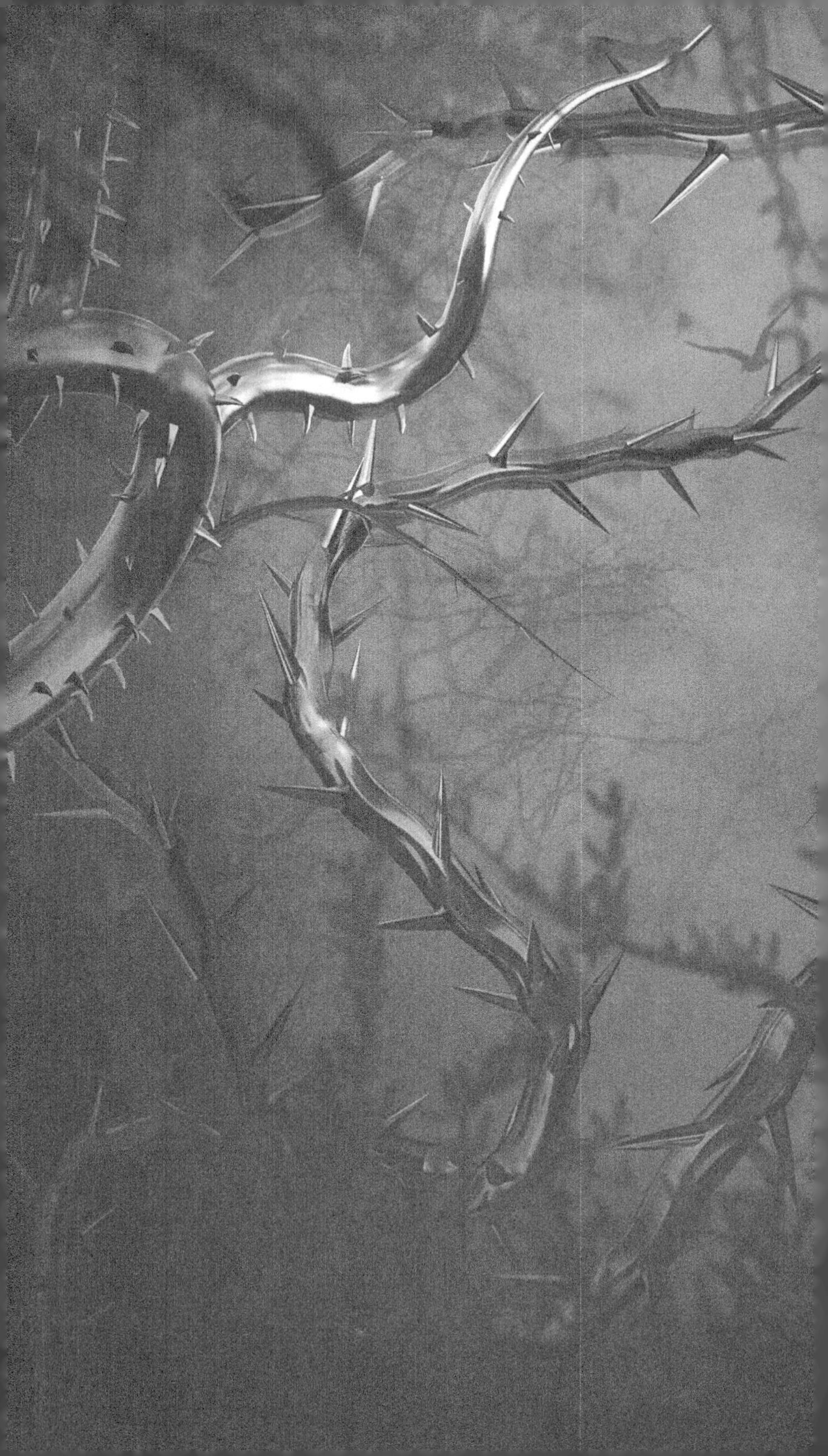

20
RAFE

Only after sending Elio and Azarius out two more times, the last of which the Malevs were nowhere to be found, was I finally able to comfortably retreat to my bed.

The fact that so many of them were traveling together is alarming, but not entirely unexpected. After all, it's no secret the power players of Orlyitha are allying themselves against the abominations. It would only make sense for them to do the same.

My dreams are a muddied blend of negotiations, slaughtering Malevs, forming new alliances, and the annoyingly vulnerable human girl. I'm hardly surprised.

Devyn.

Just the sound of her name is enough to light a fire of rage within me. She's completely useless, but for some reason, I'm intrigued by her. That infuriates me more than the sound of her name. Why would I have any interest in something useless?

Despite being descended from warlocks, she's still just a human, unable to fight or protect herself, unable to use magic or transform. She's a liability, one that somehow made Azarius and Elio fall in love with her, and she could be the reason they're killed.

Perhaps she does possess magic after all.

As I'm dreaming about standing with her in the foyer, my hands on her shoulders as I slowly pull her against me in a romantic gesture, a series of loud bangs at the door rips me out of the image and drops me in my bed.

"Who is it?" I roar out, almost hoping it's Devyn so I can take every ounce of my fury out on her.

"Elio, sir. Get up now! We're under attack!"

The blood in my veins turns to ice, and a growl rumbles in my throat. A Malev attack is the last thing I expected, but I don't have time to analyze how they managed to slip past our patrol. Or more importantly why they went through all the trouble to attack us here.

Are they after me? Information?

No. A swift realization has me groaning, a throbbing headache forming in my temple.

They're here for the human.

"What the fuck?" The words barely have time to leave my mouth before my feet are on the floor and I'm rushing toward the door. I rip it open to find Elio blocking my way. His eyes are wide, brows knitting together.

"Explain," I demand, shoving past him into the hallway. I'm only wearing a pair of silk sleep pants, but there's no time to change. We hit the stairs and take them two at a time to the second floor.

"Malevs. We think they're the group we saw, but it doesn't make sense," Elio rambles. "There was no sign of them earlier."

"It's possible they saw one of you tracking them and hid until nightfall. Where is Azarius?"

Glass shatters somewhere below us, and I curse under my breath. These Malevs are going to obliterate the mansion, the fuckers. I'll make sure they pay for every scratch.

"The foyer, holding them off."

"And the girl?" I scold myself for asking. I shouldn't care if she lives or dies, or gets taken, but for some fucking reason, a possessive urge ignites in my chest, and I feel obligated to ensure her safety.

"Azarius hid her in one of the rooms, but I don't know how much it will help. They can smell her a mile away."

"Correct. So don't let them get that far," I say as we hit the foyer floor. "Kill them all."

I take a moment to assess the situation, my eyes sweeping over the room. Azarius has barricaded the entrance with sofas from the dining room, and the Malevs have broken the windows on either side of the door.

A Malev pokes its brown, snakelike head in through one of the holes, and Azarius promptly kicks it in the face. It lets out a beastly shriek as it retreats.

"How do you want to handle it, boss?" Azarius calls as a second Malev attempts to crawl through the window. He rakes his claws across its face, spilling black blood on the tile floor.

"If they get inside, they'll destroy the place. Not to mention, it'll be easier for them to get the human," I say pointedly.

There's no need to speak carefully, because we all know why the Malevs are here. Not to mention, Devyn has spent every day of the last few weeks tromping around the mansion. Her scent is everywhere, and it's probably driving the beasts crazy.

"Let's meet them outside." I extend my hand and draw all the nearby shadows to me, assembling them in an opaque mass half the size of my body. I throw it at the window, knocking every remaining sliver of glass from the panes.

Azarius doesn't hesitate, leaping through the hole in a graceful bound. Elio dives through head-first next. Calling on my powers, I shift into gray smoke and swirl through the window, becoming solid again when my feet can touch the ground.

It's absolute mayhem.

Countless dark forms shift around us, some engaged in combat with Elio and Azarius, others moving in my direction. A few skirt toward the sides of the mansion, disappearing out of sight around the corners, and I make a mental note to go after them when I break through the mass ahead. Out of sight means out of control, and we can't let any of them get that far.

A broad Malev with a huge stomach and four arms steps in my direction, bellowing a growl that shattered the air around us. I wait while his steps turn into a sprint, and when he grabs for me, my body turns to smoke, weaving through his grasp. I reappear to the left in a flash, grabbing it by the throat and squeezing until I feel bones crunch beneath my fingers. I shove him away, watching him stumble before he crashes to the ground, unmoving.

I look up, and two more have taken his place, blocking my way from going after the stragglers. They're easy kills, but this is still taking too long.

There's an option that would make much easier work of these Malevs, but tapping into that power is risky. Unlike Elio and Azarius, who can change into humans at will, I don't have a human form. The demon blood I possess doesn't allow it.

I am a monster, and then I become something truly monstrous. Difficult to contain, impossible to predict, my other form is a force to be reckoned with. But if I'm not able to control it, I risk destroying much more than the enemy.

I risk hurting two of my most loyal followers.

I risk hurting her. My thoughts shift to the human hiding upstairs, and I'm annoyed with myself again. Since when does she take up so much real estate in my mind?

The Malevs continue closing the distance, hesitant after seeing what happened to the fat one, and I succumb to the pull of my demonic power. There's no time for second guessing.

My body contorts, elongating and gaining mass. My nails stretch into claws. The blood pumping through my veins turns to liquid fire, burning its way through my body, and when I roar, I barely recognize the menacing sound that escapes my throat. It rips through the air around us, making the nearest beings vibrate in terror.

The approaching Malevs hesitate, obviously deterred by my transformation, and I lunge forward, my claws aimed for their throats.

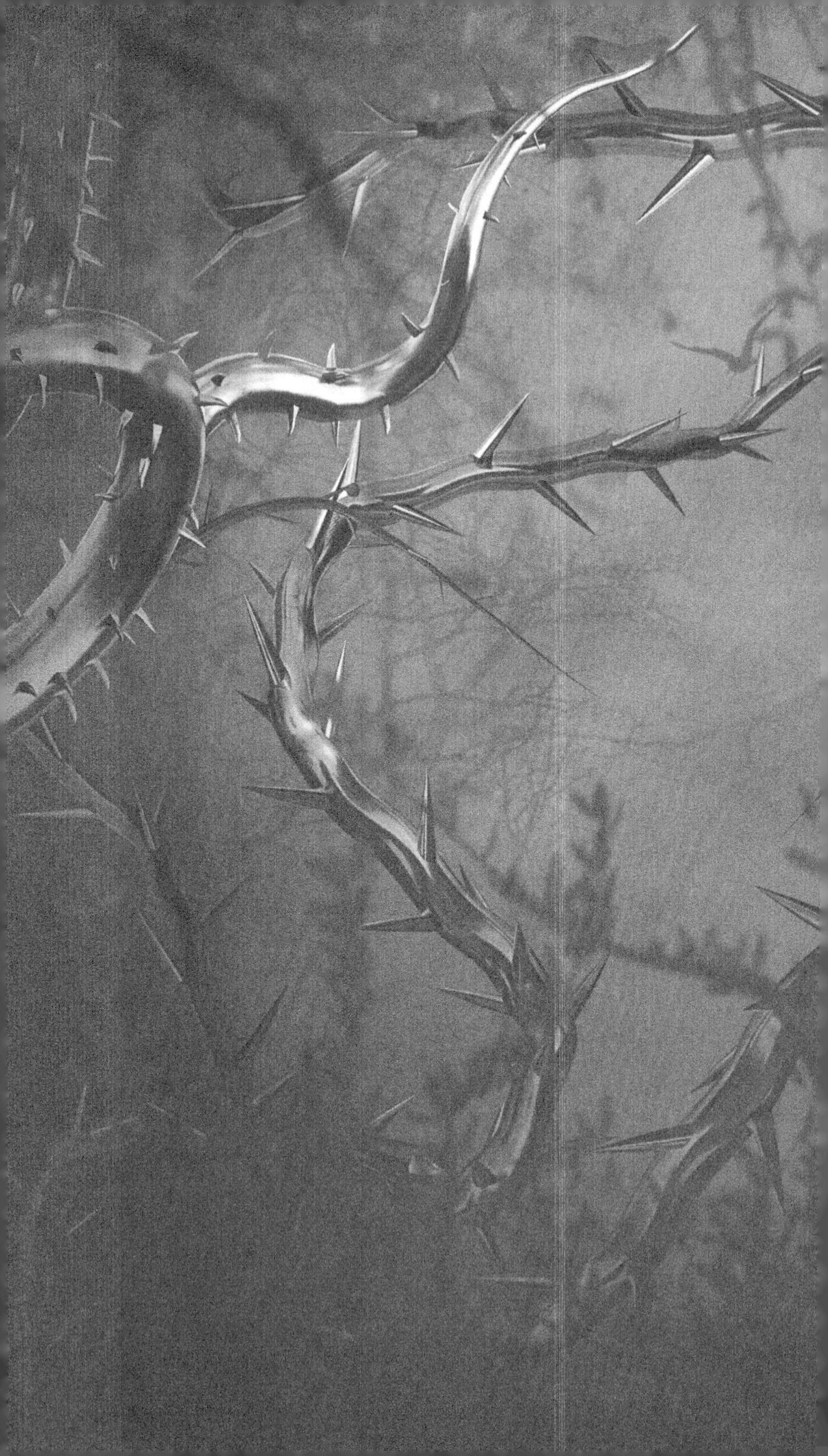

21
DEVYN

The sounds drifting up from the ground outside make my stomach turn.

Growls. Glass breaking. Seconds ago, a brutal roar ripped through the air, making the hair on my arms stand up.

It's killing me to not see what's going on, but I promised Azarius I would stay buried in Elio's armoire with a six-inch dagger after I barricaded the door. We hoped the smell of his clothes would be enough to mask my scent, but I'm not convinced. I never imagined wanting to bathe myself in nesda juice again, but that's exactly what I find myself desiring as I shift my position to appease a thigh cramp.

Despite trying not to fault myself for the Malev attack, I know I'm to blame. Azarius even said he'd never seen one of them in these woods before I got here. Now, there's a group of them beating down the door, and Elio and Azarius are risking their lives to protect me.

What kind of mate puts their lovers in danger? A crappy one. That's me.

My legs are starting to fall asleep, and I ease open the door of the armoire. A pillar of light falls through the crack, breaking up the pitch blackness I've been sitting in, and I can see straight to the window. The need to know what's happening outside swells, pulling me toward the glass vantage point, and it doesn't take long for me to give in.

I'll sneak over, glance for a second, and hurry back to my hiding place. No one will know, and my desperate curiosity will be sated.

My feet hit the ground softly as I slide off the shelf, and I hurry across the room to the window. I stand to the side, obscuring as much of my body as possible, and peer around the edge toward the ground.

I'm hit with instant regret. The dark ground is swarming with Malevs, crawling, walking, and sliding their way toward the mansion. Dozens of bodies—luckily, all Malevs—litter the ground.

I scour the scene, searching for signs of Elio or Azarius, only to find them fighting back-to-back near the front door. For every Malev they strike down, two more step up, and I can see a long trail of blood oozing from Azarius' chest, spilling over his pale white torso and dripping down his leg.

My stomach turns and I taste bile. My eyes sweep

back across the space, searching desperately for any sign of Rafe, but I don't see him. Surely, he wouldn't let Azarius and Elio face this fight alone.

I have half a mind to march my way to the third floor and beat down his door until a large, dark figure catches my attention. It darts toward the side of the mansion, easily cutting down two Malevs without slowing down, and I squint to see better.

Long, muscular limbs. Giant horns that curl forward. A barbed tail that whips viciously at approaching Malevs. The monster is unlike anything I've ever seen, and I know without a doubt who it is.

"Rafe," I whisper, watching him disappear around the side of the house.

Something crashes in the hallway, and I jump, spinning around to face the door. The lounge chair was the heaviest thing I could haul in front of it, but I don't know how effective it'll be if someone tries to break in.

I dart for the armoire, jumping inside as swiftly as I can, snapping the door closed behind me. I'm drowned in darkness again, and I scoot as far back as I can, hiding beneath as much fabric as possible.

Another crash comes from the hallway, this one muffled through the wood of the armoire. I take a shaky breath, hoping to soothe my nerves, but yet another crash makes me gasp. That one sounded closer.

My thoughts rush to Elio and Azarius on the ground. They were swamped with Malevs, barely fending them off. If one happens to make its way in here, neither of them will be able to save me. I'm on my own.

I unsheathe the dagger and hold it close, ready to defend myself. I might not be able to kill a Malev, but I'm confident I can wound one.

Something slams into the door to Elio's room, and I clap a hand over my mouth to stifle a scream. There's another bang, followed by a growl, and I tighten my grip on the handle of the dagger. For a beat, I believe the Malev will give up and move on, and I'm teased by a flicker of hope.

Then, there's an explosion outside, and I hear what sounds like the lounge chair flying across the room. I stop breathing as heavy footsteps enter the room.

"I smell the human," a voice hisses, making my skin crawl. "Find it."

More footsteps pad into the room, followed by bangs, scrapes, and scuffles of things being tossed around and searched. Movement stops in front of the armoire, and I know what's coming before the doors are ripped open.

I brace myself.

At the first sign of light, I spring forward with the knife in my hand. I swing at the Malev, slicing across his arm, and an ear-splitting shriek explodes from its mouth. My feet hit the ground and I swing again, slicing across its chest before thick hands grab me and knock the dagger from my grip.

"Feisty." The Malev clutching me bends down and smells my hair, and I fight against his grip. He's stocky, with mustard-colored skin and enormous tusks curving toward his chest. "How I'd love to taste her flesh."

"No," one of the others snaps. I can't tell who speaks, but I guess it's irrelevant. They're all ugly, hulking, and gnarly. "We can't kill her yet. Must deliver."

Without many more words, the Malevs head for the door, which has been knocked off its hinges, and stomp their way down the hall. The one that grabbed me throws me over his shoulder before following the others. His tough, knobby skin digs into my stomach, making me wince.

I have no idea where they're taking me, but they've obviously been recruited by someone to retrieve me. Whoever wants me knows about the rumors, and they think I'm a lot more special than I am.

It can't end like this.

"Elio!" I scream. It's difficult to yell loudly, being upside down and having the breath squished out of me. The Malev jostles me to shut me up, but I ignore him.

"Az!" My voice echoes off the walls.

"Shut up before I rip out your tongue." He hisses. "Boss didn't say anything about a tongue."

I clamp my mouth shut as we hit the stairs, saving my voice for when we get outside. There's not much use yelling inside the mansion anyway—the boys probably can't hear over the commotion.

We emerge outside through the back door and head directly for the tree line. I push myself up as much as I can and look around, but there's no sign of my mates.

"Elio! Az! Rafe!" I scream.

I strain my ears for a reply, but all I can hear are the steady grunts and growls coming from the other side of the house.

"Az! Elio!" I yell at the top of my lungs as the distance closes between us and the trees. It'll be much harder to catch up with us in the woods.

"Rafe!" I draw out the word until my voice cracks apart, and I slump in defeat.

The lack of oxygen from screaming has made me lightheaded, and the world sways. I swear I see a black shadow racing toward us, but it could also be that my vision is starting to fade as I slip into unconsciousness. The latter is more likely.

I hardly believe my eyes when the shadow barrels into the Malevs ahead of us, sending them flying. I push myself up again, craning to see what's happening, but it's mostly blocked by the buffoon whose back I'm on. I punch him in the side out of spite, but he doesn't even flinch.

The Malev carrying me darts forward, hurrying for the trees, but he stops short and goes rigid beneath me. Craning to look around him, I see the bottom half of an impressive black form, and I have to assume it's Rafe.

"Drop the girl." His voice is unmistakable.

The Malev releases his grip on me, and I slide off his shoulder. I barely have time to throw my arms out to avoid landing on my face, and I roll over to see Rafe snap the creature's neck. The Malev drops to the ground and doesn't move again.

I look past Rafe at the collection of bodies on the ground. He's killed the rest of the Malevs from the troupe that broke into Elio's room, all in a few seconds.

My eyes climb his body slowly, struggling to take in what I'm seeing. He's an enormous black form rippled with muscles, but he's also smoke. He seems to hover somewhere between them, and the entirety of his eyes are red.

A figment of my worst imagination. This man is fear incarnate, and he just saved me.

"Rafe—"

"Devyn!" Azarius' voice breaks through the night, and he's by our side in a second. He's covered head to toe in blood, most of it black. The scratches he obtained are already healing, closing themselves while I watch. "What are you doing out here? You were supposed to be upstairs."

Elio drops out of the sky and lands next to us a second later. "What the hell happened?"

I open my mouth to fill them in, just as Rafe turns on the spot and walks away. I watch him go, full of conflicting emotions, but Az and Elio are eager for answers and my mind is a mess.

When no words come, Azarius pulls me against him and wraps his arms around me.

"It's okay," he says with a tender voice. "We can ask questions later. You're safe now."

I bury my face in his chest, ignoring the blood all over him, and close my eyes as I try to believe him. I may be safe, but for how long?

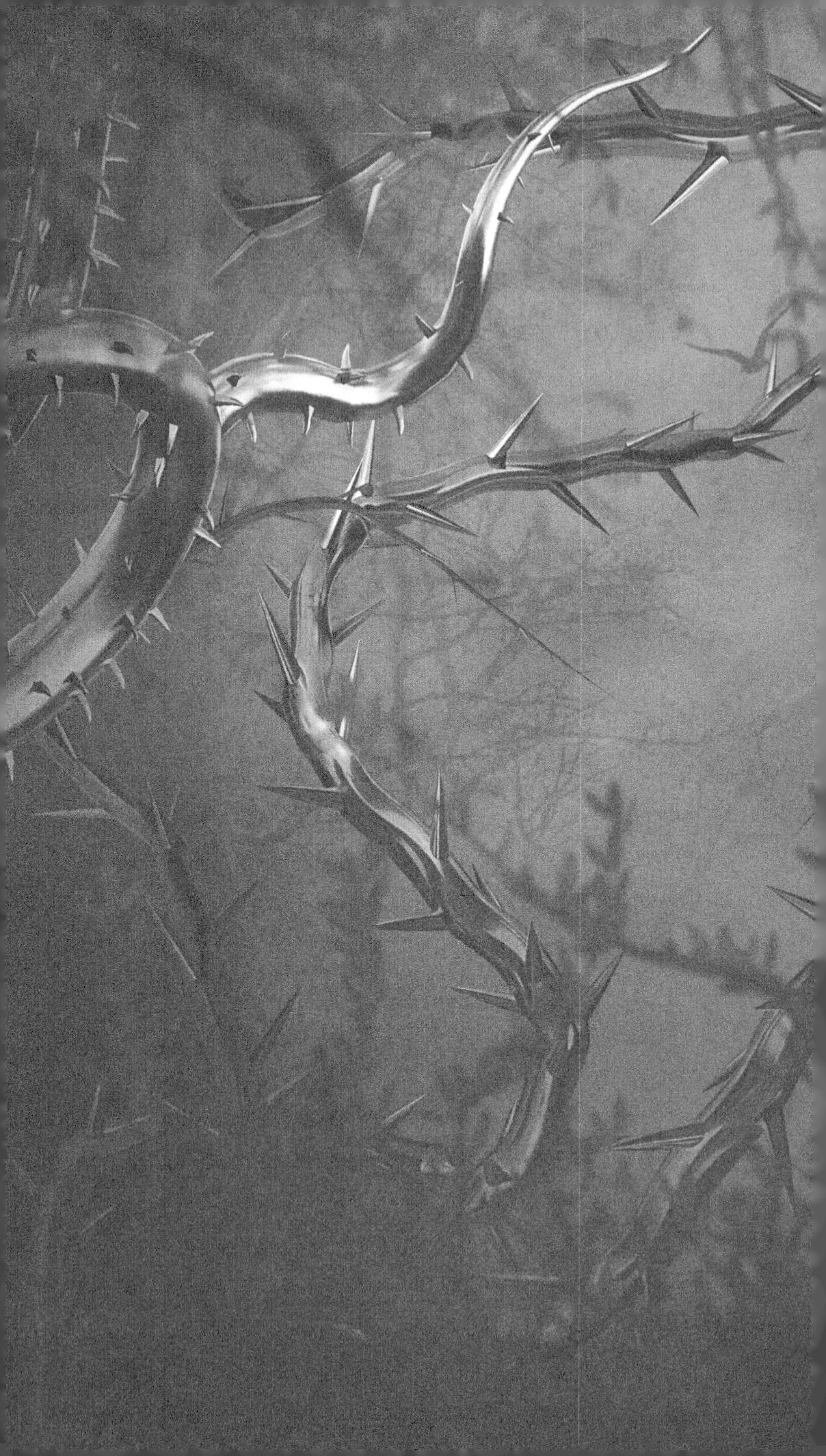

22
DEVYN

The aftermath of the Malev attack is devastating, and the cleanup is a bitch.

Corpses surround the mansion, windows smashed, doors broken, and there's blood everywhere. Elio's room is unrecognizable, and he winds up sleeping in the guest room with me for a few days until his can be put back together, not that either of us are complaining.

I help where I can, cleaning up broken glass or rehanging things on the walls, and Azarius and Elio handle everything else. They drag all the Malev bodies to a pile and burn them, rearrange the furniture that was disrupted, and start repairing the house.

Rafe's plan to assemble the monsters and drive the Malevs back into the mountains is now working at hyper speed. He left the morning after the ambush, intending to rally his allies, and didn't return for several days. In the meantime, Ignatius came to set up protective wards.

It's still a wreck, but at least we're protected from any more attacks for now.

When he returned, Rafe disappeared to the third floor, and we haven't seen him since. He hasn't sent Elio or Azarius on any errands. He hasn't even come down to check the cleanup progress. If it wasn't for my mates' ability to sense him, I would think he slipped out again to do more recruiting. Instead, he remains hidden up there. There's no telling what he's up to.

"Do you think he's okay?" I ask one evening while Azarius and I are sitting by the fireplace in the dining room. My legs are draped over his lap, while my head rests against his chest, and he's running his fingers through my hair. Elio went upstairs to shower after a long day of heavy lifting.

"I don't think he can drown in the shower."

I huff and playfully smack his leg. "I meant Rafe."

"Oh." He shrugs. "Honestly, I don't know. This is the longest he's ever isolated himself."

Lips pursed, my mind drifts up to the third floor. "I'm kind of worried."

"About Rafe?" He chuckles. "Don't be. He's fine."

Rafe's life has been turned upside down just as much as any of ours, and even though he's an intolerable asshole most of the time, he doesn't deserve to isolate himself and potentially drive himself insane with his thoughts.

I've been there, alone and cut off from everything I knew, feeling like my life was over. I know it's a dangerous, dark place. Even if he is fine and just enjoying the retreat the third floor provides, I've yet to thank him for saving me from the Malevs. He didn't have to, and even though I was screaming his name, I didn't honestly expect him to help. He proved me wrong.

"Do you think he'll kill me if I go talk to him?" I ask, sitting up on the couch.

I've already made my decision to head to the third floor, but I'm nervous. What if he doesn't want to see me? After all, this is all my fault.

"Probably not," he says, rubbing a comforting hand along my thigh. "If he wanted you dead, he would have killed you already."

"You're right." I look over to meet his eyes and force a smile.

If Rafe really wanted me dead, he would have let the Malevs have me from the beginning. He wouldn't have fought them or let them destroy his mansion.

"I'm going to try," I say, pushing myself off the couch. "If I'm not back soon, come find me."

He forces a dry laugh. "Not funny. I'll see you tonight."

I cup my hand under his chin and bend to kiss him, my lips dancing against his perfectly, the way they always do. "It's a date."

I make my way up the stairs to the third floor in a blur, and I pause on the landing.

My heart is beating in my throat, my hands trembling. Only a hallway and a wooden door separate me from Rafe, and while I doubt he'll hurt me, considering he went out of his way to save my life, the fear of the unknown still sends an icy chill over me.

He's unpredictable, a loose cannon. There's no telling what he will say or do to me now that we'll be alone. Not to mention, I'm tracking him down to talk to him, when he clearly doesn't want to be bothered.

Forcing my feet across the floor, I pass the first set of doors and make my way closer to the third, my breaths becoming shaky.

I still have time to change my mind. I can turn around, head downstairs, forget about this whole plan. As tempted as I am, I know I can't. I have to thank him, even if it's only to appease my conscience.

My hand shakes as I raise it to knock on the door. Every tap against the wood resonates through my body like a beacon of warning, but I swallow my fear.

"Enter," Rafe calls from within.

Well, at least he's alive. That's a positive.

I tentatively reach for the doorknob and push the door open, revealing what is by far the most opulent room in the entire mansion. I should have known he'd save the best of everything for himself.

All the surfaces in the room are black, but flecks of silver that shimmer in the light are sprinkled across the floor. A glossy, four-poster bed draped with an emerald-green canopy and rich green bed linens takes up the center of the room, waiting like an open invitation. There's a sitting area to my right, comprised of a wide emerald sofa and a plush black rug in front of a fireplace. The walls are covered with paintings in silver frames, and a marble statue of a woman with horns occupies one of the corners.

Rafe stands, staring out a window to my left. He's dressed in one of his pressed black suits with his back to me, and as I step farther into the room, I hear him take a slow, deep breath.

"Did Azarius send you?" he asks without turning around. My scent must have given me away.

"No. He didn't."

"I bet it was Elio."

"Nope. Wrong again."

I stop near the middle of the room, and my eyes travel toward the ceiling, where an elaborate chandelier hangs. My eyes do another lap around the room, taking it all in. How the hell did he get all this stuff into the monster realm? The thought of Azarius and Elio dragging a king-sized bed through the portal makes me laugh, but I quickly stifle it.

"Then why are you here?" As usual, his tone is sharp, no hint of the sensitive Rafe who comforted me during my panic attack. Azarius was right; he's fine and acting like his usual self.

I shift my weight back and forth nervously as I consider how to proceed. Even though I practiced my speech several times over the last few days, I'm suddenly drawing a blank.

"I needed to talk to you," I say, still trying to assemble my thoughts.

He scoffs, his eyes still glued out the window. "Then speak."

I stare at the profile of his face in disbelief. It

never ceases to amaze me just how fucking rude this man can be.

"Then turn around and pretend like you give a fuck."

It's not the smartest thing to say, and I realize it as soon as the words leave my lips, but I'm sick of being treated like the biggest inconvenience in his life. Granted, I might be the biggest inconvenience he's facing, but he could at least tell me that and stop turning his nose up like I'm nothing.

His shoulders tense, and he slowly wheels around to face me, his eyes locking onto me like lasers. He takes several steps in my direction, and I swallow hard.

"You would do well to remember who you're talking to," he says, raising his voice slightly. "I can easily make your existence a nightmare."

I'm terrified to hold his gaze, but even more afraid to look away. I knead the inside of my cheek between my teeth, contemplating how to continue without angering him further. As usual, things aren't going well between us, even though I came up here with good intentions.

So far, I'm failing miserably.

I let out a sigh, throwing my hands up before letting them fall in defeat.

"I know you hate me, and you probably regret saving me, but the least you can do is look at me when I'm trying to thank you for saving my life." The words rush out in a pleading tone, but I have to get them out before they eat me alive. "You could have easily left me to die, but you didn't, and I'm very grateful."

The pressing weight of Rafe's gaze is crushing me, making me feel miniscule. For a long moment, he doesn't say anything, just stares at me like I'm the most irritating thing he's ever seen. When I can't hold his gaze any longer, I let my gaze fall to the hardwood between my feet.

I'm beginning to think this was all a mistake. How silly of me to think Rafe might have changed because of a random act of decency.

After a whole minute of painful silence, he steps closer, and my heart rate picks up. Every footstep kicks my anxiety further into overdrive until my breathing becomes erratic. When he stops right in front of me, my head is swimming, and I flinch when he reaches out to tilt my chin up with two fingers.

Our gazes link, and my breath gets stuck in my lungs. His red eyes, which are normally hardened with rage, possess an unfamiliar softness that leaves me speechless. It's like I'm staring into the face of a stranger, despite recognizing his other features.

"You're welcome." Even his voice is soft.

He drops his hand, but our eyes remain locked. I want to burn this image of Rafe into my memory. I want to cling to the hint of compassion in his expression, because it's the first time he's looked at me with anything other than disdain. It's such a relief, I temporarily forget why I came to talk to him in the first place. I almost wish he'd look at me that way forever.

Then, in a blink, it's gone. His brows draw low over his eyes, and the typical hardness returns to his features.

"I take it you've also come to ask if you can go home," he says, his voice a little sharper. "You have to understand, there's no easy answer to your question."

I hesitate, my head spinning. That wasn't on my mind before, but it definitely is now.

Is he considering letting me go?

The thought of finally earning his trust is exciting, but I've already made my decision.

"Actually, I'd like to stay," I correct as I stare up into his intimidating eyes, searching for any hint of the softness from before. I come up short.

He cocks his head to the side and his eyes narrow. "Stay?"

"If you'll allow it."

A tense moment passes, and Rafe takes a half-step back. His eyes tear away from mine and slide across the room to the crackling fireplace. I can see the flames reflected in his eyes when he speaks.

"Why would you possibly want to stay here?" He shakes his head slowly. "Monsters and Malevolents alike are out for your blood, and our realm is on the brink of war. You're weak, and you can't survive alone. Like the day of the attack, you'll only endanger those around you."

My conviction wanes as his words dig into me like claws. Of course, he's right. I have no real place in this monster world, and I would be nothing but a burden to those around me. Can I knowingly put

Azarius and Elio in harm's way solely for the sake of my happiness?

No, I can't.

I also know I can't return home and pretend like none of this happened. I'm torn, my heart and logic fighting once again, but I know this is where I want to be.

"I can't leave my mates." I take a step to the right to get Rafe's attention, and I'm relieved when he meets my gaze again. "I've chosen them just as they chose me, and I belong wherever they are. It's true; I can't protect myself the way monsters do, but I'm not incompetent. Give me a weapon, and I'll fight."

The corner of his mouth lifts into a cocky smile. "And if you die anyway?"

"Then at least I'll die fighting for what—who—I love."

As we stare one another down, I'm struck by just how drastically my life has changed in a few short weeks. From doing whatever I could to find a way home, to doing whatever it takes to stay in the monster realm. From being opposed to dating, to having two incredible monster mates. From having no idea where my life was headed, to knowing exactly where I belong.

My entire fate is in Rafe's hands, yet again.

Damn it.

After what feels like an eternity, he slowly nods his head. "Very well. You may stay."

An invisible weight drops off my shoulders. Despite my urge to jump for joy or punch the air, I keep my composure. There will be plenty of time to celebrate later.

"Thank you so much." I press my hands flat in front of my face like a prayer. "I'll leave you alone now."

I turn to leave, but Rafe snatches my wrist in a flash, rooting me to the spot. My eyes fall to his hand, tracing his fingers against my skin, before climbing back up his form and landing on his eyes. They're gleaming with a hint of mischief.

"You're forgetting something."

I blanch, unsure of what he's referring to, but I don't have time to search my brain. He steps closer, eliminating all distance between us, leaning down so our faces are only an inch apart. The musky smell of his skin hits me in an intoxicating wave, and I'm mildly disoriented.

What the hell is he doing?

"I warned you," he says, his voice a sensual growl that plays against my eardrums. He grabs my other wrist and pins them both to my sides as I stand rigidly before him, trying to process what's happening.

Then it hits me.

You'll be bound, bruised, and brutally punished.

I suck a sharp breath, and my knees begin to shake. He leans in, his lips a hairsbreadth from my ear, and chuckles softly as he puts my hands together in front of me and holds them there.

"You want it, don't you?" His warm breath rolls over my skin like tendrils, and the hair on the back of my neck stands up. "I can sense your heart beating faster. I can practically taste the way your pussy is throbbing, begging for me. I turn you on, don't I?"

My eyes bulge. Be it his demon blood, or something else, he has me pegged.

I do want it.

The uncertainty is frightening.

Withdrawing a silk restraint from his pocket with one hand, he sets to work binding my wrists together. It only takes him a second, despite keeping his gaze locked on mine, and he steps away from me when he's finished.

I tug on the restraint experimentally, but it doesn't budge. I'm bound.

"I'd be willing to bet you're already wet for me. Am I right?"

At his words, the heat pooling between my thighs peaks, but I won't give him the satisfaction of knowing he's right. Instead, I keep quiet as he gingerly unbuttons his suit jacket and pulls it off. He carefully folds it before crossing the room, laying it over the arm of the sofa before getting to work on his shirt buttons. When he's shirtless, he returns to his place in front of me, a confident smirk gracing his face.

My eyes rake over his top half, memorizing everything I've only speculated about. He's entirely covered in tattoos, from his neck to his waist, but also scars, some thin, some long. The ink covers a lot of them, but many are still visible. I don't know how he got them—and I'm not inclined to ask—but I can tell he's been through hell at some point in his life.

"I guess I'll have to find out for myself." His voice grabs my attention, and my eyes snap back to his.

Every bit of Rafe's promise is so far out of my comfort zone, I don't even know what to expect. I've never been tied up or dominated in the way he insinuates. I try to brace myself for what he plans to do, my mind whirling with possibilities, but nothing could prepare me for the way he leans in and crushes his lips against mine.

I'm too stunned to respond at first, but as his lips move powerfully against mine and his hands dance up my torso, I relax. I follow the movement of his lips with my own, our tongues swirling together in a frenzied dance. All I want is to run my fingers up his body and tangle them in his hair, but I can't do anything.

I'm entirely at his mercy.

"These clothes are in the way." His voice is deeper than normal, laced with lust.

He grabs the hem of my shirt with both hands and tears the fabric effortlessly, revealing my bare chest. My nipples pebble as his eyes land on them. They ache to be touched, kissed, caressed by him. The smug smile on his face tells me he knows it, too.

A flick of his claws takes care of my sleeves, and what's left of my shirt falls to the floor at my feet. At least it wasn't one of my favorites.

"I've never fucked a human before," he says as he swiftly undoes the button on my jeans.

His mouth slides into a devilish grin, and he pushes my pants past my hips. After helping me out of them, he runs his hands down my thighs before lightly dragging his claws back up, slicing the blue thong I'm wearing in half. It falls to the ground to die with my tattered shirt.

Sadly, the thong was one of my favorites.

"I can't promise that I won't rip you apart," he says, drawing out his words.

I don't need reminding after how easily he destroyed the Malevs. I'm well aware of his capabilities, but that doesn't make his words any less sexy.

He grabs the cloth binding my wrists and drags me toward the four-poster bed. I think we're headed for the mattress, but he stops me near the post at the foot of the bed and raises my hands above my head. For the first time, I notice a hook hanging from the canopy, which he loops through my restraint effortlessly before stepping away.

"What are you doing?" I gasp, tugging at the hook as my heart rate spikes.

In a flash, he's against my back, pressing me between his body and the post.

"Relax," he whispers in my ear. His hands come up to place a blindfold over my eyes, and the room around me is lost to darkness. "The fun hasn't even started yet."

Without my sense of sight or the ability to use my hands, I feel lost. Like a fish out of water, I'm uncomfortable and panicking. Then I feel Rafe's hands slide over my breasts, and I catch my breath.

To be so callous, his touch is tender. He massages my chest, squeezing in time as he presses against my backside, and his lips find the side of my neck. My knees go weak at his touch, every sensation intensified with the use of the blindfold. Every kiss, nip, and caress is more pleasurable and more explosive than I've ever felt.

I need more.

His hands slide their way down my stomach before landing on my hips. He pulls me against him before dipping one hand between my thighs and running his fingers experimentally along my pussy.

"So wet. So ready," he whispers against my skin. "Do you want me to fuck you?"

I nod without hesitation, my excitement blooming at his touch. He chuckles lightly as he grabs my ass with his free hand, squeezing and grinding against me.

"If I fuck your ass?" He nips at the side of my neck. "Would you like that?"

I don't answer at first, unsure if that's an option. If Rafe's cock is as big as Azarius' or Elio's, he'll rip my ass in half. Still, my libido is through the roof, and at this point, I just want him to have his way with me.

"If you want."

His fingers dive for my clit and run circles around it, sending ripples of euphoria through my body as his hand slaps firmly against my ass. I wince at the sting, but it's quickly replaced by a pleasant warmth.

"I'm going to have fun with you," he says, raking his claws from my ass to my back. It stings a little, but seconds later, the pain disappears, and heat radiates from my skin. "I promise, no one can fuck you like I can."

His left hand finds my throat and squeezes, gently applying pressure while his fingers speed up their tiny circles on my clit.

"I want you to come for me until I'm drowning in your juices," he growls in my ear, slightly increasing the pressure on the sides of my neck.

My climax comes fast, the combination of his voice in my ear and his hand on my neck making it impossible to prolong, and I lean my head back against him as I shudder apart.

"Good girl," he murmurs, letting me recoup before moving from behind me.

He unhooks my hands and guides me to the side of the bed. I step carefully, terrified of tripping and falling in front of him, but he keeps a cautious hand on my arm.

"Lay back," he says, helping me onto the side of the bed.

I do as I'm told and lay back as Rafe's footsteps head across the room. A few seconds later, my hands are secured above my head, my legs hanging off the bed.

While I can't see anything around me, I can hear Rafe's every move. He unclasps his belt, the metal clinging as it's moved around, and his pants drop to the floor.

I'd give anything to see what he's packing right now, to know what I'm in for.

He walks back to the side of the bed and spreads my legs apart with his hands, revealing my sex dripping for him, and he doesn't hesitate to plunge two fingers inside me. I jump at the sudden fullness, and I arch my back as he pumps them in and out.

I wish I could reach out and grab him, pull him to me so I can crush my mouth against his. I want to run my fingers along his skin and tangle them in his hair. I fight against the restraint, but I know there's no use. Rafe wouldn't make anything easy for me to get out of.

"How many fingers do you think I can fit in you?" he asks quietly, his voice a low growl. He thrusts his fingers inside hard and deep as he speaks, not bothering to slow down. "All of them?"

"I-I don't think so," I say, fighting through the pleasure to speak. My body's fire has turned my brain to mush.

He quickly slips another finger inside, pumping steadily, and I begin to buck my hips. He curls them forward, hitting the spot that makes my toes curl, and I gasp at the overwhelming pleasure.

Tight pressure builds in my belly, growing exponentially every time he presses against my g-spot, until I can't stand it anymore. An impossibly strong orgasm slams into me, radiating from my center and rushing out toward my toes. I cry out against it, bucking my hips against his hand until the orgasm releases me.

"Two already," he says, tsking his tongue. "At this rate, you'll be exhausted by the time I get my cock in you. Maybe I should go ahead and give it to you."

Even though I've just climaxed twice, my pussy is still begging for attention. It wants his cock, needs it.

"Yes," I say, wishing more than ever I could take off my blindfold.

"Maybe if you ask nicely," he says as he makes his way around the bed to unhook my hands.

He can't be serious. Ask nicely? He wants me to beg for it.

If it was anyone else, I'd tell them to politely fuck off, but something about Rafe stirs my curiosity. I'm already miles outside my comfort zone.

"I will if you show it to me first."

He chuckles. "Not liking your blindfold, are you?"

I shake my head. "That's not it. I just like to look."

Grabbing my hands, he helps me into a sitting position, and I'm shocked by the wet pool beneath me. Heat scorches my cheeks as I realize I soaked his comforter.

"Very well."

He gently pulls my blindfold off and tosses it to the side. I blink several times as my eyes adjust to the light, and when my vision clears, I meet Rafe's gaze. One of his eyebrows is raised in a daring expression and he gestures downward with his eyes.

I follow his gaze, my eyes racing down his body, and when they find where his cock should be, I freeze.

There isn't one.

Instead, a foot-long, black tentacle, equipped with tiny suckers along the bottom, hangs in its place.

My mouth gapes open unattractively, and for a moment, I'm speechless.

"Wha—"

"Not what you were expecting?" he asks, taking a

step closer. The tentacle curls, the end rolling into a ball and looking a little more phallic.

"No," I admit, unable to tear my eyes away from it. "Not really."

"Do you want to see what it can do?" he asks.

A tiny voice at the back of my head is screaming for me to run. Tentacle-alien-monster dick is more than I signed up for, but if this giant wet spot beneath me is any preview of what it can do, I'm eager to find out.

"Yes," I say, nodding my head slightly.

He takes a step closer, settling himself between my thighs. "Yes, what?"

"Please."

Leaning in, he catches my lips with his for the second time, and my heart leaps in my chest.

Asshole Rafe is terrifying.

Snarky Rafe is sexy.

I have to admit, passionate Rafe who kisses me until it hurts and makes me want to beg for pleasure is pretty goddamn amazing.

He slices the fabric binding my hands, and I rub them eagerly to return the circulation. My wrists ache, and I'm fairly certain I'll have bruises in the morning.

I lay down, and he pulls my ass to the edge of the bed, positioning himself between my thighs. Unable to decide if it's safer to watch or close my eyes again, I find myself staring as his tentacle cock wiggles to life and slides itself along my sex.

It feels like a giant tongue as it teases my clit and makes its way back down my pussy, the little suckers along the bottom adding increased stimulation wherever they touch. As strange as it is, it's not unpleasant, and within seconds, my apprehension has given way to my libido.

The end curls into a knot again and I moan when he dips it inside me. In this shape, it's firmer than before and feels like a regular cock.

He thrusts into me, burying himself inside, and leans down to press his lips against mine again. Finally able to use my hands, I throw my arms around his neck and cling to him as he slams his dick into me. From this angle, he's able to hit deep, and every thrust sends a ripple of pleasure through my center.

"You're so fucking tight," he growls against my skin as one of his hands slips behind my head and tangles in my hair. He tugs until I'm on the brink of pain, then presses his lips against my neck. "I want you to come hard on my cock. Can you be a good girl and do that for me?"

All that escapes is a moan as he tugs harder on my hair and grips my ass with his free hand. He pounds me into the mattress mercilessly, and I feel my next climax building.

"That's it," he says, coaxing me on when my breathing shifts. "Come for me."

The orgasm takes hold, ripping through me like a tidal wave, and I bury my nails into Rafe's back to draw him close. He growls and drives harder, slamming into me ruthlessly until I'm finished.

His climax comes immediately after, and I'm reminded of what's inside me when it wiggles to life, filling me with his cum. I don't know how or where it came from, but I know I'm dripping with it now.

Rafe slips out of me, and I expect that to be the end. Considering how he normally brushes me off when he's done with me, I don't expect this to end any differently. I expect him to send me back downstairs with orders to never speak of this again.

Instead, he finds my mouth for another kiss.

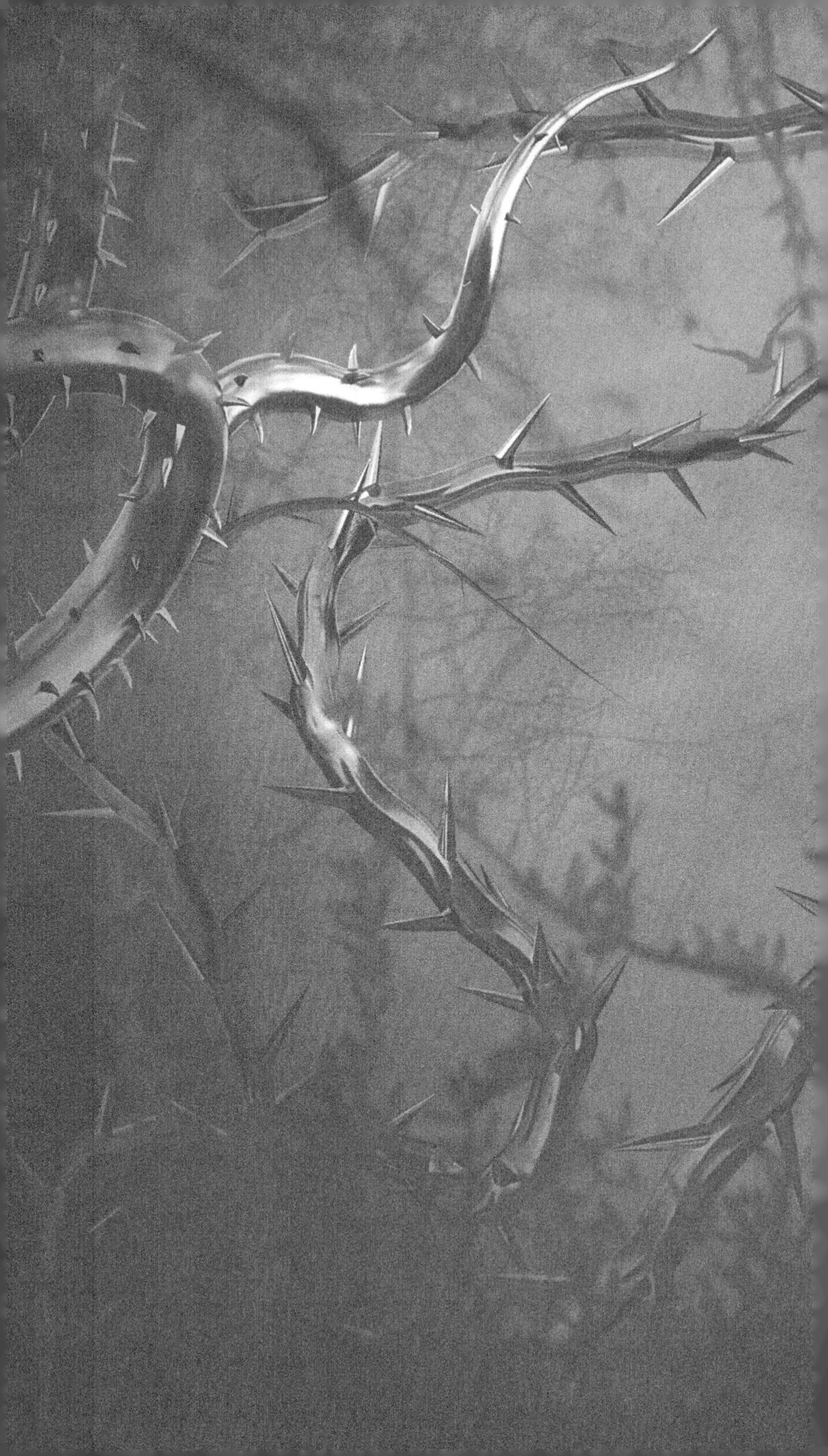

23
RAFE

I kiss her deeply, not quite ready for the moment to end, teasing her lips with my tongue and sucking on the bottom one. I hate how much I enjoy the feel of her mouth against mine, and when I pull away, her cheeks are flushed. She looks just as surprised as I do, a wild curiosity in her eyes.

Her legs are spread wide, revealing her perfect pussy, and I watch with a smile as beads of cum leak out of her. She must know I'm enjoying the show, because she wiggles her hips. I smirk, confusing thoughts clashing in my mind. Rather than voicing any of them, though, I clear my throat.

"Just remember," I say, a smirk twisting my lips, "if you come back to the third floor, this is what awaits you. Understand?"

She grins wide. "Perfectly."

"Good. Your mates are probably waiting for you." They know better than to come to the third floor unless it's a dire emergency, but that doesn't mean they aren't pacing downstairs, wondering what I've done to her. "They're probably worried I've tortured you to death. You can go."

She glances toward the door, chewing her bottom lip as the gears turn behind her eyes. I'm surprised by her hesitation—I figured she'd be eager to get away from me by now—and even more surprised by her response.

"And if I want to stay?" she asks.

I freeze, not quite sure what to say. I would have chased anyone else away, but the way a warmth settles in my chest at her offer shocks me. I can't chase the feeling off, nor do I want to. After a long moment of her batting her eyelashes at me, I answer, "I'm not kicking you out, but don't get comfortable."

"Fair." A grin breaks out across her face, and she crawls up to lay her head on a pillow, patting the bed beside her. With a smirk, I join her, pulling her into the crook of my arm and letting her rest her head on my chest.

"Is this okay?" she asks. "Is cuddling going to ruin your asshole reputation?"

I scoff, bringing my arm up to wrap around her naked body. "Not if you don't tell anyone."

We lay in silence for several minutes, my mind running rampant with untamed thoughts. I should have ushered her back downstairs so I could spend a peaceful night alone, but as I look down at her curled up against me, her cheek pressed against my chest with her eyes closed, I can't bring myself to send her away. Not yet, anyway.

Whatever magic this human possesses is something more than mere warlock blood, because I never imagined I'd come to care for someone so weak, so frail. Yet, here I am, a protective fire in my chest, wanting to keep her safe. It's strange, to say the least.

I brush a strand of blonde hair back from her face as her breaths slow and deepen, my mind wandering back to the first time I laid eyes on her. I hated her, wanted her gone from my mansion. I'd seen her as nothing more than a liability, something useless that needed our constant tending, like a temperamental flower that dies whenever you leave it alone too long.

Granted, she is still a liability. It's clear the Malevs are after her, and even though we slaughtered the ones that attacked, that doesn't mean there aren't more out there searching for her. More will come, I'm sure, but this time, we'll be ready.

Pulling the blanket up farther, I tuck her in neatly at my side before finally settling in and letting my eyes drift closed. True peace isn't something I've ever known, but I'd say this is as close as it gets. I'm sated, relieved, and content for the first time in a long time, though I expect it won't last long, not when there's an impending war and enemies at our door.

Still, even with the heaviness of what's to come looming over us, I allow myself this one brief moment of contentment. I breathe in Devyn's familiar human scent, letting it saturate my senses, and for a few seconds—it would be foolish to stay this way for any longer—everything feels right.

I don't make many promises, but I make this one to myself: I will protect the woman in my arms with every part of me, no matter what.

I'll burn this entire realm before I let anyone hurt her.

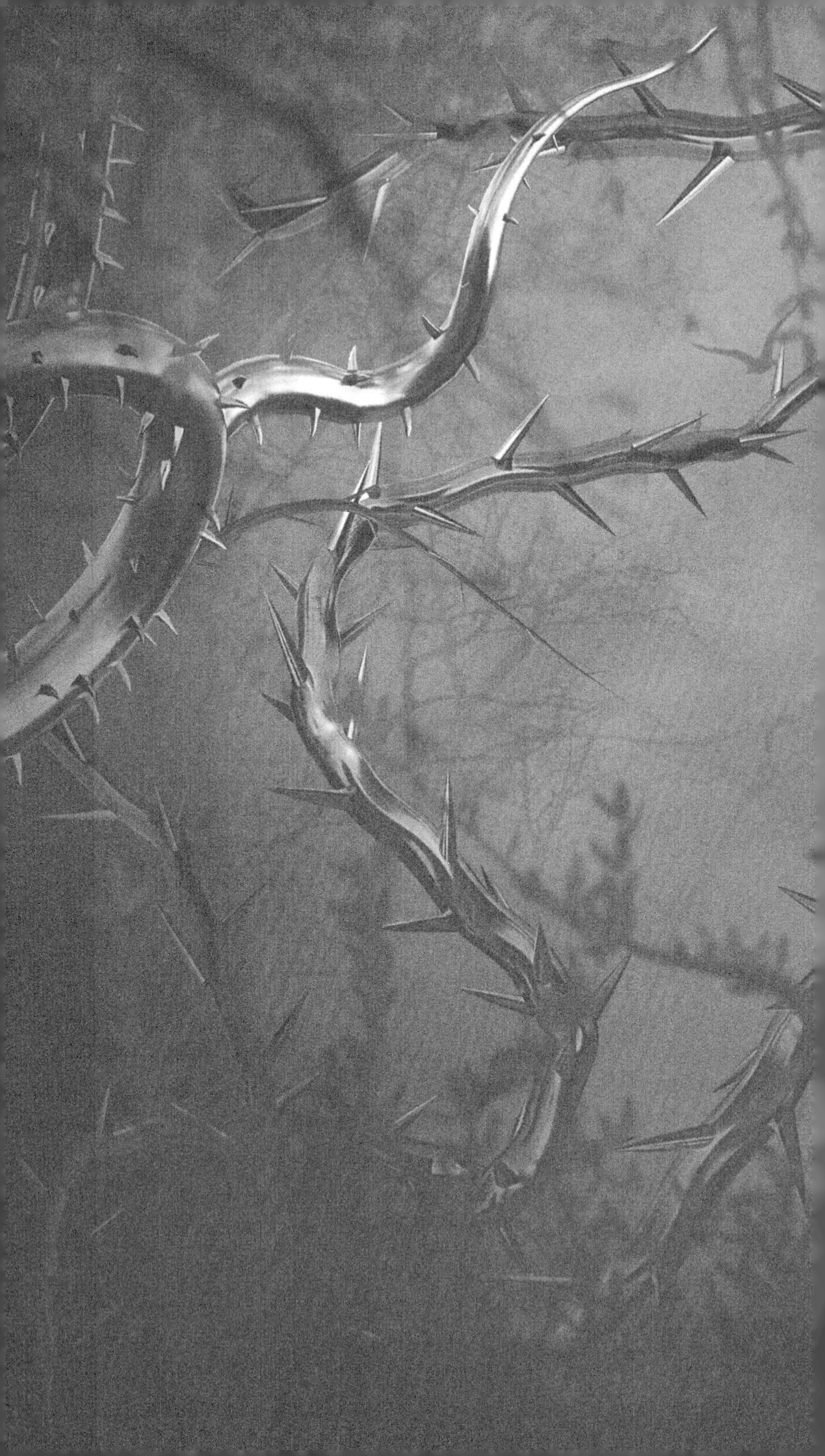

24
DEVYN

One Month Later

"Are you ready?" Azarius asks, squeezing my hand for reassurance.

I look up, my heart in my throat, and meet his familiar blue gaze with a forced smile on my lips.

He's wearing jeans and a white T-shirt, and while he looks breathtaking in his human form, I miss the black markings that normally stretch across his skin. Without his horns and tail and with a tan to his usually stark white skin, I hardly recognize him.

"It's going to be alright," Elio says on my other side, placing a comforting hand on my shoulder.

They both know how hard this is for me. I spent weeks going back and forth on whether I'm truly ready to live in the monster realm forever, and while I know this is the right choice, it doesn't make facing Cara any easier. The portal might not have killed me on the way here, but essentially walking out of her life forever after everything she's done for me just might.

Hopefully, there will be time to visit and catch up with her later, but with tensions mounting between the monsters and Malevs, war is on the horizon, and there's no telling when I'll be able to come back—if I'll be able to come back.

With a deep sigh, I nod. It doesn't matter if I'm ready or not; we're here, and we're doing it. There are moving boxes downstairs in my car, and we can't wait out here on the stoop of my old apartment forever.

"Yeah. I'm ready," I say, even though I don't believe it.

The story we concocted to tell Cara is a little rocky, but it was the best we could do. I filled her in on everything when I came back to Earth the first time, but we've practiced the details until they're embedded in my brain, just in case she decides to ask more questions. Knowing her, she probably will.

I run through the details again to soothe my nerves: After jetting around the country with Azarius and Elio on their business trips, we're moving to Florida. It's a huge condo on the beach, and they have a giant pitbull named Rafe. We even found pictures of a black dog online to make it convincing.

Simple, easy, to the point.

Then why am I so nervous?

Elio doesn't wait for more assurance before he steps forward to knock on the door. At the same time, my heart lurches toward the floor, and Azarius grips my hand a little tighter.

Cara answers with a smile on her face, her vibrant red hair piled messily on top of her head.

"Devyn!" she exclaims, rushing forward to throw her arms around my neck. She squeezes me tight before taking a step back to look me over. "It's so good to see you."

I smile awkwardly. She makes it sound like we're strangers who haven't seen each other in a few years, even though all my belongings are still in her apartment. "You too."

"Az. Elio." She acknowledges them with a nod. "Come on in."

Azarius follows me through the door, but Elio hangs back in the breezeway. "I'll be right back," he says. "I'm going to grab some boxes." Then, he's gone.

The apartment is exactly the way I remember, with a tiny living room off to the right and a small dining room table to the left. The kitchen is ahead, separated by a short wall that gives us a clear view, and a hallway after that leads to my bedroom.

My old bedroom, I remind myself. My new one is an enormous room in Rafe's mansion, dripping in pink and gold. After the Malev attack, I got upgraded to one of the other rooms and was given creative freedom over it.

Still, the room waiting for me at the end of the hall makes my chest clench. It's sinking in that this is finally happening. After all these weeks of waiting, I'm officially moving out of Cara's place. I'm going to be living in the monster realm forever.

"We won't take long if you have plans," I assure Cara, just thankful she was willing to be here between school and work while we packed. I don't think I could leave without seeing her again. It just wouldn't feel right.

"No problem," she says, grabbing a mug off the kitchen table and bringing it to her lips. "I have the evening off, so I wasn't doing anything. Do either of you want coffee?"

Coffee. The thought makes my mouth water, and my excitement must be obvious on my face, because Cara grins. "I'll make you some."

"Make it two, please," Azarius says as she walks to the kitchen. He wraps a hand around my waist and pulls me into him.

"Coming right up." Cara nods at us before searching through the cabinets for two more mugs. We'd never had many dishes, just enough for the two of us to get by, but she manages to find two coffee cups tucked up on a top shelf.

She hasn't finished pouring the coffee when Elio is knocking on the door again. I turn to let him in, four empty cardboard boxes held at odd angles in his arms. It's just enough for the three of us to carry, and I haven't even begun to think about how we'll get them through the woods to the mansion, but we'll cross that bridge when we get to it.

"Can you toss them in my room?" I ask, glancing

between him and the hall. "We'll start packing after coffee."

"Of course, princess," he says softly before heading off toward my room, being careful not to knock the few pictures on the wall down.

I turn my attention back to Cara, who's offering me a mug of coffee. She added cream and sugar, just the way I like it, and I eagerly bring it to my lips. Orlyitha may have many things, but it doesn't have coffee.

Maybe I can fix that.

"How are you liking Florida?" Cara asks, handing Azarius his mug.

My heart flutters, but I smile. "It's great," I lie. I'm sure Florida is fantastic, despite the heat and the hurricanes, but I've never been. "Definitely better than Atlanta."

Cara chuckles. "I don't doubt that. I love the beach."

After catching up briefly, Azarius, Elio, and I start going through my belongings, sorting out my essentials. They've promised me countless times that they can just buy me new things, and as tempting as the idea is, I'm attached to the few things I've managed to accumulate. The clothes, the knickknacks, all of it.

There was a time when I had nothing, and I didn't know how I would ever get out of that place. The things in this room are proof that anything is possible, so I don't plan to let them go that easily.

"Where do you want to start?" Elio asks, pulling

open the top drawer of my dresser and revealing a pile of brightly colored underwear.

I giggle. "Clothes are probably the logical place. Then we can see what we have room for."

We work through the room, and I carefully organize my belongings into the boxes, folding clothes and making sure to wrap the few breakable things in fabric. Azarius and Elio aren't much help, but I'm glad they're here in case I need them. They don't seem bored either, asking me about things I'm keeping occasionally or sharing stories about some of their previous shopping sprees on Earth.

"We should get one of these for the jet," Azarius says, pointing to a porcelain pig in a bikini that I found at a thrift store ages ago. I know he's only saying it to add to the authenticity of our story, but it makes me smile. I shake my head and shove the pig into the box.

When I've packed the first box to the brim, Azarius takes it down to the car, and I start on the next one. It's slow going, but I take my time, and Cara doesn't seem bothered. She eventually curls up on the couch in the living room to watch TV while we finish. If there was space in the tiny bedroom, she'd probably offer to help, but there's hardly room for my two beefy mates and me, much less a fourth person.

"Yell if you need me," she calls down the hall.

Elio takes the next box downstairs after I finish clearing out my dresser. Then, it's onto the desk and the closet. By the time I've finished, we've been here a couple of hours, and my stomach is beginning to growl.

"Can we stop somewhere to eat on the way?" I ask, and a grin breaks out across Elio's face.

"Of course. I'm starving." Then, he drops his voice low. "And maybe I can eat you for dessert."

I blush, unable to keep the smile off my face. "Deal."

Azarius grabs the last box and holds it beneath one of his arms. "Is this the last of it?"

"Yep. That's it."

"Okay, darling." He leans down and presses his lips against mine briefly before heading toward the front door. "I'm going to put this in the car, and then we can head out."

Elio and I follow him down the hall, but I stop in the living room. Cara pauses her show and comes over to hug me around the neck again. "Good luck with everything, Devyn. You deserve the world."

I promised myself I wouldn't cry, but the corners of my eyes prick at her words. Cara is a gem, and I can't imagine where I'd be if she hadn't let me move in and helped me get on my feet. I owe her so much.

"Thank you," I whisper, squeezing her back. "I'll be sure to keep in touch."

"You better." She smirks when she steps back, her eyes bouncing between Elio and me. "I want to hear all the stories. You hear me?"

"You got it." I laugh.

I give the apartment one last sweeping glance, a weight forming in my chest. This place has been my security blanket for the last few months while I've been in the monster realm. I always knew, in the back of my mind, that I could come back if things didn't work out. If things got too dangerous and I needed to escape, I could come home.

Now, there is no security blanket. I'm trusting Azarius, Elio, and Rafe to keep me safe until they get the Malevs under control. Until then, I'm not coming back.

After exchanging goodbyes, Elio leads the way outside, dragging me along gently behind him. Beneath the excitement of starting this new adventure, I'm a little nervous and numb. He must sense my discomfort, because he stops and pulls me into his arms.

"Are you okay, princess?"

I nod after a moment of hesitation. "I am."

"Nervous?" He leans down, but not close enough to kiss me.

Up until this moment, I'd been a little anxious. Moving to an entirely different realm is a big life change, after all. However, when Azarius and Elio started packing my things and talking about our future together, the anxiety melted away. I've never been so sure of something in my entire life.

"Nope," I say confidently, stretching up on my toes to kiss him.

The things I thought I were certain about in the past seem silly now, because being in the monster realm makes so much sense.

It's my home.

It's where I belong.

AUTHOR NOTE

**Thank you so much for reading
A Monstrous Claim: Part One!**

This was my first venture into monster romance territory, and I think it's safe to say I'm never leaving. To be honest, I never expected to fall in love with this genre or want to pursue anything more than a standalone, but halfway through I knew that wouldn't be the case. I poured sweat, tears, and countless hours into crafting this book baby, and the fact that you made it this far means it was all worth it. I'm so grateful that you picked it up and gave it a chance. Don't miss the conclusion to Devyn and her men's story in part two.

If this book made you smile, laugh, or reach for your vibrator, please consider leaving a review on all your favorite platforms so other monster lovers can discover this smut nugget and enjoy it as well.

ABOUT THE AUTHOR

R.K. Pierce is an author by day but feral chaos gremlin by night who routinely curses the blood of her enemies. While not a big coffee drinker, she does enjoy margaritas, and usually prefers socks with toes over the mitten kind. For fun, she will either read or joust. During downtime with her family, she tends to keep things low key by impersonating Elvis for funeral events or watching trashy TV shows.

R.K. Pierce's Links:

Made in the USA
Monee, IL
02 May 2025